PIT OF
AMBITION

PIT OF AMBITION

BOOK II IN
THE CASELLI FAMILY SERIES

TA`MARA HANSCOM

REATA
PUBLISHING

SIOUX CITY, IOWA

Pit of Ambition
Copyright © 2011, 2017 Ta`Mara Hanscom

Published by Reata Publishing
2900 Gordon Drive
Sioux City, Iowa 51105

www.TaMaraHanscomBooks.com

Cover design by Heidi Hutchinson
Front cover images bought on Adobe Stock
Back cover image by Ta`Mara Hanscom

Printed in the United States of America
ISBN 978-0-9844514-1-8

CAST OF CHARACTERS

JOSHUA HANSEN   Married to Mona (Spencer)

NOAH HANSEN   Brother of Joshua Hansen,
Married to Carrie (Miller)

TY HANSEN   Carrie's son by Dr. Schneider Rauwolf
aka Roy Schneider, raised by Noah

GIUSEPPE CASELLI   Married to Rosa (Rosa Matilde Rochelle)

PETRICE CASELLI   Eldest Caselli son, married to Ellie (Elaine Netherton)
Michael Petrice Caselli – son of Petrice & Ellie
Gabriella Elaine Caselli – daughter of Petrice & Ellie

VINCENZO CASELLI   Second Caselli son, married to Kate (Katlin Martin)
Alyssa Katlin Caselli – daughter of Vincenzo & Kate
Angelo James Caselli – son of Vincenzo & Kate

MARQUETTE CASELLI   Youngest Caselli son, married to Tara (D`Annenci)

TILLIE MARTIN   (Matilde Rosa Caselli) Martin – Only Caselli
daughter. Nicknamed "Angel" by her brothers,
married to Alex James Martin III

ANGELO CASELLI   Brother of Giuseppe Caselli (passed away 1964)

ALEX JAMES MARTIN, JR.   Married to Frances (Dale)

SAM MARTIN   Eldest Martin son, married to Becky-Lynn (Tucker)

KATLIN MARTIN   Only Martin daughter – married to Vincenzo Caselli

ALEX J. MARTIN, III   Youngest Martin son – married to Tillie (Caselli) Martin

BURT ENGLESON   Married to Diane Engleson

ANDY ENGLESON   Son of Burt & Diane, Pastor at Christ the King Church

GINGER ENGLESON   Daughter of Burt & Diane and lifelong friend of
                        Tillie Martin

MARIO PONERELLO*   aka Jack Nelson – married to Della (Miller),
                        Carrie Hansen's mother

ANTONIO PONERELLO   Eldest son of Mario Ponerello and his late wife

CHARISE NELSON   Daughter of Mario & Della

SALVATORE PONERELLO Brother of Mario Ponerello. Presumed dead

DR. SCHNEIDER RAUWOLF aka Roy Schneider Biological father of Ty Hansen

REATA   Ranch near Centerville, SD – Vincenzo Caselli
                        inherited Reata from Uncle Angelo, the brother of
                        his father, Giuseppe. Vincenzo and Kate live there
                        and there are many events throughout the year that
                        take place on Reata. Uncle Angelo and his beloved
                        wife, Penny, rest there.

**Mario is the arch-nemesis of Marquette Caselli. Marquette has sought Mario
since The Great Palermo Diamond Heist of 1968*

"Love does not delight in evil, but rejoices with the truth. It always protects, always trusts, always hopes, always perseveres..."

I Corinthians 13:6-7, NIV

TABLE OF CONTENTS

PROLOGUE

Giuseppe looked into Rosa's eyes as she stood in the doorway. She didn't say a word, but he knew what she was about to tell him. Quietly, Rosa closed the door and took a seat beside him.

"She spoke of him," she whispered. She looked at her lap and shook her head. "I want to tell her."

Giuseppe shook his head in adamant disagreement. "No. Let us wait—"

"For what, Giuseppe?" Rosa fought tears of frustration. She was ready to end this nonsense. "Let us go to Noah," she begged. "Let us get an explanation and bring him to Angel. I can no longer bear her sadness pressing upon my heart." Rosa's tears forced themselves from her eyes. She took quiet breaths as she sobbed, and put her hands over her mouth so her daughter wouldn't hear her crying.

"No, my Rosa." Giuseppe put his arm around her shoulders and pulled her toward his body. "I do not want to take the risk."

"Please, Giuseppe, before this thing with Alex goes any further, she should be told. Is it not more than mere coincidence that we prayed for Noah for nearly fifteen years before their *chance* meeting?"

"Disobedience combined with coincidence." Giuseppe frowned. He shook his head and locked his jaw. His Angel's heart would *not* be risked again, no matter what the explanation. Alex Martin, on the other hand, was an honorable man, and he was obviously in love. She would be safe with Alex, and her heart would mend with his charming attentions.

—Giuseppe & Rosa Caselli, September 1975

PART I
GIUSEPPE

CHAPTER 1

Rapid City, South Dakota
April, 1980

Noah Hansen pretended a frown as he watched the old business-woman. Her blue hair was ratted into a halo shape over her head, giving her a fragile appearance…but Vivian Olsen was far from incapable. *She's ruthless,* he thought as he watched her gather a bulging file from her leather briefcase, sort daintily through the pages, and hand him a small portion. He raised one sandy-colored eyebrow, and his blue eyes twinkled with curiosity…*Isn't she gonna take my offer? I'm practically giving her the place.* "So, what do you wanna do, Viv?" he asked.

"I'm gonna renew my lease."

Noah moaned, "Oh come on, Viv."

"I've gone over the figures at least a hundred times," she quipped, pursing her bright red lips and raising her black-penciled brows. "I'm better off leasing it, and you *did* give me several option periods on the original lease."

"I know it," Noah admitted. *I'm never going to unload that giant white elephant.* "All right then. Another three years?"

"Perfect," Vivian agreed as she rose from her chair, and Noah stood politely behind his desk. "I suppose your *troll* will be calling me?"

"Of course."

"Well, tell him to let me know when he's got the thing finished and I'll be over with pen in hand." Vivian held out her hand, and

Noah gave it a gentle shake. "It's always a pleasure to do business with you, Hansen."

Noah forced a smile but still sounded disappointed as he replied, "You, too, Viv."

Without another word, Vivian picked up her briefcase and her little old heels clicked their way out of Hansen Development.

Melinda appeared in his doorway. She smiled as she leaned against the casing, but Noah saw through the strained expression with which Melinda attempted to hide her foul mood. Noah sighed...*She's always mad about something. Now what?*

Melinda Smalley was Noah's personal assistant, and had been since his sister-in-law, Mona, hired her four years ago. She was smart and pretty, and newly graduated from the local business college. Long, sleek black hair, her eyes deep brown, and Mona assumed her to be a long-time Christian because they'd gone to church together for better than ten years. And while Melinda was excellent at her job, she tended to be bossy, overbearing, and testy—*especially* with Noah. She was exceptionally organized, but sometimes he wondered why he put up with her. There was just something about her that irritated him to his very core.

"Viv won't buy the place," he muttered.

Melinda nodded, though she didn't understand why Noah so desperately wanted to sell the beautiful estate he'd built on Rimrock Highway. Vivian had leased the property since 1976 and had turned it into a successful bed and breakfast she called "Angel's Place."

Noah shrugged and took a breath. "Well, whatever. By the way, what do you think of Ben Simmons?"

Melinda's expression remained strained, and she shrugged in response. *I hate Ben Simmons.* "Well, aside from being just a little over-educated for the position—"

"What do you mean, *over-educated*?" Noah frowned.

"He's going to want a substantial salary, for one thing," Melinda pointed out. "Frankly, I'm surprised he even applied for the job. He's an architect, for Pete's sake, not a foreman."

16

"But he's got tons of experience on construction crews in Chicago," Noah countered. "And you know I want to get someone with drafting experience willing to work with me and the crews."

Melinda nodded and drew in an irritated breath. "Whatever, Noah," she mumbled as she tossed some letters onto his desk. "There's your mail. You've already made up your mind. Why even bother asking me my opinion? The next thing I know, Ben Simmons will be telling me what to do."

Noah raised one eyebrow as he thought about that for a moment.

Melinda shook her head and glanced at her watch. "You've got an inspection in about twenty minutes over on East St. Pat. Don't forget about it." And with that she turned on her heel and marched out of his office.

Noah frowned and picked up the telephone next to him. He dialed his personnel manager's extension and waited for him to answer.

"Harv, here."

"Hey, Harv, it's me," Noah whispered. His frown began to melt into a smile.

"Noah?" Harv questioned. "Why are you whispering?"

Noah stifled a laugh. "Call Ben Simmons and offer him the position."

As she sat in the window seat of her living room in Sioux Falls, South Dakota, Rosa Caselli caressed the words she'd printed into the margin of her mother's Bible nearly twenty years ago. She drew a soft breath and fought her tears as she whispered in Italian, "*Venti uno Dicembre, Noah.*" She looked to the west, as she often had over the last twenty years, and prayed in her first language for a young man she'd never met. "*E questo che prego* (And this I pray), that your charity may more and more abound in knowledge and all discernment, so that you may approve the better things, that you may be upright and without offense unto the day of Christ, filled with the fruit of justice, through Jesus Christ, to the glory and praise of God."

Rosa took a deep breath and closed her eyes as she whispered, "Father, I sense danger all around him. Keep him safe." Warm tears slipped from beneath her eyelids, and she shook her head. "Why, Father? Why do You press upon my heart to pray for him? Please take this burden from me so that I may escape my sorrow and regret."

Giuseppe bit his lip and swallowed his anguish as he hid around the corner in the kitchen. In 1960, they'd learned of a little boy who was struggling with the loss of his parents and the authority of his older brother. His name was Noah, and he was only ten years old. The young child was strong-willed and disobedient, and as he grew his sins escalated into drunkenness and womanizing. For nearly twenty years they'd prayed for Noah, and they would continue.

Their only daughter, Tillie, who was nicknamed "Angel," by her brothers, had *happened* upon the man five years ago, and Rosa had begged Giuseppe to reveal their prayers to her. But Giuseppe had been stubborn...*and the thing with Alex had gone too far.* Angel had returned from a trip to the Black Hills with a story about a blackguard who'd broken her heart. She never wanted to see him again, and Giuseppe, with the kindness of a father's heart, decided to keep them apart. He buried the secret of Noah's identity deep within himself and demanded that Rosa do the same. Angel then began dating Alex that same year, and Giuseppe allowed them to marry two years later. Unbeknownst to Angel, Alex was best friends with the very Noah her parents diligently prayed for—the very Noah she'd accused of being a blackguard.

Giuseppe shook his head and swallowed as hard as he could. Of all the decisions he'd made in his sixty-three years, he regretted only one.

In nearly five years of practice, Alex James Martin III was still holding the "all wins" record—not only at his office in Sioux Falls, but at his family's branch office in Rapid City as well. Everyone looked upon Alex as the most brilliant attorney in South Dakota, and referred only the *ne plus* ultra-complicated cases to his expertise. He memorized law in a single reading, no matter the complexity, giving him a sharp advantage over everyone else.

Alex didn't have to look things up more than once. He stored information in his brain, and his colleagues were forever calling him with questions when they were stumped in a case. Interns loved to do research for Alex because he gave them the exact cite and location of the point of law he wanted to use. Other attorneys "fumbled around," according to Alex, and that was something he didn't feel his staff had the time for.

He'd set up more businesses in the last five years than his brother and father had in all their years combined practicing law. They often worried Alex would burn himself out or bog himself down, but Alex always seemed to manage, not only *without* mistakes, but with tremendous success as well. After all, he'd graduated *magna cum laude* from Harvard Law School.

And Alex was handsome. He was much like his father and brother and stood at least five inches over six-feet-tall. He had the Martins' masculine build of wide shoulders and a trim waist. His hair was so black it shone blue when he stood in the light just right, and his skin was smooth olive, without any kind of blemish. His eyes were as black as coal, and his perfect white teeth sparkled when he smiled.

Like all the Martin men, Alex dressed to perfection—from his pressed white dress shirt to the black slacks and black tie. The Martins did not wear stylish leisure suits, but rather professional, straight-cut, and pleated Italian suits that fit their handsome bodies to a 'T'.

"Alex." The receptionist buzzed in on the intercom on his desk. "Mrs. Martin is on line two. Can you take it?"

Alex set down his file and picked up the phone. "Hi, honey." He looked at his watch and frowned. "Aren't you supposed to be in class?"

"I am. I was." Tillie sighed into the phone. "Is there any chance you could pick me up?"

He rolled his eyes...*I'm so busy...I've only got about a million things to do.* "Right now?"

"I'm really sick," she answered. "And I'm so dizzy I don't think I can drive." She'd been struggling with flu-like symptoms since their return from Mexico last week. They'd vacationed there over her spring break, and both were certain she'd picked up something during their stay.

"Okay," he agreed with reluctance. "I can be over at the campus in about ten minutes."

"Thanks, Alex," she said with relief, and they hung up.

Alex collected the file he'd been working on and put it into his briefcase. He grabbed his coat and headed down the hall, stopping in his brother's open doorway. "Hey, Sam."

"Hey, Alex." Sam took off his reading glasses to focus on Alex.

"I have to give Tillie a lift. She's sick again, and I'm supposed to meet with a realtor for Noah this afternoon. Do you have time to take the appointment?"

"Sure. I've got a spot open. And you'd better get that girl to the doc. She's picked up something in Mexico. I can just about guarantee it. You know, Becky-Lynn got sick when we went to Mexico a couple of years ago. She won't ever go back."

"I know. Well, thanks for stepping in for me today, Sam," he finished, and hurried out of the office.

Tillie sighed as she climbed into Alex's Mercedes, set her books on the floor, and leaned back in the seat.

She looks sick, Alex noticed as he watched her. He put a tender hand on her shoulder and looked at her with concern. "How are you doing?"

"Terrible," she moaned. "I just want to lie down."

Alex nodded and put the car into gear. "I'm worried about you. You've been sick for about a week now. Maybe you'd better get this checked out. You know, Becky-Lynn had to go to the doctor with it."

"I know, and I'm really tired." She put her hand on the side of her face and asked, "Do I have a fever?"

Alex reached over and touched the skin on her forehead. "You don't feel hot to me, but Becky-Lynn didn't run a fever either."

Dr. Lewis couldn't fit Tillie into his schedule until the following morning. She hung up the phone, closed her eyes, and wished the room would stop spinning.

Alex frowned and put a gentle hand on Tillie's face. "Do you think you'll make it?"

"I'll be fine," she scoffed. "You can go back to the office."

Alex sighed. "I brought a file home, and I can work on it here."

Tillie smiled faintly as she looked at her handsome husband. "Thanks for sticking around. I love you."

"I love you, too." He gave her a soft kiss and tucked the covers around her. Then he settled himself into the chair beside the bed, and Tillie fell asleep. He took out his favorite file, Hansen Development, and began to review their new strategy.

Noah was amazing. After starting his little hole-in-the-wall operation four years ago, he'd grown in leaps and bounds. He developed, sold, and leased property like crazy. He was still located above the Roger Frey Paint & Supply, but instead of the small space he'd leased several years before Noah now leased the whole upper level of the building. He employed fifty people in the office alone, and more than one hundred men and women worked on his construction crews. He kept Alex extremely busy. They'd just started plans for a development project in Sioux Falls that summer.

Alex smiled. *Noah could single-handedly redevelop all of South Dakota if he were given the chance.*

Tillie's best friend from birth was Ginger Engleson. Ginger's father, Burt, was one of Giuseppe's oldest and best friends, and he had decided to retire. He sold his road construction business and made Giuseppe an offer he couldn't refuse.

For many years Giuseppe had wanted to build a second restaurant and name it "Angelo's II," however, he had never been able to find someone willing to manage it. Burt was more than willing to try his hand at the restaurant business and asked Giuseppe for his help.

"And this parcel is big enough for what we need?" Burt clarified as he and Giuseppe assessed the empty lot on the east side of Sioux Falls. He swaggered along beside Giuseppe as they previewed the land, and Giuseppe, again, marveled at the shape of Burt's body. Burt was in his early sixties, but still muscular and well-built for a man his age. He was balder than Giuseppe, but somehow, or so Giuseppe thought, it didn't make him look as old.

"More than enough," Giuseppe assured. His heart pounded with excitement as he surveyed the empty lot. *Angelo's dream was to have two ristoranti.*

"Well, it's sure nice to get in off the road. I never liked traveling that much. This way I can be home with Diane every night." Burt took a deep breath. "When do we make an offer?"

"Alex will make an offer in a few weeks. He needs some kind of an estimate from the builder first." As Giuseppe looked out at the empty lot before them, his heart stumbled. *Would that not be strange if...No, Noah would not travel all the way to Sioux Falls for something this trivial.*

Burt nodded again and breathed a sigh of relief. "I'm sure glad your son-in-law is a lawyer. He probably knows everybody."

Giuseppe pretended a smile. *Lucky me.*

Harv Meyers, Noah's personnel manager, was a short, portly man with a balding head and serious brown eyes. He wore tiny spectacles, and there was always a freshly-sharpened pencil behind his ear. His suits were always black, and the tails of his pressed white shirt seemed to never be completely tucked. However, he performed his duties in a most expert fashion, even though Melinda verbally chastised him for ambiguous errors whenever she had the chance. Dealing with Noah's personal assistant was a task he dreaded.

"Here's the paperwork on Noah's new hire," he said as he laid a thin file before Melinda and reflexively backed away.

Melinda looked up from her work and scowled at the poor man. "Ben Simmons?" she barked.

Harv swallowed so hard he was afraid she'd heard him.

Melinda reached for the file. She faked a smile and looked Harv in the eye. "When does Mr. Simmons start?"

Harv took another protective step back, cleared his throat, and answered, "He'll be in tomorrow."

Melinda gave him one professional nod and then looked back at the file on her desk.

Harv let out his breath. Her actions indicated he'd been dismissed and could leave her presence with honor. He turned and hurried from the office.

"I can't *believe* I can't unload the place," Noah moaned to Maggie May later that afternoon over lunch. "And she's got the thing so loaded up with option periods I can't sell it to anyone else." He sighed heavily and added, "She'll probably be leasing it until the day she dies. I can't believe I did such a *stupid* thing."

Maggie looked at him thoughtfully. *It wasn't such a stupid thing. You just changed your mind.*

Maggie May West was a middle-aged black woman who'd run a tough business, with the help of her sister, Estelle, for thirty-five years. Unable to acquire jobs in the late forties, the two of them had gone to work for Noah Hansen's father, Earl, in his bar. When Earl Hansen passed away, he left the bar to his son, Joshua. But Joshua was a minister and had no desire to make money from a place that sold liquor. On top of that, Joshua's younger brother, Noah, was a disobedient handful, and Joshua and his wife, Mona, had been named the boy's guardians. Considering the circumstances, Joshua *gifted* the bar to Maggie, hoping to never have to deal with it again. Over the years, however, Noah had developed a friendship with the old barfly.

"So, do you ever think about her anymore?" Maggie asked. She hadn't intended to ask about Angel, it just blurted out. Maggie still thought of her every morning when she came to work and saw the painting hanging where it had hung for the last five years.

Noah shrugged and answered with a soft smile, "Sometimes, but I've got Carrie and Tiger now, and it's like Angel didn't even happen. I guess I'm glad I met her, because she gave me the inspiration to straighten out my life, but..." Noah chuckled, "...sometimes I think maybe she was just an angel, sent by God to get me straight."

Maggie rolled her eyes and snorted. "Oh, brother, Noah. You mean to tell me that God sends His angels into bars?"

Noah laughed. "Well, sure, Maggie. He sends them everywhere." He got off of his stool and said, "I gotta get going. I'm busier than that one-legged man today, if you know what I mean."

Maggie nodded. "By the way, did you hire that new foreman you been talkin' about?"

Noah chuckled as he recalled the look on Melinda's face when he informed her of Ben's hire. "And Melinda's as mad as a little wet hen."

Maggie shook her head. "Why do you even keep that ornery woman around?"

Noah shrugged. "Well, for one thing, she takes care of tons of stuff I *hate*, like opening the mail, paperwork, and stuff. Plus, she's super-organized —"

"You mean controlling."

Noah laughed. "Yeah, well, she does a really good job holding down the fort."

Maggie sighed. "I guess that's gotta count for something." She took a stick of candy from the jar on the counter and handed it to Noah. "That's for Tiger. Make sure he gets it, and tell Carrie 'Hi' from me."

Noah slipped the candy into his shirt pocket and smiled. "I will, Maggie." And he left.

Maggie sighed and shook her head as she glanced at the haunting painting that still hung in her bar...*It was the spring of 1975, only five years ago, and she had been so beautiful*...The name of the painting was *Obedience,* and it was a very dramatic depiction of a woman, whom Angel had claimed was her mother, with an old horse. Maggie had bought it at an art show from the girl who'd claimed to be Angel. Tucked in the frame was a snapshot Maggie's sister, Estelle, had taken of Noah and Angel standing together at the bar. That had been her last night in town and Noah had fallen in love. In fact, Angel had agreed to marry him before she left.

Maggie let out her breath as she studied the painting. *Noah hasn't had a drink since you left...you'd be so proud of what he's done with his life.*

Estelle came out of the kitchen and noticed Maggie's pensive stare.

"Whatcha thinkin' about, Maggie?" she asked, even though she knew the answer, because Estelle thought about it every day, too.

Maggie slowly shook her head and looked at her sister. "Nothin', baby."

Estelle only nodded...*Why don'tcha just pray about it, Maggie, and get it over with?*

Mona's red hair glistened in the early spring sun, and her green eyes shone with delight as she gave the safety swing another push.

"Now hang on!" she said in her Southern drawl as she gave her nephew another push. "We're gonna go *really* fast this time!"

"Faster, Auntie Mona! Faster!" Ty squealed with delight.

Mona laughed as she watched him glide along in his favorite activity. His dimples gave into his giggles, and his strawberry-blond hair glowed like a halo. *What a blessing you've become!*

Three years ago, it had been quite a different story. His mother and father wanted to abort the pregnancy, but Noah talked Carrie out of it. She didn't want to give the baby up for adoption, so Noah offered to marry her and help raise the child. Carrie wasn't thrilled with the new circumstances, but she agreed to marry Noah when the father of her baby left town.

At first Carrie was openly belligerent toward Noah and his brother and sister-in-law. Even though Joshua and Mona tried to be friendly, Carrie refused to consider their affections. She wouldn't go to church with Noah, and she wouldn't spend time with Mona. However, as the months rolled by, Carrie began to soften. She started calling Mona about things like how to prepare a roast, what's involved in making a pie crust, and how to know when the noodles are done. As Mona had understood Noah and Carrie's marital *arrangement*, he was supposed to do the cooking, and she did the laundry. Why did she want to learn how to prepare food? Mona never asked. Instead, she went over and gave Carrie a few pointers on some simple meals. Carrie had never prepared a morsel in her life, and this provided for some very comical situations. It drew the two women together—first with humor and then with accomplishment—and they soon became very close. The increasing time Mona and Carrie spent together also led to the changes gradually happening between Noah and Carrie.

At first there were sweet glances and tender words between the two of them as they cared for Carrie's newborn baby. Noah was taken with Carrie's baby, whom she'd named "Tyler" but Noah called him "Tiger," after his favorite baseball team. He fed him, rocked him, and talked to him, and Carrie reminded him not to spoil the baby. Noah reassured her that everything would be fine.

Soon Noah started coming home with flowers and sweet cards for Carrie. Then he asked Mona if she and Joshua would mind watching little Ty for a couple of hours while they went to a show. It surprised Joshua and Mona, but it was fun to care for the good-natured little baby, and they were more than happy to oblige.

One night, early in the fall, Mona saw Noah give Carrie a tender kiss on their porch swing, and that's when she knew. Those two were up to something, and it wasn't just taking care of Carrie's baby. When they looked into each other's eyes that night, all that was happening between them was a dead giveaway.

By Christmas, Noah had changed his bedroom into a sewing room for Carrie, and Joshua discreetly inquired where he would sleep. Noah blushed at the question and answered, *"With my wife."*

Their hostile arrangement had little by little blossomed into a romantic marriage, where they not only fell in love with the newborn baby but with each other as well, drastically changing their original plans. Two lonely and hurting people found love in the most unusual of circumstances. Joshua and Mona thanked God every day—especially when it was revealed that Noah had led Carrie to the Lord.

Mona had promised to sit with Ty, who was now nearly three years old, while Carrie went to a doctor's appointment. The weather was warm enough, and Mona had taken Ty outside to play on the wooden swing set Noah had built for him last summer. She saw Carrie's car pull into the driveway.

"Mommy's home!" Ty yelled with a smile. He wiggled to free himself from the safety swing. "Help me, Auntie Mona!"

Mona laughed, helped him to get free of the swing, and set him on the ground. Ty pranced up to his mother, and she scooped him up to give him a hug and kiss.

"Were you good for Auntie Mona?" she asked with a smile.

"He was perfect," Mona said as she patted the little boy's back. "He is such a good boy." She looked at Carrie. "And how was the doctor?"

Carrie blushed and looked away from Mona. She set Ty back on the ground and sighed with contentment. "Mona, I'm pregnant."

"Oh, my goodness!" Mona gasped, and threw her arms around Carrie. "Have you told Noah?"

Carrie shook her head. "No. I tried to stop by the office, but he was already gone. So I'll just have to wait until tonight." She took a deep breath and said with a smile, "He's gonna be so excited."

"Oh, I can't believe it!" Mona exclaimed. She gave Carrie another embrace and cried, "Praise the Lord!"

Carrie laughed... *Yes, praise the Lord!*

"Well, I have to get going, Carrie Darlin'," Mona said as she began to back away. I have Bible study with Estelle this afternoon... but you call me later and tell me what Noah says."

Carrie smiled and nodded. "Will do, Mona."

Maggie glanced at the corner booth and shook her head. Mona had met Estelle in the bar once a week for the last two years. They read their Bibles and prayed together, and often invited Maggie to join them. Maggie always refused. She didn't believe in God and had no desire to waste her time reading about Him. She softly snorted as she watched them...*This is the dumbest thing Estelle's ever done.*

Estelle sighed and looked into her coffee cup. "I just don't understand it, Mona. I can't get Maggie to pray with me."

Mona nodded in understanding. "But the decision has to come from inside Maggie. We'll keep praying for her, Estelle."

Estelle nodded and looked into Mona's eyes. There was more she wanted to say, but something made her hesitate.

Mona smiled and patted Estelle's hand. "I can tell there's somethin' else on your mind. What is it, darlin'?"

Estelle shrugged. "Remember Angel?"

"Of course," Mona answered, blinking away the sudden emotion in her eyes. *Why are we talking about Angel again? Are we really going to have this conversation again?*

Estelle looked into Mona's green eyes. "I think of her every day, Mona. Don't know why. Just do. Every day, I dust off her pretty picture, and I find myself humming their song." She cleared her throat and sweetly sang, "Her brow is like the snowdrift, her throat is like the swan, her face it is the fairest, that e'er the sun shone on...mmmm-mmm...Annie Laurie."

Mona was taken aback by Estelle's obvious emotional attachment to the mysterious Angel. She wanted to respond somehow but was again at a loss for words.

"I miss her," Estelle went on. "I can't explain it, Mona, but I miss that person we called Angel. We talked about her every day for more than a year, and now we don't even say her name."

Mona swallowed hard and gave Estelle's hand another tender pat, responding in the same way she had for the last several months. "But Noah's got Carrie now. We probably shouldn't think of Angel anymore."

Estelle nodded. "I know, and Carrie's a wonderful girl…" Her voice trailed off into silence.

As Mona looked at Estelle, she wondered if Maggie had noticed. Estelle's long-term memory had been gradually slipping, and the only thing she consistently seemed to remember was Angel. She talked about her every time they were alone together for tea or during their Bible study.

Mona took a soft breath and bit her lip. *What's going on, Lord?*

Noah parked his old Chevy pickup by the curb in front of his house in Chapel Valley. From there, he could see Carrie swinging Ty in the backyard. He smiled. *This is the life.* He'd never once regretted his decision to make Carrie his wife and raise her child as his own. He caught Ty's eye as he walked up the drive and gave the little boy a wave.

"Daddy!" Ty squealed with delight, and Carrie turned around. "Help me, Mommy," he said as he tried to wriggle free of the safety swing.

Carrie helped Ty from the swing and set him on the ground. He sprang down the driveway and jumped into Noah's arms.

Noah laughed and kissed him. "Hiya, Tiger! How are you today?"

"Good," Ty answered. He peeked into Noah's dusty shirt pocket, familiar with the regular treats that Maggie sent home. "For me?"

"From Maggie May," Noah answered.

Ty gasped as he retrieved the precious candy stick from Noah's pocket.

"You're spoiling him," Carrie reminded.

Noah smiled into her eyes, put his arm around her waist, and gave her a soft kiss. "Just a little…Hey, Melinda said you were looking for me this afternoon. Everything okay?"

Carrie nodded, and Noah was sure he saw a faint blush.

"What's up?"

"Put me down, Daddy," Ty requested. Noah gave him one more kiss and set him down. Ty took a seat in the driveway and unwrapped his candy.

"I had a doctor's appointment this morning." Carrie chuckled and her face flushed. "Noah, I'm pregnant."

Noah's mouth fell open in surprise as he stared at his wife, who laughed at his expression.

"Are you sure?"

Carrie laughed again and nodded. "I'm positive. The baby is due at Christmas time."

Noah took her into his arms and held her close, then he released her just enough to put his hand on her flat stomach. "That's the best news I've *ever* had." He looked into her eyes and kissed her. "I love you, Carrie."

CHAPTER 2

Palermo, Sicilia

"Thank you for coming all this way to see us wed!" Bianca threw her arms around Tara and kissed her cheek. "It means the world to us to have you here!"

"We would not have missed it." Tara smiled at the young Sicilian bride before her. One of Marquette's favored Chianti informants, Alessandro Gionelli, had, at long last, decided to wed his sweetheart, Bianca. For many years now, Bianca had assisted Alessandro with his investigations for Marquette Caselli. Recently Marquette had led Alessandro to the Lord, and encouraged him to marry Bianca so they could travel together.

"Please, let us sit for just a moment," Bianca said as she gathered handfuls of her gown and adjusted it for sitting. They seated themselves at a small table not far from their husbands. Tara glanced at Marquette, who was enjoying what appeared to be a very comical conversation with Alessandro and his groomsmen just a short distance away. She waved at him and then smiled at Bianca.

The weather was warm for the season on the Sicilian coastline, and it made for a beautiful wedding. At the last moment, the bride decided to move her nuptials out of the Palermo Cathedral, and onto the Tyrrhenian Seacoast. Her parents and relatives rushed to make it happen, and the wedding was glorious. White cloths covered tables set on the private beach of the Manelli Villa. Lush oranges and tropical flowers were heaped in bowls, centered on each table. Bags of cookies marked each place setting, and the songs of a thousand birds filled the air. The Manelli staff had prepared a sumptuous feast of prosciutto, manicotti, beef and ziti, roasted turkey, sausage and peppers, fresh oysters, and a substantial, yet elegant, white cake.

"Now I have never understood completely the deception of Luigi Andreotti," Bianca began. Her dark eyes flashed with a frown. "I have waited a very long time to hear *your* side of the story. Please indulge me in this for my wedding gift."

Tara sighed with a smile. Most everyone in her childhood home of Castellina, in Chianti, Italia, knew of the falling out between the Casellis and the Andreottis, and many had chosen sides. There was still anger and resentment towards Marquette Caselli for marrying Tara D'Annenci, for she had been promised to Luigi Andreotti.

"Oh goodness." Tara took a deep breath and let it out. "I was raised in the same valley as the Casellis and the Andreottis, so I knew both Marquette and Luigi from the time of my birth. My father was dear friends with Luigi's father, Lorenzo Andreotti. They fought side by side in World War II, and in the heat of a dreadful battle my dearest father promised me in marriage to Luigi. I was three years old, I believe, and Papa wanted what was best for me. Those were hard times in Chianti, and a young lady without support would suffer many terrible things. So Papa made that hasty promise —"

"But I thought you had the right to refuse a husband that you did not love," Bianca interrupted, frowning.

Tara nodded. "I did, but *not* until I had reached the age of accountability, which was sixteen. My father passed when I was fourteen years old, and my grandmother took me to Chicago to hide me from Luigi."

Bianca bit her lip thoughtfully. "Why did you not travel to South Dakota to see Marquette?"

"He was in transition at that time. The train crash that killed my family in Roma happened at the same time Marquette and his family were on their way to America. Marquette had agreed to mail me his new address when he arrived. I knew only that they would meet a man in New York City who would help them find their way on the trains across America.

"Marquette did send a package with his location, but it was intercepted by Luigi's soon-to-be-brother-in-law, Pietro, who gave the information to Luigi's father.

"A priest in Roma hid Nonna and me in a small apartment until he could send us to America. We settled in Chicago with my mother's sister and her husband, and that is where Luigi found us. His father demanded that I keep the promise, but Nonna refused —"

"And is it true that Luigi actually attended the university with you in order to persuade you to marry him?"

Tara nodded. "We spent many long years together. He begged for my hand, and I begged him for the location of my beloved Marquette."

"And Marquette knew nothing of your location?"

Tara shook her head. "The Andreottis told Marquette's family that all of us, including Nonna and me, had perished in the crash. He had no idea that I was even alive."

"Amazing." Bianca sighed and shook her head. "But Marquette eventually found you. How?"

Tara raised a dark brow and smiled. "Chasing the Ponerellos, of course." She giggled and opened her mouth to say more.

"My love," Marquette had placed his hand on her shoulder. Tara looked up into his eyes. "Alessandro has located a man on Ustica who was present the night we arrested the Ponerellos. Come. We must seek him out immediately."

Tara nodded and rose from her chair. She extended her hand to Bianca. "And it seems we are on the move again! God bless you and your marriage, beautiful Bianca."

Bianca rose to her feet and embraced Tara one last time. "*Arrivederci, mia bella sorella in Christo*. And God bless you in your quest for the Ponerellos."

In August of 1968, Marquette Caselli and his long-time business associate and best friend, John Peters, had traveled to Palermo, Sicily, to crack the biggest case of their lives. Since 1955, Italian and Sicilian authorities had pursued the most notorious Mafia family Sicily had ever known: The Ponerello Family. Finally, in August of 1968,

Marquette Caselli broke through an intercepted coded message. The message revealed that the Ponerello Family was hiding on the small fishing island of Ustica, just off the Sicilian coast. Though The Family attempted to shoot their way free that day, all thirty-eight members were captured.

A small freighter was used to ship them back to Sicily, where they were to be jailed while awaiting trial. Still missing were fifty loose diamonds heisted from a jeweler in Palermo. The diamonds had never been retrieved.

As the freighter began its departure from Ustica, Salvatore Ponerello, Jr., escaped his bonds and threw himself upon the rocks near the shoreline. Even though a body was never recovered, it was assumed he died. Salvatore's father cursed Marquette that day and promised revenge upon him and his family for years to come.

Ponerello's curse didn't come to pass, as it was at that moment Marquette discovered that his Tara was still alive, and he and John began a search in the opposite direction. As a result, they lost the trail of the missing Ponerellos. As far as they knew at that time, only two Ponerellos had been able to escape the confines of their criminal family. They were still thought to be alive somewhere in Europe.

In May of 1975, John Peters caught a lead on the Ponerellos in the Midwest. John had been missing ever since. Marquette and Tara believed him to have been murdered by one of the missing Ponerellos, though his body had not yet been recovered.

After almost five years of dead-ends, Alessandro Gionelli had located a man named Giovanni—an old fisherman in Ustica—willing to talk about the days when the Ponerellos ruled Sicily. Marquette and Tara rushed to Ustica to interview him.

Giovanni appeared to have an accurate memory of what transpired that night in August of 1968, now nearly twelve years ago.

"There were two young Americans, one of whom was Italian by birth, and they led the police to this very harbor." Giovanni's eyes twinkled beneath the hot sun of the day. "I was only seventy years old then, and I rowed my boat out with the rest of them. We took police into our boats from larger craft hidden farther out and then rowed closer to shore…" The old man paused to laugh heartily, and Marquette and Tara noticed he had no teeth. "Those Ponerellos! They had no idea what was about to happen! They were all collected, like butterflies in a net, and sent back to Palermo. Of course, Salvatore dashed himself upon the rocks, and I am certain he sent his miserable soul straight to Hell that day." The old man laughed again, obviously relishing his memories.

"And you have never seen any of them again?" Tara questioned.

Giovanni nodded as a crooked, toothless smile spread across his face. "Sometimes we see Salvatore's ghost down by the rocks, and he yells threats at whoever will listen. We tell the children to stay away from that place so Salvatore's evil soul does not come to rest in one of them."

Marquette raised one brow. "What sorts of threats?"

Giovanni narrowed his eyes. "That he will soon return and rule Sicilia with an iron hand."

Tara swallowed hard.

"And what of the elder son?" Marquette questioned further. "Has anyone ever seen or heard from Mario, or his young son, Antonio?"

Giovanni shook his head. "And we will not, my young friend. Mario escaped the clutches of his evil family many years ago. He wanted to live a life of honor and respect, and it embittered his father to no end. And do you not know? His father revoked the rights of the elder son from Mario and cast them upon Salvatore when Mario left the family."

Marquette nodded in understanding. He was all too familiar with the old story.

Mario Ponerello's once-black hair had completely silvered, and his sharp, dark eyes were lined with age and worry. But he smiled with pride as he looked into the face of his only son.

"So he has hired you. You have done well, my Antonio. We will never forget your sacrifice."

Antonio bowed before his father and kissed his hand. "I will do everything I can to keep the husband of Carrie and their children safe. You will always be able to count on me, Papa."

Mario nodded and took a deep breath. "In a few weeks you will take your vows, Antonio. Are you ready for this commitment?"

"I am ready at this moment to take my vows, Papa. Why do you not make me the Elder Son now?"

"Because you have not reached the age, my son," Mario reminded. "The time will come very soon enough, my Antonio. There is no need to rush."

Tillie's symptoms were even worse the next day. When she awoke, she vomited for an hour, thinking she might never stop. Alex drove her to the doctor.

After drawing blood and examining her, Dr. Lewis said, "I really can't find anything wrong. But maybe something will show up in your blood work." He looked at Alex. "Why don't you take her home and I'll give you guys a call this afternoon. If it's a bacterial infection, I'll prescribe an antibiotic. But for now, she looks like she could use a nap."

They went home and Tillie crawled into bed, curling up under the covers.

"I'm missing a *huge* test today," she groaned.

Alex sat down on the edge of the bed beside her and put a loving hand on her shoulder. "Can I get you anything?"

"Please, no. I just want to take a little nap. Maybe later."

"Okay. Well, I'll just sit here for a little while and work on some stuff. Maybe the doctor will call us back pretty soon."

Tillie nodded, and Alex got his files together and resumed his position in the chair beside their bed.

Joshua was surprised when Mona peeked into his office shortly before noon.

"What are you doing here?" He got to his feet, reached for her hand, and gave her a soft kiss. "I didn't know you were coming to town today."

"Well, I had some errands," she replied, "and I needed to talk to you about something. I was going to mention it last night, but didn't get around to it with all the news about Noah and Carrie…"

Joshua noticed the worried crease between her brows. "What's wrong, Mona?" He asked as he led her to the couch near the window.

They seated themselves, and Mona gave Joshua's hand a tender squeeze. "'Course, you know Estelle and I have been doing a little Bible study together." Joshua nodded in recollection, and Mona continued, "Well, Josh, she's started to talk about Angel —"

"Angel? Angel who?"

"Angel…You know, *Noah's Angel.*"

"Oh," Joshua nodded. "What for?"

Mona shrugged. "Beats me, but it's really starting to bother me… in fact, *I've* started to think about Angel every day. And I can't explain it, Josh, but it makes me so sad."

"Why? We never even met the woman."

"I know, but I feel…" she hesitated.

Joshua frowned. "Feel what?"

"I feel…compelled…to…to pray for her," she whispered.

"For Angel?"

Mona nodded.

"Hmm." Joshua frowned and sat quiet.

"Will you pray for her with me, Josh?"

Joshua was surprised, but he clasped his hands around his wife's. "Would you like to start?"

Mona nodded, and then she began to pray.

Alex was fixing himself a sandwich in the kitchen when the telephone rang.

"Mr. Martin?"

"Yes."

"This is Dr. Lewis. How's the missus?"

"She's sleeping," Alex answered. "Did you find anything?"

"I did. Based on the information she gave me this morning, and the elevated levels of some hormones in her blood, I'd have to say Tillie's pregnant."

Alex felt as if the floor had given way. He gripped the side of the cupboard with his free hand and said, "Pregnant? Being pregnant makes you *this* sick?"

"Some gals have a hard time with the first few months, but she's young and healthy," Dr. Lewis answered. "If you can get something into her stomach, it will probably help. Give her some crackers and ginger ale."

Alex swallowed to find his voice. "Thanks, Dr. Lewis."

"Congratulations, Alex, and don't worry too much. Everything else checked out normal."

Alex hung up the phone and staggered to the refrigerator. He fumbled with the ice bucket in the freezer, found a can of ginger ale, and added a straw.

"Pregnant." He shook his head and smiled. *That's funny. We hadn't planned that yet. She won't even graduate from college until the end of the month. She won't even celebrate her twenty-third birthday until after that. This is way too soon.*

He shuffled down the hall and into their bedroom. Tillie's black curls were spread out on the white pillow beneath her head, and he stood still in the doorway as he watched her. *She still seems so young...*

He made his way to the bed and took a careful seat on the edge. He set the ginger ale on the nightstand and put his hand gently on her shoulder. She opened her eyes and looked up at him.

"The doctor called," he said, feeling the slightest twinge of excitement in his stomach.

"What did he say?" she asked in a sleepy voice.

Alex softly laughed and shook his head. "We're going to have a baby."

"What?" She lifted her head from the pillow and looked into his eyes. "Did you say —"

"Yes!" He took her into his arms, held her close, and kissed the top of her head. "We're going to have a baby."

"You mean, I'm…pregnant?"

"Yes." He laid her back on the pillow.

"Wow." Tillie smiled and looked into his dark eyes. "I thought you had to plan something like this."

"Apparently not." He reached for the ginger ale. "And the doc says to try to put something in your stomach. It'll help."

Tillie took a sip from the straw he offered. "I can't believe it." She laughed despite her nausea. "Can you imagine me and you and a baby?"

Alex could imagine a baby quite easily. He was thirty years old—it was time to start a family.

In December of 1976, Marquette and Tara had gotten a lead on the Ponerello case. A motel manager in Miami, Florida, found John Peters' file tucked between a mattress and box spring. The duo's home telephone number had been scribbled on the front of it, and the manager had called them.

Upon investigation, Marquette and Tara learned that John had picked up a trail on a man named Jack Nelson. Nelson had owned a fishing business in Miami up until 1972, when he sold it, and was never heard from again.

After visiting with Giovanni in Ustica, Marquette and Tara traveled to Miami to interview the man who'd bought the business from Mr. Nelson.

"Well, Mr. Nelson sure didn't look like *that*," the buyer, Dave Jasper, insisted in his heavy Southern drawl as he pointed to the photograph Marquette held before him—the photo of Mario Ponerello.

Marquette frowned and shook his head. "But you said he had a foreign accent —"

"Yeah, sorta like yours. But he was a way taller fella, real dark, and he had a funny mark of some kind on his left cheek…like a scar or something."

Tara raised an eyebrow…*Perhaps Mario has tried to alter his appearance.* She produced the photograph of Mario's right-hand man, Schneider Rauwolf, the German who'd helped Mario and his young son, Antonio, escape Sicily in 1964.

"How about this man?" she asked. "Was he ever around?"

Dave nodded. "He came around a couple of weeks after I bought the place, looking for Mr. Nelson —"

"Looking for Mr. Nelson?" Marquette questioned.

"That's what he said. And he was with another fella he called 'Custer' and said they were on their way to Austin to work on the big campaign."

Tara frowned. "The big campaign?"

"The Presidential campaign. I guess Custer was some highfalutin' presidential campaign worker —" Someone called for Dave from the docks. He smiled at Marquette and Tara. "I'm real sorry, but I gotta get back to work. Do you need anything else from me?"

"Did this man say how long they'd be in Austin, or how they could be reached?" Marquette asked.

Dave shook his head. "Only said they'd find Mr. Nelson themselves, and then they left. Ain't seen 'em since."

"Thank you, Mr. Jasper." Tara smiled politely.

"Yes, thank you." Marquette extended his hand. "You have been a great help to us."

"No problem," he said, and hurried down the dock.

Marquette sighed and looked at his wife. "Why in the world do you suppose Mario and Rauwolf separated?"

Tara shook her head. "That seems odd."

"Mr. Jasper could not identify Mario from this photograph. Is it possible Mario had someone pose for him during the sale of the business, in order to hide his identity?"

"Of course it is possible, but why? And why in 1972? We had no idea he was in Miami at that time. He would have had no reason to hide his identity—"

"Unless he was running from Rauwolf?"

"I suppose we could attempt to find Rauwolf on this latest lead and ask him ourselves. We still know the lovely young lady who worked on the presidential campaign in South Dakota. Perhaps she can help us track down a 'Custer' in Austin who may, in turn, give us information on Rauwolf."

"That is probably a long shot, my Tara." Marquette took her hand and began to lead her away from the docks.

"A long shot we cannot afford to ignore," Tara added with a frown.

Alex went back to the office and Tillie dialed her mother's phone number. When Rosa answered, Tillie let out a giggle.

"Is it my Angel?" Rosa asked.

"Hi, Ma`ma…it's me. I have some news for you."

"Should you not be in class this day?"

Tillie giggled again. "I was really sick this morning and had to go to the doctor, Ma`ma."

"Well, you sound fine now. Is everything all right, my Angel?"

"It's great, Ma`ma!" Tillie's stomach went over a hill and she had to swallow hard. But she smiled as she exclaimed, "I'm going to have a baby!"

Rosa gasped, and then she laughed. "Oh, my Angel! That is wonderful. I am so happy for you, my dear! When will this all happen?"

"December first!"

Rosa laughed again. "Your dreams are coming true, Angel. God has blessed you!"

"I'm calling my brothers next, so I gotta go. I love you, Ma`ma."

Tillie's brother, Vincenzo, lived on a spacious ranch near Centerville, South Dakota. He'd inherited the ranch when their Uncle Angelo passed away in 1964. Reata, Vincenzo explained to Tillie, came from the name of Rock Hudson's ranch in the 1956 movie classic *The Giant*, one of his favorite movies.

Vincenzo was in the main house with Kate for lunch when Tillie called. Kate saw that he was having a quiet conversation, and that he was smiling, so she pressed him for information as soon as he hung up the phone.

"That was Angel," Vincenzo smiled. "It seems that she has been blessed. Our little Angel is with child."

Kate didn't want to frown, but she couldn't help herself.

Vincenzo raised a curious brow at his wife. "I thought that you would be pleased. The wife of your dear brother, my sister, is having a child. It has long been her dream to be a mother."

Kate slowly nodded. "But Alex is so busy right now…he can hardly find the time for her as it is."

Vincenzo rolled his eyes. "Lovely Kate, Angel does not require the constant attention of her husband. She is a very independent spirit."

Kate didn't say anything, but she couldn't disagree more with her husband. Kate's brother, Alex, the husband of Vincenzo's beloved young sister, was far too ambitious to attend to a pregnant wife.

Tillie caught up with her brother, Marquette, through his liaison, reaching him at his hotel in Florida. She gave him the news in a quick conversation, explaining that she still had to call their brother, Petrice. Marquette pretended to be excited, but the news made him sick to his stomach.

Tara came in the room after enjoying a quick swim, to find her husband standing beside the telephone and frowning.

"What is it, Marquette?" she asked curiously. "Have you already heard back from our contact in South Dakota?"

Marquette shook his head and sighed heavily. "No, Tara. I just heard from my sister. It seems that she is pregnant."

Tara took a breath. "Oh, goodness." She sat down on the bed and looked at her husband. He'd never liked the husband of his sister. Tara was certain that the thought of Tillie carrying Alex's child would do nothing to dissuade those feelings.

Marquette sighed again. "I suppose he will not be slowing down for this event."

Tara had to nod in agreement. Alex never seemed to slow down for anything.

Marquette shook his head. "I begged my father not to allow this debacle."

"Marquette, perhaps you should give Alex a chance before you hasten to pass judgment."

Marquette locked his jaw. "I know a blackguard when I see one, Tara. What I cannot figure out is why my father never saw it."

Tillie loved children, and wanted more than anything to have them; however, her morning sickness wasn't as delightful as the promise of bringing a new life into the world. And she still had to finish the last few weeks of her senior year. Every morning she awakened with intense nausea, and Alex coaxed her into having a few soda crackers and ginger ale on ice. She still felt a little "gaggy," as she called it, but at least the snack kept her from "tossing her cookies." She forced herself to take a prenatal vitamin, loaded her backpack with more crackers and ginger ale, and toughed out another day of classes.

Naturally, every woman around her who'd been pregnant before offered their share of advice and remedies. The best counsel came from Rosa, who said, "No matter what you do, you will be sick until the end of the twelfth week. I have never seen it any different."

"And then it will be over?" Tillie nibbled on the biscotti her parents had brought over.

"Yes," Rosa promised. "And then you will be able to enjoy the babe as it grows. Soon she will move, and you will be able to see her." She gave Tillie's flat stomach a soft pat. "Right here. You will see her *right here.*"

Besides doing a Bible study with Estelle, Mona devoted one day a week to Carrie's continuing walk with the Lord. Carrie loved to read the Bible and spend time with Mona, talking about what she'd learned. So on Thursday afternoons, when Ty settled down for his nap, Carrie and Mona brewed a pot of tea and opened the Bible to whatever was on Carrie's mind.

"Okay, let me see if I have this straight," Carrie quietly mused. She squinted for a better look at the verses and read aloud, "And Peter answered Him and said, 'Lord, if it be Thou, bid me come unto Thee on the water. And He said, 'Come.' And when Peter was come down out of the ship, he walked on the water, to go to Jesus. But when he saw the wind boisterous, he was afraid; and beginning to sink, he cried, saying, 'Lord, save me.' And immediately Jesus stretched forth His hand, and caught him, and said unto him. 'O thou of little faith, wherefore didst thou doubt?'" Carrie looked up at Mona with a soft smile. "And it's your impression that this record is given to us so that we draw a comparison between the pull of the water against Peter and the pull of sin against us?"

"Exactly! When we are being pulled into sin, all we have to do is trust in Jesus, and He will pull us right out of the trouble—just like He pulled Peter out of the water."

Carrie nodded. "Interesting. I never saw it that way until now."

Mona patted Carrie's hand. "And I have the *funniest* story about that."

Carrie smiled and waited. Mona's stories were always the best.

Mona cleared her throat and began in her wonderful Southern drawl, "My sister, Charlene, had this little problem with her credit cards. Well, it was more than just a little problem. You see, Charlene loves to shop. One by one, she ran them credit cards up to their max, until she was in debt nearly twenty-two-thousand dollars. Instead of asking Jesus to pull her out of the sin of her overspending, she waited until the credit card companies cut her off. Momma and I intervened.

We confronted her about her spending and prayed over her, asking Jesus for help to pay all the bills.

"Well, soon Charlene was offered a real good job at the grocery store. She sent the credit card companies as much as she could, but secretly she prayed to Jesus to send her twenty-two-thousand dollars. Momma and I didn't know about that part.

"Anyways, one day there came a news flash on the radio. Some woman had found a sack of money in her front yard, and guess how much was in that sack of money?" Mona looked to Carrie for the answer.

Carrie speculated with a giggle, "Twenty-two-thousand dollars?"

Mona nodded. "As soon as Charlene had heard the news flash, she called Momma and claimed that the twenty-two-thousand was *hers* and that whatever angel God had sent with the money had dropped it into the wrong yard!"

Carrie laughed out loud, and so did Mona.

Mona took a deep breath and continued her story. "'Course Momma was flabbergasted by Charlene's hysteria. She told that girl that the money wasn't hers, and that there was probably a reasonable explanation for what had happened. Sure enough, when all was said and done, that money belonged to a bank that had been robbed earlier in the day. Seems the robber dropped his sack of money while he was trying to get away from the policemen."

Carrie laughed again and shook her head. "Oh, Mona, your stories are *so funny!*"

"I know…it's 'cause they're true." Mona nodded as she reached for her cup of tea.

"So, how did it all turn out for Charlene? Does she still owe money?" Carrie asked.

Mona shook her head. "No. Jesus blessed her with a second job at the gas station, and she finally got everything paid off. She keeps her eyes on Jesus now instead of on her credit limits."

Carrie laughed and looked into Mona's twinkling green eyes. *Thank you, God, for giving me this family.*

Noah Hansen chartered a small plane to Sioux Falls to have a look at the property on which Alex was ready to make an offer. He rented a car at the Sioux Falls airport and followed Alex's directions to the southeast side of town, where he was to meet with a realtor named Ed Brown. Ed would also give Noah a brief tour of the surrounding area. After that, Noah and Ed were to come to Alex's office together to discuss their offer.

"There will be several new families moving into this area," Ed explained as he and Noah walked through the grassy field of the future job site.

"And the owner will sell the entire parcel—not just pieces?" Noah asked.

"That's correct."

A white Suburban pulled onto the site, tooting its horn, and they turned their heads.

"Who's that?" Noah asked as they watched a small, dark man exit the driver's side and another taller, more-muscular man exit the passenger side.

"Hello!" called the smaller man through a thick accent and a happy smile. "We are looking for Ed Brown!"

Ed smiled, gave them a friendly wave, and whispered, "It's the restaurant owner I told you about. You're gonna love working with this guy. He's a hoot!"

As the pair got closer, Noah saw they were older, at least in their mid-sixties. When the darker gentleman smiled, his black eyes sparkled in the most familiar way.

"Is it Ed Brown?" Giuseppe asked as he extended his hand in greeting.

"Yes."

"Giuseppe Caselli," he introduced, and turned to the gentleman next to him. "This is my dear friend, Burt Engleson."

Ed shook hands with Burt and turned his eyes back to Giuseppe. "It's good to finally meet you in person." He looked at Noah and added, "I've only talked with him over the telephone."

Giuseppe's eyes fell upon Noah then, and his friendly smile seemed to fade. Noah saw the hesitation in Giuseppe's expression, but he extended his hand in greeting and offered the older man an open smile. "Noah Hansen."

Giuseppe took Noah's hand and gave it a firm shake. As he looked into Noah's eyes, he felt his regret rise from his heart and into his throat. *Oh, my God, why have You put me here this day? Why have You chosen for me to meet this man—the man I sinned against so grievously?* Giuseppe swallowed as hard as he could and forced a smile onto his face as he looked from Noah to Burt. "We are building a restaurant."

Ed nodded. "Mr. Hansen is our developer."

Giuseppe looked into Noah's eyes. *I am more sorry than you will ever know, Noah Hansen, and I still pray for you every day of my miserable old life.* "When can we take a look at a lease?" he asked.

"My lawyer is working on them," Noah answered, noticing the unusual length of Giuseppe's glance and, *again*, that familiar expression in his sparkling black eyes. "Have we met before?"

Giuseppe's pounding heart nearly stopped. "I do not believe so." And in an effort to continue the conversation he asked, "Who is your lawyer?"

"Alex Martin."

"He is the husband of my daughter."

"Oh, you're kidding?" Noah grinned. "He's practically my best friend."

In Noah's dancing blue eyes, Giuseppe saw the exact likeness of the man Angel had painted five years before—the last and *best* painting she had ever created.

"You must be Senator Caselli's father then," Noah continued, trying to somehow lighten the little man's sinking mood.

"Yes, I am Petrice's father."

"He's an amazing man," Noah complimented. "He's not afraid of anything. I'm glad he's in Washington."

Giuseppe nodded and looked at Burt. "I suppose we should be hurrying along. We just stopped to see the site."

"Well, it was nice meeting you," Ed said.

"Yes, it was nice meeting you," Noah added, giving Giuseppe one more glance.

"Thank you for your time, gentlemen," Burt said as he turned and began to walk back to the Suburban.

"Yes, thank you." Giuseppe gave Noah one last look and suddenly blurted, "Mr. Hansen, do you live around here?"

Noah shook his head. "I live in Rapid City."

Giuseppe nodded. *Thank goodness he is still three-hundred-and-fifty miles away.* "How long will you be in town?"

"Just a few hours. I need to get home to my family."

Giuseppe swallowed and nodded. *Home to his family...of course.* He caught the glint of Noah's gold wedding band and looked from the ring into Noah's smiling eyes...*My Angel should have put that ring upon your finger...* He took a soft breath and began to back away. "Well, I must be running along. Have a good day." And with that, he turned and trotted back to his truck where Burt was already waiting.

Ed chuckled. "Nervous little guy, wasn't he?"

Noah nodded, but there was just something too familiar about the rattled old man that he couldn't put aside.

"Hey, you're frowning," Ed teased, and he gave Noah a friendly slap on the back. "Do you still want to see the plat?"

Noah took a breath and brought himself back to the business at hand. "Show me the plat."

After the awkward meeting with Giuseppe Caselli and Burt Engleson, Noah and Ed went over to Alex Martin's office to prepare an offer for the owner of the property.

"Noah!" Alex extended his hand to his favorite client.

Jan, the Martins' receptionist, had to smile as she watched them. Noah was so unlike any of Alex's other clients. It was almost comical to see the two men together. Noah wore sturdy jeans, tan Carhartt work shirts, and cowboy boots. In contrast, Alex was dressed in an Italian suit and Gucci leather shoes. Noah's sandy-colored hair was always messy, while Alex's black hair was combed flawlessly into place. Noah's hands were always rough and callused, as if he'd just walked off the job site, unlike the other men in the office, who had never lifted a hammer or saw in their lives. And while Alex Martin was the most handsome man Jan had ever seen, Noah had an unpolished masculinity and charm not found in "professional" men.

She sighed as she watched Alex lead Noah and Ed down the hall to his office. *Too bad he's married.*

"So, gentlemen," Alex said as he gestured for them to take a seat in the chairs before his desk. He closed the door to his office and seated himself. "How does the site look?"

"It looked great to me," Noah answered. "I think we can go ahead and give 'em an offer, as long as it's for the entire parcel. I want to put a little mall on the west side of that restaurant."

Ed affirmed, "No piecing it out. No problem."

Alex looked at Ed. "I can have papers to your office by this afternoon." He handed Ed a file. "There's the formal offer if you want to review it with your seller."

Ed took the file and glanced inside. "All right then." He got to his feet. "Well, I guess you guys don't need me anymore." He smiled at Noah and then at Alex. "I'll take this directly to the seller and call you if something goes haywire."

"Okay," Alex concluded as he got to his feet again, opening his office door. "Call Shondra if something needs to be changed in the wording or whatever. I'll be in court this afternoon."

Ed left, and Alex took his seat again. "Wow. That was the quickest meeting I think I've ever had." He leaned back in his chair and looked at Noah. "Hey, did you buy into that foreign stock Sam recommended?"

Noah nodded with a smile, and Alex couldn't help but laugh out loud. "So did we," he laughed again. "Man, I made a bundle. How 'bout you guys?"

"Oh, man, my stockbroker bought the stuff at something like ten or twelve dollars, and we wound up selling it for over a hundred."

Alex's dark eyes shone with excitement, "And I've got some *really* good news. Tillie and I are expecting."

"No kidding? So are Carrie and I. When's your baby due?"

"December first. How about yours?"

"December twenty-fifth."

"Has Carrie been very sick?"

Noah shook his head. "Not at all. Why? Is Tillie sick?"

"Oh, boy," Alex grimaced, "she's been *really* nauseated. She had to call me to come and get her from school one day. Couldn't even drive."

"She's only got a few weeks of school left, right?" Noah asked.

"And she'll be glad to get it over with."

Noah remembered the awkward meeting with Tillie's father that morning. "By the way, I met your father-in-law."

"Where did you see Giuseppe?"

"Over at the site," Noah answered. "He was with some Burt guy."

"They're planning to branch off of the existing restaurant Giuseppe owns. They're going to call it 'Angelo's II.' Burt is the father of one of my best friends, Andy Engleson. He's a minister here in town. In fact, he married Tillie and me."

"It was quite a surprise to meet the Senator's father. He certainly has a heavy accent."

"He's always spoken that way. It's funny, his sons have accents, but they've softened with time. Not Giuseppe's. His stayed thick."

"So your wife is Italian?" Noah asked.

Alex nodded. "But she was born in America."

"What brought them to America?" Noah asked. *Something about this is really familiar…*

"Giuseppe's brother, Angelo, first came after World War II," Alex explained. "That was in 1945. He'd always begged Giuseppe to come with him, but Giuseppe didn't want to leave Italy. Finally, in 1956, Angelo got sick with heart disease, and Giuseppe made the move. The boys were teenagers, and Rosa was pregnant." Alex chuckled as he recalled, "In fact, I still remember the day they got here. My dad and Sam went to New York to meet their ship and help them get across America on the trains. They could barely speak English. My sister, Kate, was fifteen, and she fell completely in love with Giuseppe's middle son, Vincenzo. They finally got married in 1962, just a couple months after they graduated from college."

"So you've known that family for quite a while."

"We all lived on the same block. In fact, our parents are all still over there. The Englesons, the Casellis, and my parents. You can see the Casellis' front porch from my folks' front porch." Alex smiled wistfully as he recalled his childhood. "Andy and I used to pretend we were soldiers and hide in the bushes. We'd spy on Vincenzo and Kate when they were sitting on the Casellis' front porch. Kate used to get so mad at us…"

Noah pretended to laugh at the humorous story, but in the back of his memories, he was recalling another story that had been told to him five years before. A story about a *powerful warrior who fought with the Allies in Italy…Angel's father*. Noah shook off the old memory and attempted to focus on what Alex was saying. *Besides, he calls his wife Tillie, and she's studying comparative literature. Angel had planned on studying art. And, while Alex is a great lawyer and a nice guy, my Angel would have never been attracted to someone like him.*

Rosa watched Giuseppe's trembling hand as he dialed the long-distance number she'd helped him to acquire. She wondered what the outcome of this would be, and why he should even care now. After all, Angel had married Alex and was carrying his child. It shouldn't matter anymore. However, when Giuseppe had returned home after his chance encounter with Noah, he insisted on contacting the brother of

Frances Martin. Frances' brother, Mac, had been friends with Noah's brother, Joshua, since the 1950s.

As Giuseppe waited for the connection to be made, he saw Rosa's frown. "Do not look at me in such a way," he murmured.

"You should not be doing this, Giuseppe. Why torture ourselves? What can come of this?"

"MacKenzie Dale," Giuseppe said into the phone. Apparently he had made his connection. "This is Giuseppe Caselli. Yes, I will hold." He looked at Rosa and whispered, "Because I want to know."

"Know what?" Rosa whispered. "You made a decision we cannot undo. We cannot change the past, and you are playing with fire, Giuseppe."

"*Shh!*"

"Well, hello, Giuseppe," MacKenzie said into the phone. "You're the last person I ever expected to give me a call."

Giuseppe cleared his throat. "Yes, well, hello, Mac. I have some questions for you."

"Shoot."

"Well, I had an opportunity to meet the brother of your friend, Joshua Hansen. The preacher?"

"Oh, he's such a nice kid. Where did you meet Noah?"

"He will be developing a property where my friend and I are planning to put another restaurant," Giuseppe answered. "I was just wondering what kind of a fellow he is. Can he be trusted?"

"Heck, yes," MacKenzie answered with a chuckle. "He's the most popular developer in Rapid City. Everybody loves him. Why?"

"But what of his past, Mac? Is he not the boy who gave his brother such a difficult time?"

"Well, yes, he is. But he straightened out his life quite a few years ago. I thought Frances told you about that."

"She mentioned he stopped drinking," Giuseppe said. "And we are still praying for him."

"Josh tells me the poor guy was jilted back in '75, and *that's* what really straightened him out. Apparently, he asked a gal to marry him, and she agreed. Then she just up and dumped him. It nearly killed the kid. She really broke his heart."

"But he married?"

"And that was the craziest thing. The girl he married was pregnant and threatening to abort, so Noah up and married her. Everybody in town knows the kid belongs to a worthless sidewinder, but Noah treats him like his own."

Giuseppe's heart pounded hard against the walls of his chest. "Is he still married to her?"

"Yep, and from what I hear from Josh, they get along really well. In fact, they've got a little one of their own on the way. Josh says they were just two lonely people who got together and found love, and I say good for them." He paused and added, "But as far as a developer, I wouldn't go with anyone else. Noah Hansen is the best in the business. He's an honest man."

Giuseppe nodded. "Well, all right then, Mac. Please do not tell my son-in-law I called about Noah. He thinks a great deal of the man."

"Secret's safe with me," Mac said, and they hung up.

Giuseppe put the phone back into its cradle and looked into Rosa's eyes. "Oh, my Rosa, what have I done?"

Rosa put her arm over Giuseppe's shoulder as warm tears streamed down her face. "Do not fret this thing, my love. What is done is done, and we cannot go back now."

Marquette studied the old, yellowed photographs and notes with intense interest. It had always been an obsession for him. The one that got away and eluded him still. He looked at the ornate dagger in the photos and recalled vividly the time he was summoned to Sicilia to investigate a diamond robbery in 1968. During that investigation, he'd uncovered one of the biggest Mafia families their country had ever known—earning him a world-wide reputation. By the time he'd arrived in Sicilia, however, Mario and Antonio Ponerello had been gone for four years, and he'd never been able to catch up to them. He sighed as he remembered. He touched the symbols on the handle of the dagger that identified the Ponerello family. They'd put their family shield and patriarch symbol on each handle, and bragged that their enemies would be dead before they'd realized that they'd been cut.

The Ponerellos had built their lives and faith around the Greek myth of Daedalus, an inventor and builder who killed his young worker, Talos. Daedalus then left Greece for the island of Crete. There he built the Minotaur's Labyrinth. King Minos would not allow Daedalus to leave. So, Daedalus fashioned for himself and his son, Icarus, wings of wax and feathers. Then they attempted to fly away together. Icarus flew too close to the sun and his wings melted and he fell to his death. Daedalus, however, escaped to Sicilia, where he changed his name to Ponerello, and planned his revenge.

Marquette's search for the Ponerellos continued until his dearest friend, John Peters, disappeared. No one had seen or heard from him since 1975.

"*Il Dagger Del Dinastia...*" Tara whispered. "*The Dynasty's Dagger*. What do you hope to discover in reviewing these old files so intently, my love? Salvatore, Sr., is still imprisoned, and at the age of ninety-one is nearly dead. His elder son, Mario, would be sixty-one by now and, with no family to help him, is as paralyzed as his father —"

"But Antonio will soon be twenty-two —"

Tara let out a soft gasp. "The age of passage."

Marquette took a deep breath and slowly let it out. "My spirit tells me that something is afoot with our old friends the Ponerellos."

"But what if Noah finds out?" Carrie whispered to her stepfather as they watched Ty play on the swing set in the backyard.

"Antonio is very discreet. Noah will *not* find out," he assured. "In a few days Antonio will take his vows, and we will all be much safer—"

"I think we should just tell Noah, and call the cops —"

"No, we must not involve the police, for they will surely send Antonio and me back to Sicilia, and then who will care for your sister and mother?"

Carrie reluctantly nodded. *This is going to get worse before it gets better.*

CHAPTER 3

"This is interesting," Tara said as she and Marquette went meticulously through the old campaign information.

Marquette looked up to see the mysterious expression on his wife's face.

She lifted one eyebrow and tossed a paper in his direction. "This is a terribly long shot, but there *is* a Custer Thomas who worked on the campaign in Texas in 1972, and is now what I would consider highfalutin'. He is the Attorney General for the state of Wyoming and is up for reelection this November. And he fits the description of the man Mr. Jasper spoke of."

Marquette frowned as he picked up the paper and read the information.

"I think it is most interesting that this man is in Wyoming," Tara continued, "considering that is where we learned of Ranch 'A' in 1975—a place rumored for hiding criminals. We should probably try to make an appointment with Mr. Thomas. With our ties to Petrice, he may easily agree to see us."

Marquette shook his head. "That is doubtful. Notice his political affiliation. He is opposite Petrice on most issues. Most likely he will not give us the time of day." Then he tilted his head and smiled in a mischievous way. "It is so very difficult to be this famous."

Tara chuckled. "Perhaps we should use our other wiles in this instance."

Marquette nodded. "Definitely. However, this particular lead will have to wait until after Angel's graduation. We are due in Sioux Falls tomorrow."

It had been four weeks since Tillie Martin's pregnancy had been diagnosed, putting her at the magical twelve-week mark. Just as Rosa had predicted, the morning sickness left. Tillie's pretty smile and joyful spirit returned, but there was another drastic change that had begun, and no one could keep from commenting on it. A small lump had appeared just below her belly button. In fact, it had expanded so much that she could no longer button her jeans. Rosa suggested she might want to start getting some maternity clothes together.

"My goodness," Dr. Lewis said as he measured her stomach. "You must have given me the wrong date for your last cycle. This measurement shows at least twenty weeks of pregnancy. According to the dates you gave me, you should only be twelve weeks along at most."

Tillie placed her hand on her swollen abdomen, whispering in astonishment, "Five months? No way. I'm *certain* of the dates."

Dr. Lewis shrugged and helped her into a sitting position. "Well, these measurements are always just a guess, but you might want to check your calendar when you get home." He put his stethoscope over her heart and asked, "How are you feeling otherwise?"

"Really great," she answered with a faint smile, still trying to recover from the shock of possibly being five months pregnant instead of just twelve weeks.

"Everything staying down okay?" he asked as he moved the stethoscope to her lower ribcage area. "Deep breath now."

Tillie inhaled for him and answered, "The morning sickness is totally gone, and I've got tons of energy. And I graduate tomorrow."

"So what will you be doing with all of your free time?"

"Oh, I'm so excited," she answered with a smile. "Alex and I are turning his office at home into the nursery. It's right off our bedroom."

"And where will Alex's office wind up?"

"Upstairs. But there are two nice rooms up there, and he says he doesn't need much space."

Dr. Lewis gave Tillie's knee a friendly pat. "Well, don't work too hard, and keep taking those vitamins I prescribed for you. Be sure to drink plenty of water now that it's getting warmer."

"Okay."

"And say hi to that nice hubby of yours," he added as he turned and started for the door. He hesitated with his hand on the knob and turned around to look at her. "We'll see you again in about six weeks, and don't forget to check the calendar. We might have to push up that due date a little bit."

"Okay," Tillie said with a nod. Dr. Lewis left the room, and Tillie got dressed and hurried home to check her calendar.

When Alex returned from work that evening, he found Tillie trying on a pair of his jeans and one of his shirts. As Alex had very long legs, she'd rolled the pant- legs up at least twelve inches to make them fit. He laughed at the sight.

"Don't laugh," she warned as she looked at herself in the mirror. "Have you seen what's out there for maternity wear? Everything looks like it's made for a giant toddler!"

Alex laughed again. "You look really cute. Maybe you should cut the legs off and have Kate hem 'em up. By the way, how did it go at the doctor today?"

Tillie rolled her eyes, unzipped the jeans, and gave them a kick across the room. "He thinks I'm about five months pregnant."

Alex's mouth fell open in astonishment, and it was Tillie's turn to laugh.

"Yep," she chuckled, "that's right. He told me to get home and check my calendar, which I did, and I gave him the correct dates the first time around." She pointed at the little bulge just below her belly button. "Tall, like you, I guess."

Alex laughed again. He hesitantly reached out, as if he wanted to touch the baby, stopping himself just short of making contact. "May I?"

58

She reached for his hand and placed it over the very firm lump that had caused such uproar. Her stomach was warm beneath his touch, and he smiled into her eyes.

"Does she move yet?" he whispered.

Tillie shook her head. "But I'm not supposed to feel anything for a little while yet. At least that's what all the books say."

"But if the doc thinks five months…" He gave Tillie's stomach an affectionate caress.

Tillie rolled her eyes. "There's no way, Alex. If that's so, then why didn't I get sick five months ago?"

Alex raised an eyebrow. An important deduction.

"And what will I wear to graduation tomorrow?" Tillie went on. "I can't zip the skirt I had planned to wear."

Alex gave her a soft kiss on the lips. "Let's go out to the mall and see what they have. I'll bet we can find something."

Tillie Martin graduated with degrees in Comparative Literature and Russian Language. She was now qualified to teach Russian history at the high school level but, for the time being, she was content to wait for the baby and be with him or her, whenever it would happen.

They'd found a few nice things at the mall the evening before, and she wore a yellow dress beneath the black graduation robe.

Alex had planned a small reception at their house, inviting only their families and a few close friends. Tillie had been so sick earlier on, he'd been afraid to plan anything bigger. But the nausea and exhaustion had left her now, and she was back to her old, spunky self.

The ever-popular New York Senator Petrice Caselli arrived that morning, along with his wife, Elaine, and their two young children, Michael and Gabriella. Vincenzo and Kate and their children, Angelo and Alyssa, drove up from their ranch near Centerville. Marquette and Tara managed to arrive in Sioux Falls shortly before the graduation began.

All the Martins were there, as were the Englesons, except for Ginger, who was nowhere to be found. And even though Ginger and Tillie had been best friends since they were babies, Tillie would only smile and say, "I can't imagine where she is today!"

Alex and Giuseppe arranged for Georgie and Doria to prepare a few dishes and have them catered. Rosa was in charge of the punch and coffee. The Dixie Bake Shoppe prepared a white cake with white frosting and pink trim, and Alex bought a bouquet of white roses for the dining table. Alex and Tillie's little house was packed, but it was a perfect reception. Tillie glowed as she moved around and visited with her guests about the excitement of graduation and their first child.

"She and Bobby eloped," Tillie whispered to Giuseppe. "Now don't go and tell Burt."

Giuseppe snickered as he glanced at his old friend across the room, and then he whispered, "He will be steamed, as I would have been."

Tillie rolled her eyes. "You mean like you were when Patty eloped with Ellie?"

Giuseppe laughed. "You were the only one truly steamed, my Angel."

"Oh, I was not."

"And what is all of this whispering about over here?" Marquette interrupted as he and Tara joined them. He gave his sister a soft kiss on the cheek. "You look simply lovely, Angel."

"Thanks, Marq," she said with a smile. "And where have the two of you been? We haven't seen or heard from you in months."

"Oh, brother." Tara rolled her eyes. "You do not even want to know, Angel. We have had the most difficult time."

Marquette reached for the small bulge at Tillie's middle and gave it a soft pat. "And what is this? Should he be so large already?"

Tillie giggled. "That's the sole topic of conversation around here these days."

"Congratulations, Angel."

Tillie looked up to see her oldest brother joining them. It was still amazing to her how his hair had changed from just a few soft wisps of silver to an even mixture of black and gray, while Vincenzo and Marquette still had extraordinarily full black heads of hair. Petrice, at only the age of forty-one, claimed it had been his last four years in the Senate that had changed the color of his hair.

"Thanks, Patty."

"Russian language." He smiled. "Perhaps the President should have taken you to Vienna with him last June."

Marquette snorted. "Must we speak of that horrible, insidious little man this day?"

Petrice raised an eyebrow. "You still do not care for him? Can you not let it go?"

"I cannot, for I knew he was trouble on his first day in office."

"Oh, Marquette, he was trying to bring the two sides together."

"Bah!" Marquette scoffed, and Tillie had to laugh because he reminded her so much of their father.

Giuseppe laughed as he watched his sons continue with their political banter.

Tillie politely bowed out of the conversation and left them to discuss the evils of Washington and abroad. She got a cup of punch and glanced into the backyard where Vincenzo was smoking his pipe, watching the children play. She went outside and took a seat in the grass beside him.

"Hey, you," she said with a smile. "You're still sneaking off to smoke that thing?"

Vincenzo feigned a grimace. "Can you believe it?"

"What do you do in the winter?" He wasn't allowed to smoke in anyone's house, including his own.

"I get very cold." He looked at the playing children. "Did you watch my little ones on the Captain 11 Show yesterday?" The Captain 11 Show was a local children's program that aired in the afternoons. It was hosted by Channel 11's handsome weatherman who was dressed up as a sharp, galactic space captain. Children from all over the eastern part of South Dakota flocked to the television station to appear on his show.

Tillie giggled. "I saw them. I loved the part where Angelo asked Captain 11 for his autograph."

Vincenzo nodded with a laugh. "Captain 11 is a good man to put up with such trickery." His eyes followed the playing children in Tillie's backyard. "Soon, you will be watching your babe run and play back here."

Tillie sighed with a smile. "I'm really excited, Vincenzo, but I'm a little scared, too."

Vincenzo put his arm on her shoulders. "My Kate tells me it was the most wonderful experience of her life." He playfully frowned and added, "Funny. I thought meeting me had been the most wonderful thing in Kate's life." Tillie chuckled. "By the way, have Marq and Patty left already?"

Tillie shook her head. "Oh, no. They're going at it in the house. Marq still wants to hang our President, and Patty will defend him to no end."

Vincenzo shook his head. "Did you see Ellie's last column in *The Washington Post*?"

"Scathing. I wonder what kinds of discussions she and Patty have."

"One can only imagine."

They heard the deck door open and close, and turned around to see Elainc, Tara, and Kate coming to join them.

"Speaking of the political devil herself." Vincenzo smiled at Elaine.

Elaine grinned. "You must have seen my column."

"Oh, wow," Kate said as she took a seat next to her husband on the grass. "I *loved* it. Agreed with everything you wrote!"

Tillie rolled her eyes and sighed. *Here they go again.*

Vincenzo saw the sour expression on his sister's face. "Let us speak of something else; Angel has tired of politics this day." His eyes shone with mischief. "For instance, we could speak of this dreadful stallion I am having such a hard time with. I believe I will call him... *Liberal* —"

Vincenzo was interrupted by the ladies' laughter, including Tillie's.

Giuseppe refilled Burt's empty coffee cup.

"Well, it figures," Burt lamented. "That goofy kid."

Giuseppe squelched his laughter. "At least we know Bobby is of good moral character. They have waited these last five years. Perhaps they could wait no longer?"

Burt rolled his eyes and mimicked Giuseppe's accent, "My Diane will not be pleased."

Giuseppe chuckled. "What if we promise your dear wife a big reception when Angelo's II opens?"

Burt raised a gray eyebrow with interest. "I will attempt to persuade her."

Giuseppe nodded. "I will have my Angel work out the details with your *goofy* kid."

"Thanks, Giuseppe," Burt replied and then he sighed, shook his head, and sipped at his coffee.

Tillie was a little tired at the end of the day, but happy, and Rosa and Giuseppe offered to help with clean-up after the rest of the guests had left.

From the deck door, Giuseppe watched his daughter and her husband as they picked up the few paper napkins and plates the little ones had left behind in the backyard. Alex took Tillie into his arms, kissed her softly on the lips, and then tenderly placed his hand over the baby. Giuseppe smiled faintly...*It seems so perfect.*

"She shines," Rosa whispered, surprising Giuseppe; he had not realized she'd joined him.

He nodded as he watched the two in the backyard. He swallowed away the emotion in his throat and whispered, "Did Vincenzo tell you of the dreadful time he is having with War Winds' offspring?"

Rosa slowly nodded. Many years ago, Giuseppe's brother, Angelo, had given her a remarkable stallion he'd named War Winds— after the stallion in the movie *The Giant.*

"He will have nothing but trouble with that animal," Giuseppe continued to whisper. "Why does he keep it?"

Rosa swallowed and took a soft breath as she watched her daughter and son-in-law. "Because War Winds became a part of our family and because I loved him so very much."

Giuseppe nodded. "And what will come of this thing with Noah and Alex?"

Rosa shook her head. She was sick at heart for her husband, but nothing could change whatever course of events had been set in motion by his decision. She attempted to comfort him. "Nothing, my love. Do not torment yourself. God will take care of things."

"Noah saw her in my own eyes the other day. He could not help but give himself away."

"Mere coincidence," Rosa lied. She took a deep breath. "And what can be done about it now? Giuseppe, look at the two of them." And at that moment, Alex scooped his lovely wife into his arms and began to carry her toward the house. "Obviously, God intended them for each other. Let us doubt it no longer."

Alex had left his office door open and was concentrating so hard on what he was reading that he didn't see the dark-suited figure in the doorway. After several moments, he sensed someone watching him and looked up, surprised to find Petrice.

He got to his feet and extended his hand with a smile. "Patty, I thought you'd left by now."

Petrice shook Alex's hand. "Oh, not yet. In a few hours. I had to come and see you first."

"Well, have a seat. What can I do for you?"

"Well," Petrice said as he seated himself, "I did not have the chance to visit with you at the reception this weekend."

"We were a little busy."

"I have become very good friends with the governor of South Dakota, Jackson Williams. He tells me he is in need of an attorney to represent the state's interest in state-held land and leases. He needs someone he can trust. A good man. The position would require some traveling and consultation. I had wanted to recommend you but, with the baby on the way, I thought perhaps you could refer me to someone else."

"I really can't think of anyone right off the top of my head. But I'll give you a call if I come across anybody looking to get into the state's business."

"Thank you, my brother. I will look forward to hearing from you."

Melinda scowled as she watched Noah take the hand of his wife and lead her out of the office. She shook her head and gritted her teeth. *I can't believe how lucky that tramp got when she bagged Noah Hansen…I wonder if this one even belongs to him…Is somebody saying my name?*

"Melinda," a voice repeated.

She took a deep breath and focused on the figure in front of her desk. Her eyes narrowed in anger as she looked at him. *Ben Simmons… My life has gotten so hard.*

"What do you want?" she snapped.

Ben smiled sweetly and handed Melinda a full manila folder. "Noah wants these estimates copied and sent to Mr. Martin in Sioux Falls."

"Whatever. I'll get it done."

"Thank you. And also, if anyone needs to reach me, I'll be at the warehouse site on St. Joe."

Melinda frowned in confusion. "But I thought Noah was supervising that site."

Ben shook his head. "He decided to take the afternoon off with Carrie."

"Humph." *Figures. Spoiled brat.*

After they left the office Noah and Carrie went home, where Joshua and Mona were babysitting Ty. As they walked up the driveway, they noticed that Ty had roped his aunt and uncle into playing ball. When Joshua and Mona had taken Ty to the circus, they purchased an inflatable bat and ball. That one event had started a love for the game in the little three-year-old. He coaxed anyone who was willing into playing just one game.

"Look at that," Carrie whispered as she and Noah watched Joshua bend over and pitch the ball. Ty took a hefty swing. Mona was their catcher, and she stood just behind Ty to retrieve the missed balls.

Noah chuckled. "Josh is quite a pitcher."

Mona waved as she saw them approaching, but Joshua and Ty concentrated on the game. Carrie and Noah waved in return.

"By the way," Carrie said as they walked along, "Mom wondered if I could stop over tonight for just a minute. Just me. Would that be okay?"

Noah shrugged. "Sure. But doesn't she want to see the rest of us?"

"She's not feeling very well today, and she doesn't want Ty to catch it."

Marquette and Tara went to Ranch 'A' at Beulah, Wyoming, and met with the director, Stan Mitchell. Apparently Ranch 'A' was now owned and managed by the Fish and Wildlife Service for the purpose of fish diet development. Mr. Mitchell also informed them of the sale of Ranch 'A' to one of the state's governors in 1942 for the purpose of operating a dude ranch. The business venture never made money, and in 1963 the federal government purchased the property for fish operations.

"We have been told that Ranch 'A' housed crime family members," Marquette said with a frown. "Are you aware of that?"

Mr. Mitchell grinned. "Yeah, I've heard the rumors, but I really don't know anything about it. I didn't come here until about six months ago."

"Do you know anyone in the area who might be knowledgeable in this subject?" Tara inquired.

"Well." Mr. Mitchell scratched his head. "There's an old guy who lives down the road just a piece, and from what I've heard, he's ranched since the early 1900s. I've never met him, but everybody says he's friendly."

Mr. Mitchell gave Marquette and Tara directions to the Mathers' Ranch, where they introduced themselves to a man named Rusty Mathers. Apparently Ol' Rusty, as he was called, had been an area rancher since 1915, when he was a young man and had received land from his father. By now, Ol' Rusty was well into his eighties, but his mind was sharp and clear. He was more than willing to share stories about the old Mafia hideout.

His elderly wife, whom he introduced as Alvera, brought a pitcher of iced tea out to the porch, where they welcomed their guests with obvious delight.

"We ain't had nobody ask about them villains in a coon's age," Rusty informed through a toothless smile. He took off his old straw hat and scratched his bald head. "But we all know they're still a goin' at it up there in Big Eagle."

"Big Eagle?" Tara questioned, confused.

"It's a little town near the three borders," Alvera explained, and her old gray eyes twinkled with a smile. "They all hide up there now. It's loaded with gambling halls and cathouses."

Marquette raised one eyebrow. "The three borders?"

"Where Montana, Wyoming, and South Dakota meet," Rusty answered.

"It's the hometown of our attorney general, Custer Thomas," Alvera tittered.

Tara frowned with interest. "I thought his hometown was Casper."

"Oh, heavens no!" Rusty laughed and slapped his knee. "He'd like everybody to believe he's from Casper, but we been in these parts near forty years before he was even born. He's from Big Eagle all right."

Alvera leaned close enough to Tara to put her hand on her knee and whispered, "He ran for office *unopposed*, you know."

Tara slowly shook her head. "No, we were not aware of that."

Alvera and Rusty nodded in agreement.

Rusty took a deep breath. "See, when they closed down Ranch 'A,' they all had to have somewhere to go, and Custer's mother kinda runs Big Eagle. She's been hidin' bad guys up there since forever. Nobody crosses *that* family."

"There are more than just mother and son, then?" Marquette questioned.

"Custer has a stepfather and an uncle," Alvera answered. "And they keep it all real hush-hush. But all us locals know just the same."

Marquette nodded with a frown. "I guess that we will have to make a visit then to your infamous attorney general."

"Governor's office on line two," Jan called in over Alex's intercom.

"Thanks, Jan," he acknowledged. But before he picked up the call he quickly went to his office door and closed it. He took a deep breath, went back to his comfortable chair, and picked up the line.

"This is Alex Martin."

"Hi, Mr. Martin," came a loud, clear voice on the other end. "This is Governor Williams. My assistant says you've been trying to reach me."

"Yes, I have." Alex smiled. "I understand you're looking for representation for state business."

Carrie watched her stepfather's shaky hands place the ornate dagger into the waiting palms of his only son, Antonio. Antonio was on his knees in front of his father, head bowed and eyes closed.

"This day, the day of your birth, symbolizes your age of maturity, as well as the coming of time to receive a position coveted by all the men in our family." Mario took a breath, reached for Antonio's chin, and tilted his face upward. "Look at me, my son."

Antonio opened his eyes and waited for his father to continue.

"You are the Elder Son," Mario whispered. "You have a commitment and a responsibility to protect this family from any dangers that may present themselves. Do you swear, upon the oath of our family name, to uphold this duty until your death?"

"I do, Papa."

"And do you, my Antonio, promise to do whatever it takes to protect any members who join this family, regardless of their religion and beliefs?"

"I do, Papa."

Mario let out a deep breath and smiled into the eyes of his son. "Then you are ready to assume the Elder Sonship."

Carrie watched with wide eyes...*This isn't right. They should be calling on Jesus.*

CHAPTER 4

Melinda crept close to the wall so as not to cast a shadow. *If he sees me coming, he'll stop.* Ben Simmons was on the telephone in the conference room, and he wasn't speaking English. He was nearly whispering the conversation, and Melinda had to press closer to the doorway in order to hear. The only thing she'd been able to understand was "Sioux Falls," and Noah's name. *What on earth is he up to?*

When she heard him hang up, she narrowed her eyes and stepped into the doorway, running directly into him.

"Pardon me," Ben apologized in his polite way.

"What language was that?"

Ben raised an eyebrow. "Why, Melinda, English is not your first language?"

Melinda's blood boiled. "You're such a jerk. I don't know how you fooled Hansen into giving you this job, but I know you're up to something."

"My dear lady, I am up to nothing. Now please stop eavesdropping or I will be forced to mention it to our boss." And with that, Ben held his head high and walked away from her.

Melinda stomped her way back to her desk where she slammed down a file and threw herself into her chair. *I hate Ben Simmons.*

Shondra Payne had worked for Martin, Martin & Dale, A.P.C.L., since 1968, the year Alex began his studies at Harvard. She'd been a lawyer for only six years at that point but was promoted to the position of administrative manager. By now she'd been in the business for twenty years and worked exclusively with Alex Martin. She was forty-three years old and had never married. She always said that she'd chosen a career instead of a family, as she did not desire to shortchange either one.

Shondra softly knocked at Alex's office, let herself inside, and closed the door. Her gray eyes were bigger than Alex had ever seen them as she stood silently by the closed door and stared at him.

After a very long silence, Alex asked, "What is it, Shondra?"

She bit her lip and cleared her throat as she attempted a professional frown. "The governor is here."

"He's *here?*" Alex stumbled to his feet, grabbing his suit jacket from the back of his chair. "What's he doing *here?*" *I thought the ol' boy would call first! How in the world am I going to keep this from Dad? He doesn't want me in politics…*

Shondra shook her head and whispered, "I don't know, but he asked for *you.*"

"*Me?*" Alex raised his eyebrows, pretending to be surprised as he straightened his tie. "Does this look okay?"

Shondra nodded. "Do you want me to bring him back…or what?"

"Uhh…" Alex swallowed hard and looked around his office. "I guess so."

Shondra opened Alex's office door, where Sam stood with the most peculiar expression on his face. She slipped around him as he stepped into the office.

"Hey, the governor's here," Sam whispered.

"Hey, did you guys know the governor's here?"

Sam and Alex turned their heads to see their father. He held his glasses in one hand and a file in the other, and his face wore the same quizzical expression as Sam's.

"He's here to see *me*," Alex admitted, frantically searching his brain for an excuse...*I'll just tell them Petrice referred me, because he would have.*

"What's he wanna see *you* for?" Sam whispered.

"Did he have an appointment?" James inquired.

"Gentlemen." They turned to see Shondra and the Governor of the State of South Dakota waiting in the doorway.

"Gentlemen." The governor came toward them with his hand outstretched and a smile on his face. Jackson Williams was a big man, almost as tall and broad as one of the Martins, and he had a clamorous reputation that preceded him. His opinions were larger than life, and he was forever getting into highly publicized verbal arguments with other governors, state legislatures, and even his own brother, who practiced law in another Sioux Falls office. He wore dreadful, black horn-rimmed glasses, but his smile was friendly. All three of the Martins reached for his hand at once.

"James Martin," their father said as he clasped the governor's hand first. "And these are my sons, Sam and Alex."

"The famous Martin Legacy," Governor Williams said with a smile. He shook Sam's hand next and then Alex's. "I'm Jackson Williams."

"How do you do." Alex squirmed as the awkward scene played out before him...*Please don't say anything in front of them.*

"I just happened to be in town today and thought I'd stop by and see if you had a few minutes," Governor Williams said.

"I guess I thought you'd call," Alex answered, noticing his father and brother raise their eyebrows.

"Oh." The governor laughed his big laugh and slapped Alex's shoulder hard. "I don't like to do much business over the phone. I like being in person."

Alex tried to get the look of surprise to leave his eyes as he gestured toward one of the chairs in front of his desk. "Have a seat."

"I guess we'll just be going then," James said with a frown.

"It was nice meeting you, gentlemen." The governor smiled and took a seat in front of Alex's desk as Sam and his father left the office. Alex closed the door behind them.

"Your family has a very good reputation," Williams began.

Alex nodded as he walked to his chair behind his desk and seated himself. "Thank you."

"How old is your father now?"

"Dad just turned eighty-one."

Williams nodded. "And how long did your grandfather practice?"

"Sharp as a tack until he was one hundred."

"Think your dad will practice that long?"

Alex shrugged. "He's still going strong, and he doesn't believe in retirement. He thinks a man should work until he can't work anymore."

"Wonderful." Williams' eyes smiled behind his glasses. "But, as you know, what I really came to talk about is *you*."

Alex raised his eyebrows. "I'm extremely busy right now, and Petrice told me the position would require some traveling. My wife is expecting, and I'm not comfortable leaving her alone too much. She's already had somewhat of a difficult time with it."

"Well, Mr. Martin, what if I could arrange for a state charter to fly you into Pierre, say once a week? We could review whatever was needed, and you could be back in Sioux Falls by the end of the day."

Alex's expression was thoughtful as he considered the governor's offer. "Why don't you give me a chance to talk to my wife and see how she feels about this?"

"No problem." Williams got to his feet, extended his hand, and Alex did the same. "Tell you what, you talk to your wife, and then you give me a call before the end of the week. Let me know what you can do for us."

"I don't know if it's such a good idea." Alex's father shook his gray head. After the governor had left, James, Sam, and Alex had gathered in James' office, where Alex reiterated the substance of his conversation with Jackson Williams. "If Tillie wasn't so darn young," James went on, biting his lower lip, "I might tell you to go for it, Alex, but she just turned twenty-three."

"But she feels *great*," Alex persisted.

"We talked about this when you decided to take such a young lady for your bride," James reminded.

Alex sighed. He remembered the conversation well and rattled off the familiar speech in his head...*He's seventeen years older than Mom, and curbed his own career to be a good husband to the woman he chose to have children with...blah, blah, blah.*

"I don't know," Sam said. "Tillie keeps pretty busy, and she's terribly independent. She might not mind so much."

James nodded. "Alex, you're thirty years old. You'll have to make this decision on your own, but talk to Tillie first. See what she says about the whole thing, and let her know, *honestly*, how often you'll be gone."

"Governor Williams says only one day a week," Alex replied.

James' frown deepened. "Well, I'm sure you'll be putting in quite a bit of time here at the office trying to keep up with all of those state-generated leases. There's gonna be late nights and maybe weekends. And what about Hansen Development? Sam tells me Noah's got a job in Sioux Falls now. There will be inquiries about him, and he'll need more time as well."

"Well, I'll talk to Tillie and see what she says —"

"Alex," his father interrupted, "don't take advantage of her and talk her into something she's not comfortable with. She's done *every-thing* you've asked of her, including finishing school, when we all knew very well that she would have rather worked part-time for Giuseppe and puttered around in her house, or started a family—"

"She *needed* to finish school," Alex shot back.

Sam raised his eyebrows and looked from his father to Alex and back at his father. *This is gonna get pretty hot in a couple of minutes.* He stood from his chair. "I'll let the two of you be alone for a minute." He walked toward the door. "Let me know what you decide."

"Alex," James sighed, "I can't tell you what to do. I can only give you advice and pray to God that you'll take it. You've got an extremely heavy work load the way it is. Why on earth would you want to get into the state's business?"

"It would give me some exposure...*politically*."

"Oh, brother." James rolled his eyes and shook his head. "You know how I feel about that. A man cannot serve both a constituency and a wife, and you chose your wife *first*."

"Patty does it," Alex stubbornly argued. He got to his feet and shook his head. "Just because you gave up your life for Mom, doesn't mean that everybody has to do the same thing."

"Petrice Caselli is a different sort of a man," James scolded as he watched his son move closer to the door.

Alex turned with narrowed eyes. "Well maybe I am, too. You know, Dad, you just might want to support me for once." He opened the door and slammed it as he left.

James shook his head. Alex had always been driven by that calculating ambition, even when he was a little boy. James had thought it had ebbed quite a bit after he started to court Tillie, but that old, evil shadow of aspiration had reared its ugly head again. However, this time Alex had a pregnant wife to consider. James leaned back in his chair and closed his eyes. Hopefully, this little *desideratum* of Alex's would soon pass.

Alex left his car in the small, private parking garage and walked down the sidewalk on 10th Street. He was angry, and it was a feeling he did not experience often. He had never been given to having a temper or becoming irate when things didn't go his way, and he didn't understand people who did. He'd rather see the logic in all situations and work from there, but the situation with his father was *different*.

He shoved his hands into his pockets as he walked. He watched the traffic and people pass by, going about their own lives and doing what *they* wanted to do, uncontrolled by James' opinion and theology. *What does he mean, Petrice Caselli is a different sort of a man? I obediently followed the wishes of my father, worked my butt off, and graduated* magna cum laude *from none other than Harvard Law. Does it even make a difference?*

He shook his head and kicked a small pebble out of the way as he turned the corner and crossed onto Phillips Avenue. He saw the Bechtold's Jewelry Store and continued on his way. *I can do this*, he encouraged himself, *and Tillie won't mind. Sam's right. She's incredibly independent, like the rest of her family, and she'd never dream of holding me back from something I want. She loves me as sincerely, devotedly, and passionately as I love her, and we can work this out together.*

Alex stopped at the glass door of Bechtold's and peered inside. *Of course, there's nothing wrong with a little persuasion.*

When Alex pulled his Mercedes into the driveway less than an hour later, he saw Tillie's plumping figure on the back patio. She was dressed in a pair of oversized, bright yellow overalls and a white t-shirt. She was turning something on the grill, and he noticed that she'd set the table on the patio for a romantic supper. He smiled. *She truly loves me and she'll understand.*

He got out of his car, and she waved. He smiled and walked toward her with a single white rose.

"For me?" She smiled into his eyes and put her nose into the blossom. "What are you up to, Alex?"

He handed her the small velvet box. "I just thought maybe you might like this."

Tillie's eyes opened wide with surprise as she looked from the box and into her husband's eyes. "Thanks, Alex, but you didn't need to do that."

"Open it up. See what you think."

"Okay." She opened the box and gasped when she saw the heart-shaped diamond pendant inside. "It's beautiful," she breathed, noticing the pendant was attached to an expensive gold chain. She looked up into Alex's handsome dark eyes. "Thanks, I love it."

He kissed her and said, "You're welcome." He lovingly touched the place where their baby had grown even more. "How are things today?"

"*Great*," she smiled, taking the new pendant out of the box and turning around for Alex to fasten it. "I think I felt her move today."

"*Her?*" He clasped the chain and placed his hand over her little belly.

"Well, I don't know," Tillie chuckled. "I guess I just don't want to say '*it*,' even though we don't know, you know, boy or girl. Tomorrow I'll probably say '*he*.'"

The anger toward his father began to melt, and Alex folded her into his arms. "Tillie, I have to ask you about something."

"Hansen's men are doing a fine job," Burt Engleson observed as he and Giuseppe walked through the construction site.

Giuseppe nodded in agreement, but his tone was downcast. "Remarkable. I am surprised they have been able to put things together so quickly."

Burt noticed Giuseppe's demeanor and put his hand on his old friend's shoulder. "What's the matter, Giuseppe? You seem a little down today."

"Do I?"

"Yep. You seem worried about something."

Giuseppe nodded with a heavy sigh. "I *am* worried, Burt. I made a decision many years ago, and now it has come back to haunt me in the worst way —"

He was interrupted when a young gentleman approached them with a smile and an outstretched hand.

"Giuseppe Caselli and Burt Engleson, I presume?" he asked as he shook their hands. "I am Ben Simmons, and I wanted to introduce myself. I work for Noah Hansen, and will be supervising this site off and on over the summer months."

Giuseppe took the hand of a very tall, dark man. His smile was open and friendly, but for a fleeting moment Giuseppe saw something eerily familiar in the young man's black eyes.

"And why is that?" Burt questioned. "Where's Mr. Hansen this summer?"

"His wife is expecting, and he does not wish to make many trips away from her," Ben answered cordially, hoping not to let on that he saw the spark of recognition in Giuseppe's eyes.

Giuseppe squinted as he looked at Ben. "Have we met?"

Ben smiled and shook his head. "I am certain we have not."

Giuseppe nodded again, but in his heart he had the feeling this man was deceiving him...*but for what reason?*

"I need to check on an equipment order," Ben explained with another open smile, "but if either of you need anything at all or have any questions, you can find me in that white trailer over there."

"Thank you," Burt acknowledged, and Giuseppe nodded.

Ben turned and headed in the direction of the trailer.

Burt frowned. "What's wrong, Giuseppe? Why did you give the kid such a hard time?"

Giuseppe let out a heavy sigh and shook his head. "He is very familiar. It seems to me that I should know him from somewhere."

Burt shook his head. "That's not it. Something else is on your mind. Why don't you tell me about this decision that's haunting you?"

Giuseppe's black eyes filled with tears as he looked at his oldest friend. *How I wish my brother Angelo was here.* "Burt, there is a sin on my heart."

Burt swallowed hard. "I'm sure it's not that bad...unless you've been cheating on Rosa. You haven't cheated on Rosa, have you?"

"Oh, heavens no!" Giuseppe took a breath. "I could never cheat on my Rosa, and yet it is much worse than even that. I cheated on our God. I prayed a certain prayer for fifteen years, and when the answer came, I did not like it."

"So what did you do?"

"I ignored God's perfect answer and manipulated my own desires, and now I am waiting for the other shoe to drop."

"Does Rosa know about this?"

Giuseppe nodded. "It was her idea to begin the prayer! She begged me to obey, but I refused. I was so certain I had misunderstood

God, or perhaps there was coincidence involved. I made excuse after excuse—"

"Just what on earth is going on, Giuseppe? Just give it to me straight."

Giuseppe shrugged. "I do not even know where to begin, my friend."

"At the beginning." Burt put his hand on his friend's slumped shoulder. "There's nothin' you can't tell *me*, Giuseppe."

Marquette wore his best black suit and tucked his long pony-tail beneath one of his hats. He'd covered his handsome eyes with large mirrored sunglasses and fastened a fake goatee to his clean-shaven face.

Tara was dressed in a similar black suit and had borrowed one of Marquette's hats so that she could also hide her hair beneath it. She wore matching sunglasses. Their identities would be sufficiently disguised.

After a lengthy investigation in Big Eagle, Wyoming, Marquette and Tara went to the state's capital city, Cheyenne, for a personal interview with Wyoming's Attorney General, Custer Thomas. Allegations had been made against Mr. Thomas with regard to the illegal gambling in Big Eagle. And, as Marquette and Tara also learned, Thomas was the central figure in a federal cocaine investigation. His suspected partner in crime, a man named Wes Stuben, was also partnered with Mr. Thomas' wife, Ashely Worhal Thomas, in a law firm in Casper. As Rusty and his wife had warned, Mr. Thomas was well-connected throughout Wyoming. As such, Marquette and Tara decided to "use their professional wiles," and they headed for Mr. Thomas' downtown Cheyenne office for a short visit.

"We need to see the Attorney General," Marquette said as they stood before Mr. Thomas' receptionist.

"He's very busy." She looked at the suspicious duo. "And you don't have an appointment."

"Oh, but we do," Marquette insisted.

"Then give me your names," the woman pressed.

Marquette laughed. "Tell him Wes sent us over."

The woman's face showed her surprised, and she began to nod. "Let me see what I can do." She hurried through a door, and Marquette nodded at Tara. They quickly followed the woman into an office, surprising Custer, who was seated behind his desk.

"Hello, Custer," Marquette greeted as he and Tara strolled over to the desk and took positions on either side of the man.

The attorney general looked from Tara to Marquette, and then to his receptionist.

"I'm sorry, sir," she apologized.

"It's okay, Becky," he said with a nervous smile. "Why don't you leave us alone for a moment?"

Becky nodded, left the office, and closed the door behind her.

Custer leered at Tara's body and reached over to put his hand on her hip as he said, "So Wes sent you over?"

The instant his hand touched Tara's hip, she produced a switchblade and snapped it open. He jerked his hand away and slid back in his chair, staring with surprise at Tara.

"You misunderstand our visit," she warned.

"I would not do that if I were you," Marquette advised. "She is very quick."

Custer bit his lip as he looked at Marquette. "You told Becky that Wes sent you over. What's goin' on?"

"On occasion, we lie," Tara answered with a cynical smile, giving the switchblade a delicate wave beneath his nose.

"But only professionally," Marquette added. "And we know about the drugs. We also know about your wife's law partner."

Custer cursed and demanded, "Who are you? Your accent is really familiar."

"It does not matter who we are," Marquette said, and then he gave Custer's face a soft slap. "And you must not use profanity in front of a lady."

Tara almost laughed, but she bit her lip and concentrated on a more serious expression.

"What do you want?" Custer questioned.

"What do you know of a man named Schneider Rauwolf?" Tara asked, with a wave of her blade.

Custer wrinkled up his nose as he looked into her mirrored glasses. "You are so familiar, but I don't know anybody with that name."

Marquette produced Rauwolf's photo. "You were seen with him in Miami, Florida, in 1972. You were looking for a man named Jack Nelson."

Custer looked at the photograph. He nodded his head and looked back at Marquette. "The Wolf, and we never found his friend...at least *I* never did. I went to Austin shortly after that. The Wolf went somewhere else, and we never talked about it again."

Tara pressed her blade softly against Custer's chin. "I highly doubt you are telling the truth. Where is the Wolf now?"

Custer took a delicate breath as he turned his eyes toward Tara. "Sometimes he stays up in Big Eagle. That's all I know. If I want to contact him, I leave a message at the front desk of the Big Eagle Hotel."

Marquette was satisfied with Custer's answer. "Do not attempt to warn the Wolf." He nodded at Tara, and she closed her switchblade as they started to back out of the office together.

"Think about what we have said," Tara warned. Marquette opened the door for his wife, allowed her to pass through first, and then he looked back at Custer.

"You are nothing but a blackguard, sent by Satan to do his evil work upon the earth. May God have *no* mercy upon your soul." With that, Marquette stepped through the door and closed it on his way out.

Custer jumped to his feet and sprinted to the door. He pulled it open and looked out, only to see Becky standing in the middle of the room.

"Who were they?" he demanded as he continued to curse and storm. His face had become as red as fire.

Becky shook her head.

"Well, find out!" he roared. "Where did they go?"

Becky shook her head again and answered, "They told me I couldn't watch them leave."

"No, Carrie, darlin'," Mona giggled as she reached for the controls on her stove. "Don't ever boil the lids and bands. We only want to keep them hot."

"Oh." Carrie nodded with an understanding smile. "I see what you're saying now."

Mona giggled again. She was teaching Carrie how to make and can strawberry jam, and Joshua had volunteered to take Ty to the park. It was a hot summer day, and Mona's June strawberries were ready for picking and canning.

The kitchen was warm from the boiling pots of jam, and Mona's red hair hung in damp strings across her forehead. Carrie couldn't help but smile as she watched her sister-in-law take a giant glug from her tall glass of iced tea.

"Whoo!" Mona gasped as she reached for her ladle. "It's hotter than Hades in this house."

Carried nodded as she reached for her own glass of tea. "Okay, so once we've canned this stuff, how long will it last?"

"Oh, years, but Josh and Noah usually eat up the jam so fast you'll be lucky if it makes it till next spring!"

"Noah really loved the apple butter we made last fall," Carrie said. "*This* is even better."

Just then Joshua came through the back door, with Ty on his hip.

"Mommy!" Ty exclaimed.

"Hey, guys!" Carrie smiled in their direction. "You've been gone for a long time."

"We went to the Dairy Queen after the park," Joshua explained. "Hope that's okay."

Carrie shrugged. "I'm sure Ty didn't mind."

"Not at all," Joshua answered as he gave the little boy a kiss on the top of his head and then handed him to his mother. "But I think he's getting tired."

"We're making delicious strawberry jam," Mona informed as she stepped over to Joshua and gave him a kiss on the chin.

"I see that—and *smell* it!" he answered. "You're always teaching somebody how to cook something."

"Yes, well," Mona laughed and turned back to her stove, "it's my ministry."

Joshua nodded, and in his brown eyes Carrie saw the glint of humor. He raised a brow and asked, "Has Mona ever told you about how she's tried to teach her sisters to cook?"

"Oh, she doesn't want to hear about that," Mona replied.

Mischief danced in Joshua's expression, reminding Carrie of Noah. "None of Mona's sisters can cook," he began with a sly grin.

"Oh, Josh!" Mona admonished with a frown. "Don't go into this."

"I have to." He laughed. "Anyway, she's got three sisters, you know, and none of them cook. But Mona is always trying to teach them something. Keep in mind, these gals are all in their mid-thirties and early forties." He paused to roll his eyes. "Well, a couple of years ago we went down to Atlanta for Christmas, and Mona decided she was going to teach the girls how to make Christmas candy. The fudge turned out pretty good, and the almond bark wasn't bad, but when they got to the divinity, the whole scheme fell apart —"

"Divinity is extremely complicated," Mona interjected as she began to ladle her strawberry jam into the hot jars.

"I'll say," Joshua chuckled. "Anyway, you have to hold the electric beater in the bowl while you add this boiling stuff to the mixture, and you can't stop beating, no matter what, or you risk ruining the candy. So Mona's little sister, Mary Jo, is just whipping the daylights out of the mixture in the bowl, and Mona announces that it's time to add the boiling stuff. Mary Jo holds her mixer steady, and Mona pours. Mary Jo is so intent on keeping the mixer in the bowl that she doesn't realize it's spinning on the countertop and getting really close to the edge—" Joshua laughed. "Poor Mona turned around to put the pan back on the stove, and just like that, that bowl spun right off the counter and landed *right side up* on the floor! Mary Jo followed that bowl all the way to the floor with her mixer—" He was interrupted by Carrie's giggles.

"There was divinity all over Momma's kitchen," Mona grimaced. "It took us days to get that stuff off the walls."

Carrie laughed again, and Mona smiled at her. "It's a true story, ya know."

"I know, Mona," Carrie tittered. *"That's what makes you so fun!"*

"Oh, goodness," Burt breathed. He stared into his half-full espresso cup and then looked into Giuseppe's forlorn face. Giuseppe had just confessed what he considered to be his worst abomination: that of keeping Noah and Tillie apart. "I don't know what to tell you, my friend."

Giuseppe shook his head. *"I should have known.* After all, Rosa and I had prayed for the man for fifteen years. It was His perfect answer to our prayers. It was more than mere coincidence they were thrown together in such a way." He sighed and added, "I saw the kindness in his eyes, and that is when I knew he was meant for my Angel."

Burt nodded thinking, *I imagine you're right, Giuseppe, but I don't know what you're gonna do now.* He cleared his throat and attempted a smile for his friend. "Listen, we're gonna pray about this, and it's gonna be okay. Don't get so tied up over this thing. Alex is a great guy, and he'll take good care of her." But Burt didn't even believe his own words, for Alex had already proven himself unfaithful to Burt's son, Andy. For years the boys had planned to go to Vietnam together. But when the time came, Alex secretly registered at Harvard in order to avoid the draft, and Andy went to war alone.

Giuseppe sighed and looked into his cup. "Say what you will, my friend, in order to comfort me, but I know what you are really thinking. I have made a mess of my daughter's life."

CHAPTER 5

Reata, Summer 1980

Vincenzo had a firm hold of the saddle horn but it was of no use, as he flew hard into the side of the barn. The stubborn stallion had thrown him again. He stumbled to his feet and dusted off his backside.

"You evil monster," he muttered. He looked around for his hat and saw his foreman, Bill Mitchell, with it...and Bill was laughing. "Do not laugh, my friend," Vincenzo warned with a scowl for the miserable stallion. "That beast will soon become a gelding if he does not change his ways."

Bill laughed and handed Vincenzo his hat. "I can't figure it out, Vincenzo. You've never had a problem with one of your animals."

Vincenzo put his hat back on and glared at the stallion. "He is as crazy as the day is long. There is something wrong with that beast. Had he not come from War Winds' lineage, I would have shipped him off to the glue factory by now."

Bill laughed and slapped Vincenzo's back. "Come on. Kate sent a hand down a little bit ago. They've got our dinner ready. You'll feel better after you've had something to eat."

"Bah," Vincenzo growled as he shook his head and started for the house with Bill. *I have half a mind to get rid of the beast...*

Noah had purchased a pontoon boat and put it in Pactola Reservoir. He and Carrie had talked about doing it for the last couple of summers, but were concerned about Ty being too little. This year, however, the young sailor fit into his small life vest perfectly, and they bought the boat of their dreams.

Joshua and Mona couldn't have been more delighted, and they joined Carrie and Noah many times on Pactola to fish or cruise romantically under the beautiful blue skies of the Black Hills. Carrie made them all bright-blue t-shirts with the words *Hansen Yacht Club* embroidered on the left side, telling everyone they had to wear them whenever they were on the boat. Noah surprised them all one night when they went up to the lake for a sail. He'd had the words *Hansen Yacht Club* painted in the same shade of blue across the back of the boat.

Into the first month of summer, Carrie's pregnancy began to blossom. Her eyes began to shine with delight and expectancy as the baby became more visible to the outside world. It was a happier and more contented occasion for her this time. She thanked God for the goodness in her life when she felt Noah's child move within her.

They glided leisurely across Pactola, watching the sun set behind the western ridge and thinking of names for their new baby. Ty curled up in Auntie Mona's lap and fell fast asleep, while Joshua steered the boat. That was his favorite place.

"What will it be this time?" Noah asked as he laid a curious hand upon her stomach. His heart almost stopped with the thrill of movement from the unborn child. It was just small, soft flutters now, but he could feel them if he was patient enough to wait.

"I think a boy," Carrie smiled into his eyes.

The baby made a very sudden movement, and Noah almost jumped. "I think a boy, too!" he whispered. He laughed, and kissed Carrie tenderly on the lips. Life had certainly changed for Noah.

Giuseppe sipped his espresso as he gazed out of the front window of his living room, unaware that his wife watched him from behind.

What is he thinking now? she thought as she watched him gaze toward the west. She cleared her throat to get his attention, and when he turned around she noticed he hadn't finished tying his tie.

"You will be late this morning," she chided as she stepped close enough to finish the tie.

"I have plenty of time," he grumbled.

"Did I hear you say Vincenzo called?" she changed the subject abruptly as she made the perfect knot.

Giuseppe nodded. "He is having trouble with that stallion again."

Rosa *tsked* and finished the tie, gave it a soft pat, and looked into her husband's eyes. "Vincenzo's colt may have come from a good stallion, but the mare he chose was flawed. She was very beautiful to behold but her temperament was detestable. Vincenzo would do well to admit that he made a mistake in that breeding and perhaps just sell the beast."

"It would be very hard to part with the colt," Giuseppe reminded. "You know how much War Winds meant to all of us."

Rosa smiled wistfully as she recalled the memories. War Winds had been a gift to her from Giuseppe's brother, Angelo, in the summer of 1960. War Winds' raven-black coat and the clever glint in his eyes had reminded everyone of Delia, Rosa's beloved horse that she'd had to leave behind when they left Italy. Only Vincenzo and Rosa had been able to manage the young stallion, and he'd lived on Reata until his death in 1974. But before he died, War Winds fathered several fine colts and fillies, all of which Vincenzo had kept and bred. Every one of them had worked on Reata except for the most recent, a two-year-old fathered by War Winds' very last colt. He refused to be broken and wreaked pure havoc on the ranch.

Rosa blinked away her tears. "I suppose he thinks that to let the colt go would be like letting a little piece of our family slip away. But what he doesn't see is how very much the colt will hurt his family if allowed to continue its reign on the ranch."

Giuseppe sighed as he sipped at his espresso. He shook his head and looked again out the window. "Vincenzo's mistake is easy to mend. But, I wonder how much longer before mine falls apart?"

"You guys *have* to come out and see my new boat," Noah tried to persuade Alex over the telephone one morning in the middle of July. "You gotta bring some leases out anyway. Why don't you and Tillie just fly on out for the weekend? Carrie and Mona will make us up some sandwiches, and we can fish."

"I just can't," Alex interrupted, and Noah heard the shuffling of papers in the background. "I'm too busy. I've already put those leases in the mail. You'll have them by tomorrow."

Noah sighed. This had been his third attempt to get Alex to come to Rapid City to see his new boat and get their wives together. He was certain Tillie and Carrie would hit it off. After all, he and Alex had gotten to be great friends over the past few years.

"By the way," Alex said into the phone, "I received an inquiry for you. A gentleman by the name of Scott Allan wants you to put up a little strip mall over on the east side of Sioux Falls. He really likes your spot over on Sycamore —"

"I'm not starting anything else until after summer," Noah interrupted.

"But it would be good exposure," Alex retorted, surprised that Noah would refuse the work. "You *do* still want to expand into Sioux Falls, don't you?"

"Well, sure, but it's summer, and I like having the time off with Carrie and Tiger —"

"Who's running your business?"

"Melinda and Ben," Noah answered abruptly.

"Melinda and Ben." The displeasure in Alex's voice was not disguised.

"Well, I go in in the mornings and stuff, and Ben's been checking my site in Sioux Falls," Noah answered, trying not to snap at Alex. *What's with this guy lately anyway? He's so busy running like a chicken with his head cut off, back and forth between the governor in Pierre and Sioux Falls that he doesn't even have time to come to Rapid City for a simple ride on a boat. He really ticks me off...* "You know what they say, Alex, 'all work and no play,' and you need to sniff some roses too."

"Listen." Alex sighed. "Just take a look at those leases and let me know what you think."

"You must know by now I don't look at that stuff." Noah snapped. "That's what I pay you for! Why do you send it out here anyway?"

"Noah," Alex ordered, "would you just read the stupid leases for once?" And Alex slammed the phone down.

Noah heard the line go dead on the other end. He shook his head and hung up the phone.

Alex threw his pencil across his office. *What's gotten into him anyway? We've been building his business at a fantastic rate of speed, and then the ol' boy decides to go out and get himself that stupid boat.* Alex shook his head. *I'm not about to get on that thing. What a worthless waste of time. Sniff roses? Unbelievable!*

"What happened?"

Sam's voice interrupted Alex's thoughts, and he looked into the open doorway to see Sam frowning.

Alex rolled his eyes. "That *stupid* Noah Hansen. He's gotten himself a boat, and it's all he can talk about. I've got a guy who wants to give him some business, and Noah would rather sail around the reservoir. Can you believe it?"

Sam raised an eyebrow. "How much coffee have you had today?"

"Probably not enough."

"How are things with Tillie?"

"Good." Alex rubbed his forehead and looked down at the mountain of files on his desk. "I'm taking tomorrow off to go to the doctor with her."

"That's good." Sam smiled faintly and looked at the heap of files on Alex's desk. "Is there anything I can do to help you out a little, Alex? I know you've been working late quite a bit."

Alex shook his head. "I've got everything under control. And I'll have some spare time now that Noah has decided to send his business down the tubes."

Sam laughed. "He's not *sending his business down the tubes;* he's just taking a little time off."

"Whatever." Alex reached for a file.

Sam looked at Alex with concern. "I'm glad you're going to spend the day with Tillie tomorrow. In fact, why don't you go home early this afternoon? You guys could go over to Angelo's for supper. Maybe catch a show."

Alex frowned. "What are you talking about?"

"Taking some time off for your *dearest friend.* Isn't that what you used to call her?"

Alex swallowed, and felt his frown begin to relax. He looked into his brother's dark eyes and nodded.

"How's she taking all of this anyway?"

Alex shrugged and looked away from Sam. "She feels sorry for me."

"Oh, boy." Sam rolled his eyes and shook his head. "Get home and see your *dearest friend* for a little while. And then call Noah and apologize. I heard what you said."

Alex sighed. "I can't believe I treated him like that. He's just such a good ol' boy that it drives me crazy sometimes."

Sam nodded. "And if you need help with anything, please don't be afraid to ask. We've got tons of associates to help us out."

Alex nodded, but he wouldn't be letting *an associate* handle his work.

Noah rolled his eyes and shook his head again. *Whatever, Alex,* he thought as he tipped himself back in his chair and put his feet up on his desk. He picked up the thick wad of papers Melinda had left for him to "read." *I s'pose I should take a look at this stuff.*

He'd started to thumb his way through the first few pages when he heard Melinda's angry voice barking at someone in the outer office.

He glanced over the top of his sheaf and saw Ben Simmons smiling down at Melinda, obviously attempting to defuse whatever problem she was having.

"I apologize, Miss Melinda," Ben began, but she cut him off.

"Stop calling me that! I *hate* it when you call me that!"

"Very sorry," he began again. "Now what would you like me to do with these small equipment orders?"

"I told you," Melinda stormed. "Emily is in charge of the small equipment orders."

The two of them had been so intent on their argument, they hadn't noticed Noah walk over to them.

"Is there a problem?" he asked.

Melinda gritted her teeth and explained in a very strained voice, "He can't remember who gets what orders. He's driving me *crazy,* and I can't believe you hired him!" And with that, she spun around on her heel and stomped out of the office. The rest of the staff around them pretended to put their heads into their work, as if nothing had happened.

Ben smiled at Noah. "I think it is her lunchtime. Maybe she will feel better after she has a bite to eat."

Noah faked a smile in return. *Nothing will ever make that woman feel better. Maybe I should just fire the battle axe...*He cleared his throat and commented, "I thought you two were getting along a little better these days."

Ben shrugged. "Some days are better than others. But really, Noah, I do not mind her. She is, at times, a bit of a challenge, but nothing I cannot work through."

Wow...patient guy, Noah thought. "Well, if she gives you too much trouble, just let me know. You don't have to put up with that."

Tillie was hanging wallpaper in Alex's new office upstairs when she thought she heard his car in the driveway. *That's strange. It's still early in the afternoon.* She dried her hands and hurried, as much as she could hurry these days, down the stairs and into the living room. Alex was just coming up the front steps with a bouquet of roses. She squealed with delight and flung open the front door.

"What are you doing?" she said with a giggle as he walked into the house. He appeared to be exhausted, but he smiled.

Alex looked at his dearest friend and smiled into her eyes. She was so sweet in her pretty green sundress. Her crazy, curly hair was tied to the top of her head with what appeared to be a rag, and there were a few flecks of white wallpaper paste on her forehead.

"These are for you, beautiful," he said with a smile as he presented her with the flowers and gave her a tender kiss on the lips. "I just missed you today and thought I'd stop by and see what you were up to." He looked at her tummy and nearly gasped. It was as if it had grown since that morning; the sun dress was almost out of room.

Tillie took the flowers and laughed. "Well, I'm almost done with your office, *and* I had your favorite painting reframed." She reached for his hand. "Do you want to see it?"

Alex followed her up the stairs, wondering how in the world she managed to make it so effortlessly with the extra weight she carried on her middle. The portrait of *Obedience* sat on the floor at the top of the steps, framed in cherry wood. The old frame had been oak, he remembered.

Tillie had painted two of the same dramatic scene of her mother with her favored pet, the old horse named Delia. The paintings were inspired by an old photograph Giuseppe had taken on the day they left Italy in 1956. Rosa's hand rested beneath Delia's chin as she watched her family pack their few bags into a relative's car. Tillie had named the portrait *Obedience*, because that is how she saw her mother's actions in having to leave her precious friend behind in order to follow her husband. The painting had always been Alex's favorite and, unbeknownst to him, it was also beloved by his friend Noah Hansen. The second painting still hung in Maggie May's, where it had hung for the last five years.

"I like it," Alex said. "Where are you going to put it?"

"Right over here," Tillie answered as she led him into the new office that she was redecorating. "And we'll put your desk over there."

Alex looked upon the transformed little room with amazement. *She did all this? When did she have time for this?* "Wow. When did this all happen?"

"Over the past few weeks."

"Did you do all of this on your own?"

"Vincenzo did the wainscoting, but I stained everything and hung the paper. I would have been finished today…" Suddenly she stopped talking, and her face held a very surprised look. "Alex," she whispered, her eyes big and round. *"He's moving!"*

Alex smiled with surprise and reached for Tillie's incredibly large stomach. He placed his hand on it and waited patiently for the baby to pass by. It wasn't too often he felt the baby lately.

"Oh," he breathed as he felt his child move inside of her. "I can't believe it." He looked into Tillie's eyes and questioned with a smile, *"He?"*

"Well, who knows." Tillie laughed, and it seemed to make the baby move even more. "By the way, what are you doing home so early?"

Alex smiled into her pretty eyes and felt the stress of the day fade away. "Sam thought maybe I should come on home, take you out to dinner and a show."

"Will you still get tomorrow off?" she interrupted excitedly. Alex nodded, and Tillie practically jumped. *"Well, finally!"* She put her arms around his neck and gave him a soft kiss on his cheek. "I thought they were gonna work you to death!"

From the back room, Maggie heard the soft trill of Estelle's voice. She paused to listen. *Is she singing?*

"Her brow is like the snowdrift, her throat is like the swan, her face it is the fairest, that e're the sun shone on…hmmm, hmmm…" Estelle's singing had paused, and Maggie heard her admonish herself,

"Why'd ya go and forget the words now? Let's see, how'd that go again?" She cleared her voice and tried again. "Her brow is like the snowdrift, her throat is like the swan, her face it is the fairest, that e're the sun shone on…hmmm, hmmm, Annie Laurie, hmmm, hmmm."

Mel, Maggie's faithful cook, paused beside Maggie and leaned over to whisper, "She's been singing for a while now…but she always gets stuck in the same place."

Maggie nodded and came out of the back room to see Estelle dusting off Angel's painting, *Obedience*. Estelle heard the footsteps and looked at her sister with a smile.

"She looks prettier than ever today, Maggie May."

Maggie nodded. "But what were you singing, baby?"

"Oh," Estelle giggled softly and shook her head. "I was singing their song."

"Whose song?"

"Noah and Angel's song," Estelle answered as she gave the top of the painting a tender stroke with her feather duster. "'Annie Laurie' was their song, and I thought if I sang it to the Lord, He'd bring her back."

Maggie's jaw almost hit the floor. She managed a breath for recovery and asked, "Why on earth would you want Angel to come back now, baby? Noah's got Carrie, and there's a little one on the way."

Estelle's eyes showed a moment of surprise, but she covered with a smile. "Oh, that's right. I guess I was just…I was just…I was just praying for Angel. Me and Mona pray for Angel."

Maggie couldn't hide her surprise. "When did you start doing that?"

"Oh, I've prayed for Angel for a long time, but me and Mona been praying together for Angel for a couple of months or so." Estelle's eyes opened with expectation. "I know, Maggie! Me and you should pray for Angel!"

Maggie frowned. "I don't pray, and you know it."

"Come on, Maggie," Estelle coaxed. She stepped closer to her sister and reached for her hand. "Let's pray! It's so wonderful."

Maggie pulled her hand gently out of Estelle's tender grasp and shook her head. "No, baby. I don't pray." And then she turned and went to the back room.

Estelle shrugged and looked at her beloved painting. "Now, where was I?"

Dr. Lewis seemed to become faint when he walked into the small examining room to see Tillie. He stopped in the doorway and stared as she smiled back at him. Alex was there with her, and he caught the old doctor's worried expression.

"Well, goodness," Dr. Lewis managed in a quiet voice. He closed the door and reached for the cloth tape measure on the counter. He helped her lie back on the table and measured her stomach with a frown. "This says thirty weeks," he commented as he repositioned the tape measure and tried again.

"What's that for?" Alex asked in a curious tone.

"Well," Dr. Lewis explained, "theoretically, each inch is a week of pregnancy, and it's supposed to help us predict when the baby will be born. Forty inches would mean the pregnancy has come to term." He looked down at Tillie with a serious expression. "Tillie, you're measuring thirty weeks. You must have given me the wrong dates. You should only be measuring around eighteen to twenty weeks."

Tillie frowned at Dr. Lewis. "I'm *positive* about my cycle. I keep track on a calendar."

Dr. Lewis took a deep breath, put his stethoscope in his ears, and began to listen to Tillie's stomach. If the baby moved, he moved with it, listening in different places before he came to a startled stop and listened for a very long time.

"Well, I'll be," he said so quietly Tillie and Alex almost didn't hear him. He chuckled as he continued to listen, and then he murmured, "I'm gonna send you two down to our ultrasound lab. In fact, I'm coming down with you." He shook his head, stood up, and pulled the stethoscope out of his ears. "I think you've got twins in there."

Tillie thought she might roll off the table. "What?"

"Isn't your mother a twin?" Dr. Lewis asked with a smile as he helped Tillie into a seated position. He glanced at Alex and noticed that his dark complexion had yellowed and his mouth hung open as he stood beside his surprised wife.

"No," Alex answered with a shake of his head. He didn't remember his mother having a sister at all. *Uncle Mac wasn't her twin...was he?*

"Not you," Dr. Lewis laughed at Alex and clarified, "Rosa's a twin, isn't she?"

Tillie took a deep breath and nodded, but no words came out. Rosa had lost her twin sister Edda during World War II.

"Well, come on," Dr. Lewis said. He reached for a blanket and kindly wrapped it around Tillie's shoulders. "There. That'll cover you up a bit."

Alex helped Tillie from the examining table and they followed Dr. Lewis down the hallway and to a doorway that said *ULTRASOUND LAB*.

"It's so handy to have one of these around," Dr. Lewis said as he led them through the swinging doors and up to a desk where a nurse was doing paperwork.

"Is there a tech in the lab?" Dr. Lewis inquired politely.

The nurse nodded. "You can go in if you want."

"Thank you." Dr. Lewis led them a little farther along until they reached another set of swinging doors that took them into a darker room with what appeared to be a large television.

A technician told Alex to help his wife onto the table while he got what he called "*echo oil*" warm under the spigot at the sink. Dr. Lewis adjusted dials and switches at the television while Alex helped Tillie onto the higher table and then into a laying position. He covered her with the blanket Dr. Lewis had given them.

"Twins," she whispered, looking into Alex's eyes as he stood above her, holding her hand.

Alex shook his head and smiled back down at her. "No way. You're just further along, that's all. Don't worry."

The technician returned with the warmed oil and stood above the table. "Okay, now lift your gown, but you can keep the rest of yourself covered with the blanket."

Tillie lifted the gown to a modest level above her stomach, and Alex helped her to keep everything else covered.

"I'm going to put some of this on the baby and then we'll have a look," the technician said with a smile as he spurted some of the warm liquid onto Tillie's abdomen.

"You mean we'll be able to *see* him?" Alex asked curiously.

The technician nodded his head as he spread the warm liquid over Tillie's stomach and then reached for a piece of equipment. "Now, watch the screen and you'll see baby pretty soon." As soon as the technician's equipment touched the place above the baby, the screen came to life, revealing two perfectly formed little babies, folded around each other. Alex and Tillie gasped at the same time, and Tillie felt Alex's hand tighten around hers.

Dr. Lewis laughed out loud as he flicked a switch, and the room was filled with a rapid pounding noise.

"That's their hearts beating," the technician informed.

"Their hearts," Alex whispered, feeling a strange emotion come over him.

Tillie was just very quiet as she watched the screen in awe, praising God every moment for the miracle before them. *How had He gotten two babies in there?*

"Give me a view of each of them separately if you can," Dr. Lewis instructed with a smile, watching the screen carefully.

The technician began to move his instrument around on Tillie's stomach, stopping when only one baby filled the screen. He paused for Dr. Lewis to take a good look, and then moved to the other.

Dr. Lewis laughed again and pointed to the screen. "See this?" He pointed to something Tillie and Alex could not make out. It was positioned just above the head of the baby they were looking at. "That's a foot. They're tucked in there just perfectly. One up. One down. They'll turn naturally during delivery." Dr. Lewis instructed the technician, "Let me see 'em again, together." The technician brought the two babies into view, and Dr. Lewis nodded with approval. "Two placentas. Probably fraternal twins, which would mean that it took two separate eggs to achieve this particular pregnancy. Maybe you'll even get one of each."

"So," Alex said as he looked at the doctor with confusion, "when will they be here?"

"I'm leaving your due date at December first," Dr. Lewis answered. He smiled at Tillie and said, "Apparently you *did* give me the correct dates, because these babies are only about eighteen to twenty weeks."

"I knew it," Tillie said, satisfied that at least she had been right about the dates of her own cycle.

"I'll bet you're going to be a lot busier than you thought you'd be," Dr. Lewis laughed.

"A lot busier than I thought I'd be," Tillie muttered as she and Alex strolled through the Vern Eide car dealership. Neither of them had spoken much after leaving the doctor's office, except that Alex had mentioned wanting to trade Tillie's Mustang for something more practical for babies. That's how they wound up looking at cars.

Alex shook his head and gave Tillie's belly a tender pat. "Two babies, maybe one of each. That's probably why you can never decide to say boy or girl."

Tillie nodded thoughtfully. "What will our families say?"

"Probably 'Way to go, Angel.' After all, it was *your* eggs." He looked at her mischievously and winked with a smile. "Why didn't you tell me there were two eggs on the loose in there?"

Tillie laughed. "Well, now we've got to try to fit *two* cribs into that little room."

"Yep." Alex nodded and stopped beside a black Mercedes wagon. "How 'bout this?"

"Nice," Tillie said as she looked at the expensive car. "But what about the cost?"

Alex rolled his eyes and waved at a salesman. "You have to have a comfortable car, and Mercedes is the best."

CHAPTER 6

For seven long days during intense heat and unusual humidity, Marquette and Tara watched the tiny hotel in Big Eagle that Attorney General Thomas had referred them to. They saw several suspects in the government's cocaine case come and go, but Schneider Rauwolf was nowhere to be seen.

"At least none of them seem to carry guns," Tara whispered as she watched the doorway through her binoculars. "And that is a relief."

Marquette looked through his own set of binoculars and smiled at the memory of Tara with the attorney general. "I had no idea you could handle a switchblade so gracefully."

"Nor did I. And I am quite sure Custer was surprised as well."

Marquette chortled, "I still cannot get over the look on his red face when you snapped it open."

"What surprised me is how easily we were able to coerce information out of the man."

"He would probably sell his own mother down the river if it meant keeping himself out of harm's way."

Tara giggled in response, and then she suddenly gasped, "There he is, Marquette!"

Marquette focused on a tall, thin, red-headed man sauntering into the hotel. *John Peters' killer...* "Schneider Rauwolf," he whispered as they watched the man enter the hotel and disappear from their view. He lowered his binoculars and looked at his wife. "We have caught him at last." He took a deep breath and frowned. "That blackguard knows what has become of John."

With great stealth and grace, Marquette and Tara crept up the old fire escape along the back of the hotel. They were certain of what room the tall redhead occupied after having watched the place for so many days. The hotel was small and their clientele limited, which left only a handful of possible rooms.

The two wore their mirrored sunglasses and black hats, and Marquette even pasted on the fake goatee. They could no longer afford to be recognized because of their relationship to the famous Senator Caselli.

"You are in excellent shape," Marquette whispered to his wife as they inched along a deficient landing on the fire escape.

"As are you, my love," Tara whispered politely in return, but focused on the dreadful duty at hand. She had always hated this part of their livelihood.

"For two people now thirty-nine years of age, I would say we are quite remarkable," he added as he gave her a gentle hand up onto the next landing.

Tara agreed in silence as she grabbed a tight hold of the iron railing. She pressed her body close to the brick of the building, looked apprehensively at her husband, and whispered, "This is a strange conversation you have started at this particular time."

Marquette peered into the window they stood beside and then he looked into his lovely wife's eyes. "Do you think I need to cut my hair when I turn forty?"

Tara frowned with confusion. "Have you chosen this moment to break down on me, Marquette?"

He shook his head. "He is in there, my Tara. Do you have your friendly little knife?"

Tara nodded, and with that Marquette leaped through the open window. The man in the room attempted to scramble for the door, but Marquette lunged at him and forced him up against the wall. He pulled out his pistol and put the muzzle between the man's eyes.

"Come in now, my love," Marquette called.

Tara gracefully stepped through the window, onto the bed Marquette had cleared in his single bound, and then to the floor.

"How do you do?" she greeted with a smile as she strode toward the man Marquette held against the wall. She flicked open her switchblade; Marquette had to keep from laughing. This was his favorite part.

"What do you want?" Rauwolf asked as perspiration beaded on his forehead.

"John Peters." Tara touched the man's jaw delicately with the blade of her knife. "What can you do to help me?"

"I have no idea who John Peters is."

"Is that so?" Tara said with a coy smile. "But with my own eyes I saw John follow you and a blonde woman from a place called Maggie May's, and that was the last time I ever saw him."

"Maggie May's?" Rauwolf's tone was sincerely confused. "In Rapid City, South Dakota?" Tara only nodded in response, and Rauwolf seemed to search his memory. He swallowed hard and began to nod his head. "I did a job out there about five years ago."

"What type of a job?" Marquette's voice was gruff as he pressed the gun into Rauwolf's forehead.

"There was a guy following my boss —"

"Mario Ponerello was your boss?" Marquette interrupted.

Rauwolf's pale complexion lost whatever color it may have had, and he pretended in a jagged breath, "What are you talking about?"

Marquette tapped the gun between Rauwolf's eyes and snarled, "Do not attempt to deny that you know the man, Rauwolf, for it was *you* who helped him escape Ustica in 1964."

Rauwolf squinted into Marquette's sunglasses, attempting to see through the mirror finish and asked, "Is that you, Caselli?"

Tara covered Rauwolf's lips with her knife and questioned, "Did you kill John Peters?"

"I *had* to," Rauwolf admitted, speaking carefully through the blade of Tara's knife. "My boss was terrified of him."

Marquette swallowed his grief. "Where is the body?"

"I have no idea," Rauwolf answered. "My boss and his kid took care of it."

"Can you find out where the body is?" Marquette questioned further.

"I think so."

"Will you take us there?" Tara questioned.

Rauwolf shook his head. "There is a...I have to...You can't go with me...I will have to go alone."

Marquette shook his head and made a *tsk* sound. "Is it in South Dakota?"

"I don't think so."

"And when will you bring us the information?" Tara asked.

"It's gonna take me a couple of days," Rauwolf answered.

Tara shook her head and allowed the blade of her knife to rest upon the man's neck. She looked at her husband. "*Tsk, tsk, tsk*. I do not know about this, my love. Perhaps he is trying to escape. Perhaps we should call the police."

"No. No!" Rauwolf panicked. "Custer will have me killed! *Please*, just let me get the information and bring it back to you."

Marquette nodded his head and looked into the man's eyes. "What foreign languages do you speak, besides German and Italian?"

Rauwolf shook his head. "None."

Marquette nodded again and then he looked at Tara and began to speak in Chechen. He and Tara had strengthened their language abilities over the last seven years, Chechen being their most recent study. "This is similar to the situation we ran into in Kazakhstan. What was the name of that delightfully corrupt little town?"

"Makinsk," Tara answered as she remembered.

"Please recall," Marquette continued in Chechen, "the overlord there had several of our informants killed, and we walked away empty-handed." He sighed. "The attorney general of this state has proven to have that kind of power, and John's body may lead us, eventually, back to the Ponerellos."

Rauwolf's eyebrows went up. *Ponerello? It's Caselli for sure.*

"And we do have to break off for a few days to testify before the Senate Subcommittee, but what if he escapes?" Tara questioned.

"He may," Marquette acknowledged. "But at least we will know he is alive somewhere, and that is better than having him dead and able to tell us nothing."

Tara had to agree. She sighed. She then looked back at the man her husband held and spoke in English, "You will tell *no one* you have met with us. Is that understood?"

Rauwolf swallowed very hard and nodded his head in the affirmative.

"We will meet again in two weeks," Marquette instructed. "Right here, in this very spot."

"And if you do not show up," Tara said as she brought the blade of her knife to press against the man's throat, "then may our God have *no* mercy on your soul."

"Well, Maggie won't pray," Estelle complained to Mona during their Bible study. "I just can't figure it out, Mona. She wanted Angel to come back as bad as I did."

Mona nearly choked on her tea. "Estelle, Noah doesn't want Angel to come back anymore. He's happy with Carrie."

For a brief moment Estelle's eyes were wide with surprise, but she covered with an open smile and said, "I know that, Mona. I just think we should pray for Angel…That's all I'm saying."

Mona nodded and covered her own doubts with a smile. *Estelle is really forgetting things…I'm going to have to talk to Maggie about this…*

After several grueling days of being questioned before the Senate Subcommittee, Marquette and Tara returned to their home at Tyson's Crossing. Had they had the time, they would have opted to visit Como Lake instead. The heat in Washington was dreadful this summer, and Tara could hardly stand it.

"It reminds me of Miami," she grumbled as she thumbed through the mail that had piled up in their absence.

"Now, about my hair," Marquette pondered as he lay on the couch watching a news program.

Tara shook her head and frowned at her husband. "Cut your hair when you turn forty? Are we back to that?"

"Yes," Marquette answered. "I am reaching an age where perhaps I should suffer myself some dignity."

Tara giggled. "Do not dare touch a hair upon your beautiful head. It gives you style and grace, and I love it." She smiled and began to walk toward him with a pink envelope. "You have received something from Angel."

Marquette sat up, took the letter from her hands, and opened it. Tara took a seat next to him and peered at the words.

Marquette laughed as he read, "Angel is expecting two babes now instead of just one."

"Two babes?" Tara questioned, trying to skim the letter.

"It seems the Lord has blessed her with twins."

Tara's pretty face clouded over and Marquette looked into her eyes, where he saw the familiar tears.

"Why did the Lord not bless us with babies, Marq?" she asked in a soft voice.

Marquette put his arm around Tara and held her close. "He has blessed us in other ways, my love. The Lord, my Tara, has chosen a different path for the two of us; a path where children cannot come."

The July sun was hot in western South Dakota, forcing the fragrance of pine into the air. The wind carried it from deep in the hills into town.

Carrie Hansen pitched the inflatable ball to her son, while he made several clumsy strikes. Noah was checking a building site but had promised to come home before lunch so they could head up to Pactola for the afternoon.

She heard a car in the street and turned to see who it was. It didn't appear to be Mona's car or anyone else's she recognized. Since it parked across the street, she turned around and pitched Ty another ball. The little boy missed and turned to chase the rolling ball across the yard, and Carrie laughed.

When she heard footsteps in the driveway, she turned around to see a tall, redheaded man walking slowly toward her. Her stomach felt like she'd gone over a hill, and her mouth fell open in surprise. *I didn't think I'd ever see him again.*

"Hey, Carrie," he casually greeted, as if he saw her every day. "How ya been?"

"Fine," she answered without expression. *What does he want?*

Rauwolf's eyes followed the redheaded little boy as he scampered through the backyard. "He's mine, isn't he?"

Carrie shook her head. "He belongs to Noah."

Rauwolf looked at Carrie's little belly and frowned. "Noah Hansen? I thought you were done with him."

Carrie narrowed her eyes. "What are you doing here, Roy?"

He looked into her eyes and wondered briefly how life might have turned out had he done things differently. "I need to know where that body is, Carrie."

Carrie swallowed hard again and clenched her jaw. "No." She turned away and began to walk toward the backyard where Ty waited for a pitch. Rauwolf grabbed her arm roughly and turned her around to face him.

"Listen, Carrie," he said, his expression angry. "You tell me where that body is. I'm in a lot of trouble."

"Well, that's just too bad," she retorted as she yanked her arm out of his grasp. "And you'd better get out of here before Noah comes home. If he sees you here, he'll kill you."

"Oh, please." Rauwolf rolled his eyes and shook his head. "That little drunk couldn't fight his way out of a wet paper sack." His eyes narrowed as he scolded her, "And I can't *believe* you married him, especially when you knew the kid belonged to *me*."

Carrie looked at the stranger she'd claimed to love only a few years before and shook her head in disgust. *I never loved you.* "I had to make some pretty tough decisions," she snapped. "You were never gonna change your life, and I didn't want to live that way anymore."

Rauwolf sighed and shook his head. "Listen, Carrie, I didn't come all this way to get into it with you. Caselli and his wife found me —"

"What?" Carrie gasped in a whisper. Her heart started to pound. *If Caselli finds us...*

Rauwolf nodded. "Custer must have tipped 'em off —"

"Is that why you need the body?"

He nodded again. "And there's more to it than you're going to want to hear. Do you remember Angel?"

Carrie's breath caught for a moment, and she covered her mouth with her hand. She'd *never* forget Angel...*the girl Noah had planned to marry.*

"Well, we weren't going to tell you this," Rauwolf continued, "but she's Tillie Caselli Martin —"

"*Caselli?*"

"Marquette's sister and Alex Martin's wife," he confirmed dryly. "So if Noah and Alex get any friendlier, there are going to be big problems, *especially* for you. And if they all manage to get together, they're going to start drawing lines straight back to you, because you left Maggie's with me that night, and apparently Caselli's wife saw the whole thing." He took a deep breath and frowned. "So where's the body, Carrie?"

She shook her head. "I was high that night. I don't remember. Why can't you ask Jack?"

"Because he won't tell me —"

"What are *you* doing here?" a man's voice boomed from somewhere behind them, and they turned to see Noah storming up the driveway. Noah knew Rauwolf only as Roy Schneider, a man who'd worked for Carrie's stepfather, Jack, several years ago. The man who had fathered Ty.

Rauwolf took a few steps backward. He tried to smile at Noah. "I just came by to see my boy."

Noah looked at Carrie. "Are you okay?" Carrie nodded and watched the expression on Noah's face. She didn't remember him ever being capable of so much anger.

"Take Tiger into the house, Carrie," Noah said through clenched teeth as he reached for Rauwolf's shoulder and slowly walked him toward the garage. Carrie hurried to where Ty was still waiting with his bat, gathered him into her arms, and hastened him into the house.

The moment they were out of sight, Noah grabbed Rauwolf by both shoulders and slammed him hard up against the side of the garage, where no one could see what was going on.

"He's not *your boy*," Noah growled. "Now, what are you doing here?"

Some of the wind had been knocked out of Rauwolf, and he attempted to regain his breath. "Listen, Hansen, I'm sorry you got stuck with the kid—"

"I didn't get stuck with anything." Noah gave Rauwolf another hard slam into the wall of the garage.

Rauwolf winced from the pain and raised his hands. "Okay, okay. Just let me go, and I won't come back anymore."

Noah frowned into Rauwolf's eyes as he thought over the offer. "Carrie put *my* name on the birth certificate."

Rauwolf shrugged. "I don't care. If you want the little bastard, that's your business."

Noah's anger took control at that point and he punched Rauwolf in the face, knocking him to the ground. Rauwolf scrambled to his feet and started to back down the driveway.

"You're such an idiot," he said as he hurriedly backed away from Noah.

"You come back again and I'll call the cops," Noah threatened.

Rauwolf threw his arms into the air and trotted to his car, got in, and drove away.

Noah shook his head and wondered with despair, *what on earth is going on? Did he come back to get his son and...?* His stomach turned at the thought, and he headed for the back steps, taking them two at a time. He came into the house through the kitchen door and found Carrie and Ty sitting at the table with some animal crackers. She looked up at him, and he saw the tears in her grief-stricken eyes. His heart beat with the anxious anticipation of what she was about to say. He sat down next to her and took one of her hands gently into his.

"Please don't leave me," he whispered as he pulled her into his arms. "He's worthless, and he's *never* deserved you —"

"Noah, I'm not going anywhere." Carrie reassured as she looked up into his worried eyes. "That's not why he was here."

Noah sighed with relief and held Carrie close. "I love you so much."

"Noah," Carrie sniffed her tears away, "I've gotta tell you a couple of things."

Instead of going to Pactola that night, they told Joshua and Mona they wanted to see a show. Conveniently, Joshua and Mona offered to babysit, and Noah and Carrie left by themselves. They parked Noah's pickup in the Harney Baseball League lot, just off Fairmont Boulevard, and hiked through the darkness into the trees below the diamonds. Once a city dump, the area had since been transformed into a baseball and softball complex in recent years.

"Back there," Carrie whispered in the dark. "Roy lost his cool that night and slit his throat. He was dead before we could get him to the hospital. Jack panicked and sent Roy home, and then Jack and I brought the body back here and buried him." She shook her head. "We thought he was working for Jack's relatives in Sicily, but it turned out he was just a private investigator. Jack and Tony are both illegal aliens. They've tried to outrun Jack's family for years, and we couldn't afford to be tied to that dead body and draw attention to ourselves."

"Oh boy," Noah whispered as he took a tight hold of his wife's hand. "And you've never told anybody?"

Carrie shook her head. "There's a certain dagger that Jack's male family members all receive when they come of age. And if it's used to spill innocent blood, it must never be used again. The dagger is buried with the body, and it can identify Jack. He would be deported immediately—"

"Leaving Charise without a father," Noah finished, and Carrie nodded.

"Noah, I'm so sorry," she whispered. "I can't believe the things I've done."

He took his trembling wife into his arms. "Don't worry about it, Carrie. It's not like *you* killed the guy."

"What will you do?"

"This land has been for sale for years," Noah replied. "First thing in the morning, I'll make an offer."

Mario frowned as he sipped from his brandy snifter, and Antonio shook his head.

"But I need that information, or I'll be forced to find somewhere else to hide," Rauwolf insisted.

"You will only draw attention to us, Rauwolf," Antonio calmly rebuked. "You are better off getting away from Custer Thomas anyway. Why do you not settle down here in Rapid City with us? We could keep you safe, and you would not have to run these errands of evil."

Rauwolf shook his head. "You guys just don't get it. We *can't* settle down. Sal is always about two steps behind us, and now Caselli is hot on my tail —"

"Sal is *not two steps behind us*," Antonio argued with a dark frown. "He believes to have killed me in Chicago in 1976, and he is not even aware of Carrie's marriage. He believes she died of a drug overdose—a death you helped to purport. He does not know of Charise's existence, and he believes Papa and Della to have left the area."

Mario held up his hand. "Please, Rauwolf, let us not be anxious about this anymore. Carrie will be certain to keep things quiet."

Rauwolf persisted nervously, "But if Noah and Angel are ever able to connect—"

"They will not," Mario assured. "Noah's loyalty lies with Carrie now, and he no longer desires to find the Angel."

Rauwolf sighed and shook his head. "But one slip of the tongue—"

"Carrie will not let that happen," Antonio said with certainty. "My sister has changed a great deal since you have been away. She loves Noah, and she will not risk him."

CHAPTER 7

Giuseppe's black eyes filled with tears as he watched Noah check the progression of the construction site. *Patient, kind, thorough...all the characteristics of a knight...how could I have been so wrong? How was I so misled? By my deceitful, old heart, of course.* He sighed heavily and shook his head. *And now my Angel is alone...*

Noah had noticed Giuseppe's white Suburban pull onto the site, and he wondered why he didn't get out and have a look. In his friendly way, Noah strode to Giuseppe's vehicle and held up a yellow hard hat.

"Hi, Mr. Caselli. Wanna get out and take a look? It's coming along real nice...I think you'll be happy with it."

Giuseppe smiled faintly. "Hello, Mr. Hansen —"

"Please, just call me Noah. Everybody does."

"Very well then, Noah, but I do not wish to be in your way."

Noah smiled. "Oh, you won't be in my way. Come on, I'll show you around."

Giuseppe nodded reluctantly and got out of the truck. He took the hard hat from Noah and fell in beside him as they walked toward the site. "How is your missus?"

"Oh, she's doing real good," Noah answered with a smile. "In fact, she and our little one came to town with me this time. We thought it might be nice to get away for a few days, and she's never been to Sioux Falls. She and Tiger are at the hotel in the swimming pool."

"That is good. And I understand from Alex you are expecting?"

Noah's expression beamed. "We sure are. The baby is due on December twenty-fifth."

"That will be a wonderful Christmas present."

"It would be fun if he came on my birthday," Noah mused. "And Carrie says that's okay with her because my birthday is four days before her due date."

Giuseppe's eyes flew open in surprise. *Venti uno Dicembre.* *December twenty-first.* Rosa had heard about Noah on that very day in 1960 and had written the date in her Bible. Poor Giuseppe stumbled just then on a stray two-by-four, but Noah's strong hand caught him and kept him from falling.

"You okay, Mr. Caselli?"

"Of course." He pretended to smile as he caught his balance. "I am fine, Noah. Thank you."

Noah frowned curiously into the older man's expression. "Are you sure you're feeling all right, Mr. Caselli? You seem a little under the weather today."

"Oh," Giuseppe scoffed with a wave of his hand, "I just have so many things on my mind, what with planning to open this second restaurant and my daughter—" he stopped himself, swallowed hard, and prayed Noah wouldn't ask.

"Your daughter? Alex said she's been sick. Is she having more problems?"

Giuseppe shook his head and chuckled. "No, no...she is doing well. But have you not heard?"

Noah shook his head with a curious smile.

"They are expecting twins," Giuseppe said. "She is very excited, but her mother and I worry."

"Well, that's understandable." Noah took a breath and put a hand on Giuseppe's shoulder. "Hey, why don't you walk across the street with me and I'll buy you a cup of coffee? I was just getting ready to take a little break, and it sure would be nice to have someone to share the time with."

Giuseppe's heart sprang with unexpected delight at the offer, even though his head told him to maintain some kind of a distance with Noah. *But what could one cup of coffee hurt?*

"I would like that very much, Noah."

111

Rosa and Tillie stood back to admire their work. They had just assembled another small crib, successfully fitting two of them into the nursery.

"It's perfect." Tillie smiled with satisfaction.

Rosa agreed as she looked around at the room Tillie had designed for her babies. She'd chosen pink and blue for her colors, and then asked her family to pray for one of each.

"And what if you get two of the same?" Rosa teased her daughter with a giggle.

Tillie chuckled. "Then I guess we'll have to redecorate."

"Oh, no!" Rosa protested with a smile and a wave of her hand. She turned from the room and started down the hallway. "Come, my Angel, let me get you a delicious iced tea. You must be parched by now."

Tillie smiled and followed her mother into the kitchen. Rosa pulled out the pitcher of iced tea she'd brewed earlier that morning, filled two glasses with ice, and then poured Tillie's favorite flavor over them.

"Mmm." Tillie sipped at the cool drink. "Orange and spice. You do this *perfectly*, Ma`ma."

"Thank you, my dear. Now, how about we sit beneath your wonderful old tree in the backyard?"

They headed outside and took seats in the cool grass beneath the leafy shade. The heat of the summer had broken for a short spell, and a cooler breeze made the day more comfortable.

"It is a lovely day," Rosa remarked as she sipped her tea.

Tillie nodded, but inside she knew what her mother really wanted to talk about. Rosa only spoke of the weather when she was working up the courage to ask about other things.

"What's on your mind, Ma`ma?"

Rosa sighed as she reached for Tillie's pronounced abdomen. "Are they moving today?"

Tillie guided her mother's hand to a more active spot, and her black eyes sparkled with delight. "They move all of the time now. I don't think they ever get any rest."

"And how about you, my Angel? Are you getting enough rest?"

"Oh, plenty. I get eight hours in every night, and I usually have an afternoon nap."

"Well, that is good, because you will need every ounce of your strength to deliver those babies." Rosa took a breath. "And how has Alex's schedule been these days?"

Tillie raised her eyebrows at her mother and offered a small smile. "This is what you really want to talk about —"

"Now, Angel, I am your mother. Naturally I will be concerned about such things." She frowned into Tillie's eyes. "Is he gone a lot?"

"It's not so bad, Ma`ma. He works late quite a bit, though, and I do get lonesome."

"Have you talked with him about it?"

Tillie nodded. "And things will slow down a lot after the election. He's helping Governor Williams, you know."

"Yes, I saw him on the news last night." Rosa had seen Alex Martin III stumping for Governor Williams. *As if Williams does not already have the election in the bag. Does he really need my son-in-law, with the famous "Martin" name, to go out and gin up more votes?*

"Didn't he look great?" Tillie sighed contentedly. "He's so awesome, Ma`ma, and he's *so* smart."

Rosa pretended to nod in agreement, hiding her disappointment behind a sip of her tea. Angel seemed happy…*but something does not feel right. Alex should be with her during this time.*

Conversation with Noah came easily for Giuseppe. They talked about Noah's business and his projects, Giuseppe's restaurant, and how excited Burt Engleson was to be getting into the business. When they discussed their families, Giuseppe was very careful. He spoke openly about his sons, of course but, when it came to his daughter, his information skirted around only that she had just graduated college and was very pleased to finally be starting a family.

"So how'd you get into the restaurant business?" Noah asked curiously.

"My brother, Angelo," Giuseppe answered with a smile.

"Alex tells me the two of you were in the war together."

Giuseppe's black eyes twinkled with pride, and Noah was again struck with his familiar expression.

"We were powerful warriors…" Giuseppe began, but Noah lost track of his words after that.

Powerful warriors…Noah frowned as he was drawn deep into the old memory. The words Angel had spoken to him five years before suddenly played back in his mind: *He and my Uncle Angelo, that was his brother, fought with the Allies in Italy…*

"What's your daughter's name?" Noah interrupted.

Giuseppe's smile faded, and he swallowed hard. *I have said too much. What did she tell him about me?* He cleared his throat. "Her given name is Matilde Rosa, which was her maternal grandmother's name. The mother of my wife was named after an Italian noblewoman, *la Gran Contessa, Matilde of Canossa.*" He paused to pretend a chuckle. "But Alex calls her Tillie."

"But do you call her anything else?" Noah questioned.

Giuseppe feigned another chuckle. "Why do you ask, Noah?"

Noah sighed with a smile and shook his head. "I don't know…I met this girl once, and you're going to think I'm really weird, but you remind me of her. She said that her father and her Uncle Angelo were *powerful warriors* in Italy…" he hesitated and looked thoughtfully into Giuseppe's eyes. "And you *do* look an awful lot like her. Your eyes remind me of her."

Giuseppe hid his surprise behind an open smile. "How did you meet this girl?"

Noah sighed with an embarrassed grin and looked away. "Believe it or not, we met in a bar, but she wasn't like that at all. A couple of her friends had gotten a little liquored up, and she came in after them. And to make a long story short, we spent some time together and decided to get married, but I don't know what happened. She was supposed to meet me someplace, but she never showed. Never called either. Guess she got cold feet." He took a breath and finished with a smile. "But it doesn't matter anymore anyway, 'cause I've got a really nice wife and a great life."

Giuseppe listened to Noah's story, knowing only too well the details of his horrible misfortune. Before he realized what he was saying, he blurted out, "Do you ever miss her?"

Noah shook his head. "I don't even think about her anymore."

After his break with Giuseppe, Noah hurried over to Alex's office in order to check on some other properties that were coming available in Sioux Falls. As usual, Alex was neck-deep in paperwork.

"I'm very sorry for the way I treated you on the phone the last time we spoke," Alex said as he shook Noah's hand. "Please forgive me for losing control."

Noah was pleasantly surprised at Alex's overture, and nodded with a smile. "No problem. Just forget about it. Everybody gets a little cranky from time to time."

Alex smiled when he realized all had been forgiven, and motioned for Noah to take a seat. He handed Noah two files and began to explain, "Those are inquiries for jobs near your Sycamore site. I thought you might be interested."

Noah opened the top file and glanced at the proposal. "Ben will probably be doing most of the supervising. He's enjoyed his last couple of trips to Sioux Falls."

"Sure," Alex agreed. "And did he mention that we met the other day?"

Noah shook his head.

"I ran over to the site to meet with the realtor, and Mr. Simmons was there." Alex replied. "By the way, where's he from? I noticed his accent right away."

Noah raised an eyebrow. *Accent? Ben doesn't have an accent, does he?* "As far as I know, he was born and raised in Chicago." He smiled and shook his head. "I guess I never noticed any accent."

"Well, you know my wife's family is from Italy," Alex went on. "And Mr. Simmons does a really good job of speaking around it, but it's there all right. He doesn't use contractions."

"Well," Noah scoffed with a smile, "that's probably the Lakota influence. We all have a little bit of an accent out West."

Alex nodded because he didn't want to argue with Noah, but he was *certain* Ben Simmons had an accent, and it definitely wasn't Lakota.

Carrie and Ty had played in the pool at the hotel for two hours before they came back to their room. They changed their clothes, ordered sandwiches for lunch, and then bundled into the bed for an afternoon nap. Ty had fallen asleep immediately, but Carrie lay awake thinking about the horrible circumstances she'd suddenly found herself in. Noah was over at Alex's office. *What if Angel decides to "pop in" and see her husband while Noah is there?* Carrie shook her head and attempted to blink her tears away. *Maybe I should just ask Noah if he ever thinks about her anymore...maybe I should just tell him... No, I can't do that. If I tell him about Angel, then I'll have to tell him about Caselli.*

The telephone beside the bed rang, and Carrie reached for it. She glanced at her sleeping boy and sighed with relief. It hadn't awakened him.

"Hello."

"Hello, Carrie. It is Antonio."

"Hi. What's going on?"

"Carrie, dearest," he began in a sullen tone, "Sal has found us at last."

Carrie gasped as she sat up on the edge of the bed. "How do you know?"

"He came looking for Papa while we were out. Apparently he has known about your mother and our sister for quite some time. He wants the dagger, naturally, as he always has —"

"Can't you just give it to him? For the life of me, I don't understand why you just don't let him have it!"

"There is much to explain," Antonio quickly continued, "but you must listen to me now, Carrie. Your mother has been hurt very badly. Papa found her cut and lying at the bottom of the cellar stairs. She is still alive, but in a very bad condition."

"Oh," Carrie breathed. "What are we going to do?"

"We have already figured everything out," Antonio replied. "Dr. Schneider has signed a certificate of death, and he will also sign as the funeral director —"

"No. This is against the law —"

"And we will confine her to a small nursing home in the southern Hills," Antonio went on. "She may never walk again —"

"Are you listening to me?" Carrie protested in an angry whisper. "I'm not going to tell my husband that my mother is dead just so you can get away from this guy —"

"Yes, Carrie, you will," Antonio calmly demanded. "You must do this in order to protect my father and your sister, and your mother as well. Sal will believe that Papa has left the area in order to retrieve the dagger. He will believe that he has killed your mother, and Papa and Charise will slip into seclusion —"

"And how is this all going to happen?"

"We felt that Sal was getting closer a few months ago, and Papa was able to secure a small acreage in Rapid Valley —"

"You mean they're not even really leaving the area?"

"No. Now listen to me, Carrie, for this is most important. Papa will be forced to dump his finances in order to sweep his trail clean. You must find a way to get him some money —"

"You mean *steal?*"

"It is most necessary at this time." Antonio took a deep breath. "And Sal still believes you died of a drug overdose. He is completely unaware of your marriage and your child. You will be quite safe as long as you maintain your distance for a time. He does believe to have killed me in Chicago in 1976, which is what leads him to believe that if your mother is out of the picture, he can persuade Papa to turn over the dagger."

"Then why not give it to him?"

Antonio sighed. "Because, Carrie dearest, the handle is filled with fifty loose diamonds. When Sal attempts to fence them he will be caught for certain, and rest assured he will not go to jail alone. He will identify Papa and me, and Charise is too young to be on her own."

"Charise can stay with me and Noah."

"And Noah would connect the dots when photos of Angel's very high-profile brother and his family are paraded before our very eyes when Papa and I are captured." Antonio took a breath. "When Marquette Caselli caught the bulk of our family in Ustica in 1968, every newspaper in the world ran story after story about Mr. Caselli, his family, and their tale of immigration from Italy. Angel's identity will be compromised and, as a result, your marriage as well."

Carrie felt as if someone had punched her in the stomach, and she began to nod her head. "Okay. What do you need?"

Giuseppe parked his white Suburban in the driveway and strode up to the front porch. With a heavy sigh he dropped into one of the comfortable chairs, and looked toward the Martin home just up the street.

Rosa had heard his vehicle in the driveway and wondered why he hadn't come into the house. She went to the front door for a look. Finding him on the porch, she went outside and took a seat beside him.

"You do not look well, Giuseppe." She reached for his forehead as if to check for a fever.

"I have never been more miserable in my entire life, Rosa, my love."

"Giuseppe, whatever is the matter?"

He sighed again and shook his head. "I had an extended visit with Noah Hansen today." He was interrupted by Rosa's surprised gasp. He glanced her way and nodded his head. "Do not fret, my love; I did manage to keep our torrid little secret."

"Oh, thank goodness," she breathed with relief, patting Giuseppe's knee and looking into his sad black eyes. "Why on earth do you torment yourself this way? And why on earth would you have an *extended visit* with this particular man?"

"It was an accident," Giuseppe explained. "I went out to check the site, and he was there. He asked me for coffee, and I felt compelled to oblige him."

"You felt *compelled?*"

Giuseppe nodded. "He is a most wonderful man, Rosa. I could not seem to help myself." His breath caught for an instant. "I know *he* was intended to be our son-in-law." He shook his head and looked into Rosa's eyes. "I do not know how I will ever make amends for my sin."

He'll probably call Joshua first thing, Carrie thought as she watched Noah saunter from his vehicle up to the hotel. *I have to make this as believable as I can.* She sighed with regret. *I hate doing this to him.*

In a few moments she heard his key in the door, and he let himself inside.

"Hey you," he greeted with a smile. "How's everything?"

She shrugged with a strained expression. "Tiger's still napping," and she looked toward the bed where their little one was still curled up in the covers.

"Oh." Noah lowered his voice in understanding, and then he looked back at his wife. Her expression was strangely tense, and it made him frown. "What's wrong, Carrie?"

She swallowed hard and began, "Tony just called a little bit ago… Noah, Mom fell down some stairs today and hit her head."

Noah took his wife into his arms. "Oh, Carrie, I'm so sorry to hear that. Is she okay?"

Carrie shook her head, thankful that he held her close enough so she didn't have to look him in the eye while she lied. "She passed away. We need to get back as soon as possible."

"Oh, Carrie, I'm so sorry," he repeated, holding his beloved wife as closely as he could. "I know the guy who runs the charters between here and Rapid. We can get on a flight after supper and be home before eight or nine o'clock. How does that sound?"

"That sounds great," she whispered, feeling the tears of deception fall from her eyes. He was the last person in the world she wanted to lie to. No one was as good or as kind as Noah Hansen.

"And I'll call Josh, too," Noah added. "That way he and Mona can start getting the church ready for the funeral."

"Okay," she nodded in agreement. *'Cause we're gonna need a real-looking funeral.*

Carrie laid a yellow rose atop the casket and stepped back into Noah's arm. Her sister, Charise, who had just celebrated her fifteenth birthday, stepped closer to the casket and laid her rose next to Carrie's. She stepped back, and Jack approached with a bouquet, knelt before the casket, and gave the side of it a soft kiss.

"We will miss you so very much," he whispered, and Noah just about cried. He held Carrie just a little tighter as the scene played out before him.

Noah had watched the strange funeral, beginning the middle of that morning, when the funeral home brought over the closed casket and Jack refused to open it. He had also refused to have any kind of a visitation at the funeral home, even when Joshua had suggested that it might help the family to say good-bye. Jack insisted that viewing the dead body was against his religion, and that a Christian service and burial were as far as he was prepared to go.

Noah was surprised at Jack's lack of grief during the whole episode, especially knowing how he would react if something should ever happen to Carrie or Ty. Charise and Carrie didn't seem that upset either, and they didn't seem to think anything of it when their stepbrother, Tony, didn't show.

After the interment, Noah, Joshua, and Mona visited together, while Carrie stepped away to visit with her family.

"They are *so* weird," Noah whispered to his brother and sister-in-law. "I can't believe Jack wouldn't let them open the coffin."

Joshua shrugged. "It's just their way, Noah. Don't be so hard on them." He smiled sadly in Carrie's direction. "I know what she's going through. It was hard to bury Dad because I knew he wasn't a Christian. I imagine she's going through the same thing."

Noah looked at the sad little group assembled just a short distance away from him. They were speaking with one another, but he couldn't hear what they were saying.

"It will be all right," Jack assured as he gently placed his hand on Carrie's shoulder. "If Sal believes her to be dead, and that I, in turn, have fled from the area, he will not come back. I think we have shaken him for good. Antonio and Charise and I will stay close, and you will have nothing to worry about."

"And Noah has made certain the body is never found," Carrie reminded him. "He signed the final papers on the land yesterday."

CHAPTER 8

Reata, September 1980

Angelo and Alyssa rode ahead and into the orchard on their ponies, while Vincenzo and Kate lagged behind. Vincenzo had decided to saddle up Liberal, and Kate was on poky old Muffin, her favorite horse on all of Reata.

"Why do you ride him?" Kate chuckled as she watched the beautiful stallion prance.

"He challenges me. He has spunk."

"Spunk." Kate laughed and nodded. "Well, whatever." She looked ahead and said, "I talked to your father this morning, and he says everything is ready to go for our 19th Annual Apple Picking Party. Georgie and Doria will bring the meat out early that morning, and you're supposed to have the pit ready."

"And what of the water barrels? Were you able to locate extra?"

"Yes. Tracy has made arrangements to bring ice in from Truck Town."

"Your ma`ma tells me she and Mrs. Engleson will make their delicious chocolate cakes." Vincenzo closed his eyes with a smile. "Mmmm. I *love* those two women."

Kate chuckled. "Everything is ready to go. Your brothers will be here the night before. Patty and Ellie and the kids will stay with us, and Marq and Tara are going to stay in town with your parents." She sighed and shook her head. "But my brother will not be here this year."

"Sam?"

Kate shook her head. "Alex. Angel is coming alone."

"What is that all about?" Vincenzo frowned.

Kate shrugged. "Apparently he's got some big meeting with Williams in Pierre, and he won't be able to get back until that night." She snorted. "I told him to reschedule the stupid meeting, and he hung up on me. Can you believe that?"

"Oh, Kate, you cannot tell a man to do something like that. Especially not Alex. He is very busy, and his job is very important —"

"His *job* is taking care of your sister, especially with two babies coming along at once."

"Angel is a very free, little spirit," Vincenzo reminded her. "She needs her space. And besides, a man must work."

Kate shook her head in adamant disagreement. "You have never left me alone as often as Alex has started to leave Angel. Your brothers take their wives everywhere. Patty bought a plane for goodness' sake, and Marq and Tara are inseparable."

"Oh, Kate, Angel is different from the rest of us. She will be okay—"

It was at that moment Liberal came to a sudden stop and began to pound his hooves into the ground, interrupting Kate and Vincenzo's conversation.

"Oh, do not *dare*," Vincenzo warned. He took a tight hold of the saddle horn and pressed his thighs tightly around the horse's middle.

Kate's horse began to back away from the spirited stallion and reared slightly with alarm. She stroked the neck of old Muffin, and the dependable mount settled down. Liberal, on the other hand, began to buck viciously, and Vincenzo flew through the air, into the trunk of a nearby tree.

Kate gasped and dismounted. She rushed to the place where he had crumpled, knocked into a daze.

"Vincenzo!" she exclaimed. She put her hand on his face and looked at his closed eyelids. "Oh, Jesus, help us!"

"Kate," Vincenzo managed to whisper, struggling to open his eyes. "I am all right."

"Where are you hurt?"

The commotion brought Angelo and Alyssa riding back to see what the problem was.

"Get Bill!" Kate shouted at the two, and they charged off on their ponies.

"I do not need Bill," Vincenzo frowned as he attempted to get himself into a seated position. "Help me up, my love."

"But what if you're hurt?" Kate cried as she assisted him into the position he desired.

"I do not believe I am hurt," he replied with a rub to the back of his neck. He looked into Kate's eyes with a faint smile and assured, "He just winded me a little."

"You were knocked unconscious. I wish you would geld that animal or get rid of him. He's of *no* use on Reata."

Vincenzo took a deep breath. *This is getting out of hand, even for me.*

Rosa was on her way out of the laundry room with a full basket when she heard a ripping noise coming from Tillie's old developing lab in the basement. *What in the world?* She opened the door to the old lab and saw a small man in the darkness. He had his back to her, but he appeared to be unwrapping one of Angel's paintings. *The ones of Noah!* She gasped and dropped her laundry, nearly darting up the stairs in fright. But the man heard her commotion and turned in the shadows, revealing his identity.

"*Giuseppe!*" she scolded in quiet fury. "I thought you were a burglar! I had no idea you were even in the house! What are you doing at home at this time of day? You should be working!"

"I should be retired," he retorted as he turned back to the painting and lovingly caressed the painted strokes.

Rosa shook her head. "What are you doing to yourself, Giuseppe?"

"Contemplating my regret and guilt."

Rosa swallowed the hard lump in her throat. "Whatever for?" *We must get past this, my love… There is nothing we can do about it now.*

"Alex is far too busy, and our little Angel is left alone to grow those two babies and fend for herself. Noah would *not* have left her like this. Imagine the joy they should have shared. He should have fathered his own children, instead of having to settle for someone else's."

Rosa let out her breath and stepped further into Tillie's old lab. She looked at the beautiful painting they'd hidden in their basement three years ago. Tillie had taken a black and white photograph of Noah beside a waterfall and had turned it into a stunning portrait she'd entitled *The Perfect Knight.* She reached for Giuseppe's hand in an effort to comfort him, but gasped when she found the old photo clutched in his fingers.

"You told Angel you threw those away!" she whispered.

He nodded his head in guilty admission as he uncrumpled his shaky hand from around the photo taken of Tillie and Noah in front of the bar. His black eyes glistened with tears as he looked at their smiling faces, and he sighed with regret. "And he sees her still in the reflection of my own eyes."

"Oh, Giuseppe," Rosa breathed sorrowfully. She gently took the precious photo from his palm, and tears filled her eyes. "You must stop with this, my love," she whispered. "What can be done at this point? Angel has vowed the rest of her life with another man, a man you granted blessing." She slipped the photo into her apron pocket and cried softly, "Now hide those paintings and never speak of this again."

She turned away from her husband and left him alone in the lab. He heard her heavy, sad footsteps go up the stairs and shook his head. *I have made a terrible mistake, and my Rosa knows it.* He reached for the old shoebox that he'd hidden beneath one of Angel's work tables and retrieved the rest of the photos he'd claimed to have thrown away. He tucked them into his shirt pocket and wiped the tears from his face.

Mona sipped her coffee at Maggie's bar while the two of them watched Estelle dust the beloved painting.

"It started later in life with our mother," Maggie explained, "but Stellie definitely has all the symptoms." She looked at Mona and added, "But there's something different…" She raised a black eyebrow. "It's almost as if she *chooses* to remember Angel, and everything else falls by the wayside." She shook her head. "I don't get it, and neither does her doctor. It's *like* dementia, just a little bit different."

Mona swallowed hard. *Hardening of the arteries.* "How old is Stellie?"

"She just turned fifty last month." Maggie looked toward her sister as she dusted off the painting. "One thing she *never* forgets, and that's Angel. She remembers it every day, like it happened the day before." She shook her head and looked at Mona. "Sometimes she forgets Carrie, but she never forgets Angel."

Mona took a hesitant breath and whispered, "Does Noah notice?"

Maggie shook her head. "Not yet, and I don't think Carrie's noticed either."

Mona reached for Maggie's hand and squeezed it. Maggie looked at Mona and saw the tears glistening in her eyes.

"Please," Mona whispered, "if you need anything at all, just let me and Josh know."

Maggie managed to choke back her own touched emotions. She softly patted Mona's warm hand and nodded her head. "Will do, Mona."

Noah brushed the dust out of his hair as he and Ben walked into their downtown office. "Well, I'll see if I can get a hold of Alex this afternoon," he said with a frown. "But I'm pretty sure they can't jack us around with the lease like that."

Ben scowled, "For the life of me, why do they not want to cooperate?"

"Rich folks are so tough to get along with," Noah muttered.

Ben couldn't help but smile at Noah's simple explanation.

They approached Melinda's desk to check for messages. She regarded Noah with a warm smile but sneered at Ben.

"Good morning, Miss Melinda," Ben greeted politely. "Do you have any messages for the two of us?"

Melinda deliberately looked away from Ben and spoke only to Noah. "Norman Costello called. He received the proposal from Mr. Martin, and he's satisfied. He's putting it into the mail today. Also —"

Melinda was interrupted suddenly when Noah caught sight of Carrie coming out of the conference room, Ty on her hip. He smiled and stepped away from Melinda's desk to put his arm around his wife.

Ben chuckled at Noah's abrupt actions. Melinda was obviously miffed by his accidental rebuff.

Noah's blue eyes danced with delight at the surprise of seeing his wife at the office. "Hey, what are you guys doing down here?"

Melinda watched Carrie look into Noah's eyes. She obviously adored her husband, and it made Melinda's blood boil. What was even more irritating was how Ty reached for Noah and said, "Daddy!" Noah took the little tyke into his arms and planted a loving kiss on the top of his head.

Melinda rolled her eyes. *And it's not even his.*

"I had to come down and sign some stock papers for Mr. Taylor's office," Carrie replied with a smile. "You know, the ones you had put into my name."

Noah nodded. "Well, do you wanna go to lunch?"

"See Miss Maggie?" Ty asked with a sweet smile.

"Sure," Noah agreed. Then, as if he'd forgotten something, he turned and put his hand on Ben's shoulder. "Carrie, have you met Ben Simmons yet? Ben, this is my wife, Carrie."

Carrie smiled cordially at Ben and stretched out her hand in greeting. "How do you do?"

"Very well, thank you," Ben replied as he grasped her hand.

As Melinda watched the introduction, she saw the familiarity between the two. *They already know each other…wonder why they're not saying.* She glanced at Noah, who was still gazing at his beautiful wife, oblivious to whatever Melinda had observed. She shook her head disgustedly. *Poor Noah's about as dumb as a box of rocks.*

"Things are coming along very well," Burt observed as he and Giuseppe inspected their new building.

Giuseppe nodded. "So well, in fact, I have scheduled our grand opening for November first."

"Two months," Burt mused. "Do you think the help will be ready?"

Giuseppe tensed and muttered with a frown, "Of course. Why would you worry on that account? Georgie and Doria will have them ready and as fit as fiddles."

"Okay, okay," Burt replied with a smile. "I won't worry." He took a breath and put a hand on Giuseppe's shoulder. "And how are *you* doing, my friend?"

"Oh, the same," Giuseppe answered. "I am afraid that I am beginning to hate my own son-in-law and I am about ready to pull the plug on my secret."

"Wow." Burt took a breath and suggested, "Maybe we should talk about that."

Giuseppe took a photo from his shirt pocket and handed it to Burt. "Just look at the two of them, Burt. Surely they were meant for one another, and I have interfered with God's will. Certainly this thing will go from bad to worse."

Burt looked down at the photo. There was their developer, at a younger, obviously more rebellious time of his life, looking into the eyes of Giuseppe's daughter. "Good picture," was all he could say.

"And you should see the paintings," Giuseppe went on. He clutched his chest as if in pain. "It makes my heart ache to see the beauty that came out of her hands when she was in love with him."

Burt frowned curiously at Giuseppe. "Maybe you shouldn't be obsessing over this so much. I mean, carrying around their pictures and stuff. You could get caught with this, Giuseppe, and then there'd be some explaining to do."

"I know, but I cannot seem to help myself. I just cannot get over this."

"Have you discussed it with the Lord?"

"Of course I have," Giuseppe retorted. "He has remained silent on the matter."

Burt nodded and promised, "I will pray for you, Giuseppe, but for now I would like you to keep this secret. I don't think you should be confessing anything to anybody just yet."

Giuseppe relented with a sigh. *I do not know how much longer I can wait.*

Marquette and Tara had laid their extensive information out on two long tables in a conference room in their home on Como Lake. After two weeks of waiting for Rauwolf to arrive for his promised meeting, they left Big Eagle with the realization that he wasn't going to show. In a final effort to possibly put the pieces of their mystery together, they collected all of their old files and the files belonging to John Peters and brought them to their home in Italy, where they'd planned to relax before Vincenzo's fall party.

"So," Tara began with a deep breath, "we know how Mario and Antonio escaped from Ustica —"

"With Rauwolf, who has friends in the U.S. government," Marquette added.

"Yes, who helped them all obtain false identifications. One of these identifications is, presumably, that of Jack Nelson."

Marquette flipped through a notebook. "And we know that Jack Nelson owned a fishing company in Miami until 1972, when he sold it. But Mr. Jasper could not identify Mario's photo, and there are no more IRS records after that—not even a capital gains filing for the sale."

"Schneider Rauwolf and Custer Thomas were looking for Mr. Nelson *before* November of 1972," Tara interjected. "We know this because Custer mentioned he was working on the campaign, and Election Day is not until November."

"Rauwolf had apparently separated from Ponerello at the time," Marquette mused, "but they must have been reunited by May of 1975 because Rauwolf referred to him as 'boss.'"

Tara nodded. "However, it would appear that Rauwolf left Ponerello *again* after 1975, because he was not aware of where the body had been buried."

"Nor was Mr. Thomas aware that Rauwolf had found Mr. Nelson."

"Also," Tara proffered, "it seems terribly strange that Custer Thomas was unaware of Mr. Nelson's true identity. Should he not have known that Mr. Nelson was actually Mario Ponerello?"

Marquette shrugged. "Perhaps Rauwolf felt it better to hide Mario's true identity. As we have learned, Custer Thomas commands great power. Maybe Rauwolf was concerned for their safety."

Tara nodded and took a breath. "So, we may safely assume that it was Rauwolf who hid away in Wyoming, *not* Ponerello, because Custer would have given up that information."

"Undoubtedly."

Tara sighed. "So, where did the Ponerellos *go?*"

Marquette shook his head. "We can only imagine they were in Rapid City, South Dakota, for a time. However, by now I fear they have long gone. Perhaps they changed their names again once they reached Rapid City."

Tara bit her lip thoughtfully, and was about to respond when a loud knocking began on the other side of their conference room door.

"Yes?" Marquette responded.

The door opened and a tall gentleman dressed in a black suit stepped inside. He bowed politely and smiled at Marquette and Tara. "Mr. and Mrs. Caselli, forgive this intrusion."

"Of course, Carmine," Marquette acknowledged their butler. "Do you have something?"

"Your liaison is on the telephone," Carmine explained. "She requests communication at once."

"Wow, twins!" Ginger laughed and patted Tillie's ever-growing stomach. "And look at how *cute* this nursery is. Did you do all of this yourself?"

Tillie nodded with a weary smile. "Well, Ma`ma helped with the cribs." But everything else had fallen on Tillie's shoulders. Alex was seldom home anymore. In fact, he hadn't even seen the nursery yet, but Tillie kept that to herself.

The tea kettle whistled from the kitchen, and Tillie started down the hall. "Come on," she said over her shoulder. "Let's have tea."

A short time later, they were enjoying their tea in Tillie's wedding china and discussing Ginger and Bobby's new move. Bobby had been offered a great job in Las Vegas, and they would be relocating soon.

"Mom says Las Vegas is hot and sinful." Ginger giggled and rolled her eyes. "Not every place can be *perfect*, you know." Tillie smiled and nodded, but didn't comment. In fact, she hadn't said anything for much of the day. Ginger noticed the downcast expression in her eyes. She frowned and set down her cup. "Hey, what's bothering you? You feeling okay?"

Tillie nodded and took a sip of her tea. "I feel great. It's like a textbook pregnancy. Everything is perfect."

Ginger nodded but continued to frown into Tillie's black eyes. She'd known Tillie long enough to read her expression. "You seem a little sad today. Everything okay with you and Alex?"

At the sound of his name, Tillie's eyes filled with tears and she nodded her head. "He works a lot, Ginge. He hasn't even been home this week. He flew to Rapid City this morning to help Hansen Development through a land deal, and he'll be in Pierre tomorrow."

"But that's Vincenzo's apple-picking party," Ginger remembered as she reached for Tillie's hand.

Tillie felt her tears spill onto her face. She cried a lot lately, and she assumed it was from the pregnancy. "My brothers will be here tonight, and I don't know what I'll tell them when Alex doesn't show up tomorrow." She sniffed and attempted to dry her eyes on her napkin. "And I think Papa's mad at Alex. I don't know."

"Well," Ginger tenderly suggested, "have you tried to talk to Alex about this?"

Tillie nodded, and more tears spilled onto her face. "I have, and he says he's training some associates to handle the extra workload, but I haven't seen any difference. I don't want to be a nag about the whole thing, it's just that things have changed so drastically. Maybe I'm spoiled."

Ginger laughed and gave Tillie's hand a pat. "You have *never* been spoiled, Tillie Caselli." She giggled and corrected herself. "I mean, Tillie Martin." Her eyes began to sparkle with mischief and she whispered, "Maybe we should tell Marquette."

"Oh no," Tillie shook her head and smiled through her tears. "I wouldn't wish that fury on my worst enemy, let alone my husband. I love Alex." She sighed wistfully and added, "Sometimes he's gone in the morning before I even get up, and he never comes home before I go to bed. It's been so long since I've held his hand or just looked at his face. I wish I could spend more time with him, especially now with the babies coming. We won't have much time to ourselves once they get here."

Carrie stared at the haunting picture in Maggie's bar. The small snapshot of Noah kissing Angel was more than she could bear at times, and she found herself wondering if she could find a way to get rid of it. She never once saw Noah even so much as glance in its direction, nor did he ever comment about those times. He seemed very happy in their marriage, and he daily reassured her of his love.

"Mommy, can I?" a small voice beside her insisted, and Carrie turned her gaze to the small wonder on Noah's lap.

"I'm sorry, Ty," she said with a smile. "What do you want?"

"Miss Maggie's candy stick. Can I have one?"

"Sure," Carrie replied. "But only one."

"Oh, goodie!" the little boy exclaimed, and Maggie and Noah both chuckled.

Carrie smiled faintly as she watched Noah with her son. He loved Ty, no matter the circumstances. *But would he change his mind if he knew about Angel?*

As quickly as they could, Marquette and Tara traveled to Chicago to meet with FBI special agents. They explained that the matter was of an urgent nature, directly related to their old Ponerello case.

"Our liaison informed us of a $250K wire transfer from Rapid City, South Dakota," Marquette informed FBI Special Agent Michel. "Banking authorities were able to track the transfer to a bank in Chicago and then onto Zurich, where they have lost sight of it. And as you are aware, the Treasury Department and Secret Service flagged the original transfer, as it was made by a deceased person named Carrie Miller into an account in the name of Antonio Ponerello."

"Carrie Miller died of a drug overdose in 1972," Agent Michel replied as he passed Tara a copy of the death certificate.

Tara glanced at the doctor's signature at the bottom of the document. *Dr. R. Schneider...what is so familiar about that name?*

Marquette sighed and shook his head. "And now we know for certain that the Ponerellos have gone to Europe after all. No wonder we have not been able to find them in America."

Tara drew in a surprised breath, and Agent Michel and Marquette looked at her.

"Dr. R. Schneider," she replied with a quizzical expression. "Could this be Dr. Schneider Rauwolf?"

CHAPTER 9

Since September of 1962, Vincenzo and Kate had hosted Reata's Annual Apple-Picking Party. Now 1980, this was the nineteenth time the event was scheduled, and preparations proceeded as they always had. Rosa, Tillie, and Kate, along with the foreman's wife, Barbara, got together the weekend before the event and baked buns for roasted meat sandwiches. They made delectable pies for dessert, created from whatever apples had been frozen the year before. Frances Martin and Diane Engleson prepared twelve of their chocolate sheet cakes. Doria and Georgie made great tubs of coleslaw and pans of baked beans.

Giuseppe ordered the restaurant closed, as he had from the beginning, so everyone could attend the apple-picking festivities. There was still the storytelling contest for the men as well as the apple pie contest for the ladies. Top prizes of fifty dollars were still offered for the best pies and the biggest fibs.

In 1962, the entrance fee onto Reata was fifty cents, and each family could have all of the apples they could carry out of the orchard. In 1970, Vincenzo raised the fee to two dollars, and everyone still thought it was quite a deal, including Vincenzo, who would have had to hire someone to pick the apples and sell them for him in lieu of having an apple-picking party. He got rid of the apples, and after he'd subtracted out the cost of the meat for the sandwiches, he always made a small profit on the side.

The entire orchard was opened to everyone, except the special place beneath some smaller trees on the west end. That place was roped off and no one was allowed there, for that was where Uncle Angelo and Aunt Penny rested.

When Uncle Angelo was still alive, he and Vincenzo designed a roasting pit from memory nearly identical to the one their neighbors in Italy, the Andreottis, had. As in years past, Doria and Georgie would use the pit to roast two hogs and a side of beef. They sliced the meat thin and laid it into the fresh buns the ladies had prepared.

Each time the special event was held, the sun warmed the day. There was never a time when Reata's Annual Apple-Picking Party had to be canceled because of rain, and this year would be no exception, though the weather was cooler. In 1980, the grand event took place on the third Sunday in September. It attracted hundreds of apple-pickers from Centerville and the surrounding counties.

Vincenzo designated and mowed a large portion of grassland where the participants could park. That way cars couldn't come too close to the main house where the eating, pie contest, and storytelling took place. Two young hands were mounted on prancing geldings at Reata's entrance gate, directing the large amount of traffic as it wound its way in and out of the ranch.

Great barrels of water and ice were set on the property and in the orchard, to protect the people from dehydration while they picked apples on the late summer day.

Vincenzo's special roasting pit was hot and fiery, and Georgie and old Doria had taken up their regular positions. A long line of apple-pickers waited patiently for Rosa and Guiseppi to hand them one of the delicious sandwiches. Long lines stood at the chocolate cake tables as well, as Diane Engleson and Frances Martin dished up their famous dessert.

Angelo, who was almost eight years old, and his sister Alyssa, still at the eight-year mark herself, were instructed to help the elderly and the young apple- pickers with cups of water and napkins. They moved through the crowds of people, dressed in western wear, complete with small Stetsons, smiling and helping where they could.

Kate, Tara, and Elaine sliced buns in the kitchen as quickly as they could, while they tried to keep an eye on four-year-old Michael and three-year-old Gabriella. Elaine took a huge platter of sliced buns into her arms and smiled at her children.

"Okay, guys, let's go find Papa," she said as she led them out the kitchen door.

"And the horrible blackguard never showed up as he promised us he would." Marquette passionately relayed his and Tara's story of the tall, redheaded man they'd *leaned on* in Wyoming. Vincenzo, Petrice, and Tillie listened to their brother with animated interest while they sipped lemonade at a table by themselves.

Tillie frowned and cleared her throat. "But he admitted to working for Ponerello in 1975?"

Marquette nodded. "And I think we *nearly* had them. Our liaison was contacted by Swiss authorities only a few days ago. They monitored a wire transfer of $250K directly to a Swiss account in the name of Antonio Botticelli, a known alias of Antonio Ponerello, originating from a bank in Rapid City, South Dakota. The transfer was traced back to a Carrie Miller. So Tara and I went to Rapid City to interview the banker who performed the transfer. He gave us a Xerox copy of Carrie Miller's *current* Illinois driver's license.

"But when Tara and I attempted to find Carrie Miller, we turned up only a birth certificate and a death certificate. Even the current address on the driver's license proved to be false. It was merely the address of a warehouse in downtown Chicago. She was born in Miami, which is where Mario obviously settled for a time, and her death took place in Chicago, Illinois, in 1972, shortly *before* the sale of Jack Nelson's fishing business. And enormously curious about this is that a Dr. R. Schneider signed Miss Miller's death certificate. We can only suppose Dr. R. Schneider is actually Dr. Schneider Rauwolf, the same man who helped the Ponerellos escape Sicily. American Secret Service went to Zurich, but the cash transferred to the Swiss account was turned into a cashier's check, and authorities have now lost track of it."

"*Lost track?*" Vincenzo questioned.

Marquette nodded. "It is extremely difficult to trace cashier's checks at this point. Hopefully someday the banking industry and the government will realize how idiotic it is *not* to be watching high-profile criminals transfer their money around the world." He took a breath and shook his head.

At that moment Petrice's children came running and giggling onto the scene. Michael jumped into Petrice's lap, and Gabriella carefully wriggled into her auntie's arms.

"Hello, you," Tillie smiled into her niece's eyes. She gave the little girl a warm snuggle and a kiss on the head.

Vincenzo stretched his legs out in front of him, and Tillie saw him wince with pain. "You okay?"

"I took a dreadful fall just a few days ago," he moaned. "Liberal has thrown me again, and Kate wants him gelded immediately."

"Why do you not do that?" Petrice frowned. "That animal has given you nothing but trouble since this past spring."

"Because he comes from War Winds," Tillie reminded her brothers.

Vincenzo smiled. "Perhaps he will grow out of this."

Marquette and Petrice shook their heads in disapproval. Vincenzo's love for animals would surely be his undoing.

James sat down next to his son, Sam, at the picnic table. Becky-Lynn had been there, but was called away to help at the apple pie contest. Sam was sitting alone and James decided to take advantage of that.

Sam glanced at the unusually large slice of chocolate cake on his father's paper plate, and he grinned. "Mom's cake is better than ever this year."

James nodded and stuffed a huge bite into his mouth. "Where's your brother?" he asked through a muffled mouth of cake.

Sam looked away. "Pierre, I think."

"Thought he told us that he'd changed his mind about meeting with Williams."

Sam nodded, but said nothing.

"So, did he lie to us, or did something really serious come up?"

Sam shrugged. "He's at some barbeque in Pierre with Williams. That's all I know."

James stuffed another bite of cake into his mouth. "He's really screwing this up for himself. He's gonna make trouble between us and the Casellis before it's all over."

"The Casellis will be okay, Dad," Sam attempted to assure. "They like us—"

"Marquette has never liked your brother," James interrupted.

"Well…" Sam pretended to scoff, "He's hardly ever in town anymore. He won't be making any trouble for Alex —"

At that moment, Marquette walked up to the picnic table with a smile.

James pretended an overly-friendly smile. "Well, speak of the devil!" He held an empty lemonade pitcher in the air. "Would you have my Kate fill this for me?"

Marquette smiled. "Certainly, Mr. Martin." He took the pitcher from James and obediently trudged toward the main house.

Sam frowned at his father. "It's not right to treat a forty-year-old man like an errand boy. And if you're worried about making trouble with the Casellis —"

"I'm eighty-one years old and I'll do as I please." James gave Sam a half- smile. "Besides, I wasn't done talking to you."

Kate carried her tray of sliced buns to Rosa, who was still making sandwiches as fast as she could.

"I have to slice some more," Kate explained. "But do you need me to help you first?" She glanced around. "Where's Papa?"

Rosa nodded toward the orchard, and Kate followed her gaze. There was Tillie, walking hand in hand with her father into the orchard.

Rosa gave Kate a wistful smile. "They have gone to visit Angelo and Penny."

It was almost chilly. The early South Dakota fall wind blew through the leaves on the trees, carrying the smell of apples through the air.

"How are you feeling these days, my Angel?" Giuseppe asked.

"Great, Papa." She gave her father a smile and looked at the orchard.

"And Ma`ma tells me you have the nursery all ready to go?"

"Maybe you should stop by and see it next week. It's really cute, and we were able to fit two cribs into the room after all."

"That is good." Giuseppe took a breath. "Angel, how often is your husband away?"

"Papa," she replied as she shook her head, "it's gonna be okay. He's training associates —"

"My Angel, would you like me to speak with his father?"

"Tell on Alex?" she said with a frown.

"I suppose, if that is what you choose to call it. Perhaps he just needs a little guidance from his father. You know, my Angel, as fathers sometimes we have difficulties with our sons. They are best spoken about between one another, rather than allowing a certain problem to fester, prompting someone else to interfere."

Tillie laughed. "You mean Marq?"

Giuseppe nodded. "Your brother is very passionate where you are concerned."

"He'd better not interfere in my marriage," she said with more authority than Giuseppe had ever heard in her tone. "It's one thing to sneak around in the bushes when I was seventeen, but I'm twenty-three years old now and I can take care of myself. He hasn't said anything to Patty or Vincenzo, has he?"

Giuseppe shook his head. "I made him promise he would not. But, as you are well aware, Marquette's promises are sometimes very difficult for him when it comes to matters of the heart."

"I do miss Alex, Papa. I miss the way he used to hover over me, and I miss that little thrill that used to be there when he looked into my eyes." She sadly shook her head. "You know, I haven't seen him in nearly a week."

"He should be sharing this time with you, Angel."

Tillie felt the tears begin, and she laid her head against Giuseppe's shoulder as they walked along. "I just can't believe everything could change so suddenly. Papa, Alex *loved* me. Everyone could see it."

Giuseppe put his arm lovingly around his daughter and kissed her head. "He still loves you, my Angel." *But Noah would have loved you more.*

Marquette came through Kate's kitchen door where she was slicing the rest of the buns alone. She smiled at him, and he held the empty pitcher in the air.

"Your father could use some more lemonade," he said as he set the pitcher down on the counter. "Or would you rather I helped to slice a bit?"

Kate smiled and pulled a thawed can from the refrigerator. "Here you go," and she set the can on the counter beside Marquette's pitcher. "Four cans of water—"

"And stir it up. I can handle that." He opened the can, poured its contents into the pitcher, and turned on the water.

"So," he said as he watched Kate slice the buns at the counter, concentrating on a very casual tone. *Will she think me strange for asking about her brother? Or has everyone possibly forgotten about our lifelong feuding?*

"Where is Alex this day?" he blurted.

"I think he's in Pierre," she answered as a dreadful plan began to brew in the pit of her heart. *Remain calm, focus on your tone…You don't want him getting the impression you're about to send him after your own brother…but nobody else will do anything.*

"Oh?" He paused as he pretended to focus on stirring the lemonade, as if it were the most important thing on earth. "This must be the first apple-picking party he has missed since his graduation."

Kate nodded and glanced at Marquette, surprised to see him looking at her. His tone had remained so cool, but his eyes gave him away. She frowned and looked out the window, into the yard. *Not a family member in sight.*

"Marquette," she whispered as she turned her eyes back to him, "Alex hasn't been home in nearly a week. In fact, he's gone *all* the time. Dad and Sam have both talked to him about this, but your family is too polite to say anything."

Marquette stared at his sister-in-law with surprise. *Tara will certainly disapprove of this conspiracy. For some reason, she holds a soft spot in her heart for the worthless blackguard.*

"Kate, how is Angel feeling about this?" he asked.

"How do you think?" Kate whispered with an angry frown. "She's pregnant and should be sharing this wonderful time with her husband, but instead she's left alone, day after day. If Vincenzo had done this to me, I would have been devastated. Pregnancy can be a very emotional time for women, and they need their husbands." She slammed her fist down on the counter to emphasize her words. "I know Tillie's a grown woman and a free spirit…blah, blah, blah, blah, blah. But the reality is that she's still *very* young, and this thing Alex is doing to her could really affect the way she feels about him in the future."

Marquette raised a malicious eyebrow. *We can only pray…*

"Kate, I do not know what to say. You know I have had my difficulties with Alex, and I am quite astounded you chose *me* to give this information to—"

"Will you talk to my brother?"

Marquette hesitantly began to nod his head. "But you must not breathe a word of this to my father or my wife, or any of our siblings, for they would surely disapprove."

Kate gave him one certain nod. "Agreed."

Marquette gave Tara and his parents an excuse that he had an errand to run the following Monday before they left town. Tara, being quite content to go with Rosa to Tillie's house to see the nursery, didn't notice the masked tension stirring itself up within her husband.

"Alex Martin," Marquette said to the receptionist as he removed his hat.

"Well, if it isn't the famous Marquette Caselli," Jan said with a smile. "I don't think you've ever been up, have you?"

Marquette slowly shook his head and gave her another charming smile. "This is the first. Is he in this morning?"

"Well, I'm sure he won't mind if you want to just pop in for a minute. Do you know where his office is?" Marquette shook his head, and Jan directed, "Straight back. Second door on the right."

"Thank you, ma'am." He strode past her desk, through the swinging wooden doors, and down the hallway. He paused before the closed door and took a deep breath. Thinking he should pray, he quickly dismissed the idea. *This is righteous. I do not need to call upon God for such a trivial matter*. He opened Alex's office door, and Alex looked up with surprise. Marquette offered him a forced smile, entered the office, and closed the door.

Alex got to his feet, forced his own smile, and extended his hand in greeting. "Marquette," he said, and Marquette took his hand in a firm shake. "This is a surprise."

"I am certain it is." Marquette clenched his jaw and strode to the windows. "We missed you this weekend."

Alex sighed and shook his head. *First Dad, then Sam. I know why you're here. You've just been waiting for an opportunity to tear into me*. "Listen, Marquette, I don't want to get into it with you."

Marquette turned from the window. "Well, it is about to happen!" he snarled as he stepped toward Alex's desk. "Why are you not sharing this wonderful time with Angel?"

Alex frowned. "I'm working on it, Marquette. I'm training associates to handle the extra workload. Things will really slow down after the election."

"I do not want my sister to wait another moment, let alone until *after* the election."

Alex narrowed his eyes. "Does Tillie know you're here?"

"And why is that important? What matters is that you are not being a good husband—"

"I'm a good husband. Besides, what do you know of being a *good husband?* You drag your wife all over the face of the earth. God only knows what you've exposed her to."

Marquette lost control, and a few long strides brought him to the other side of Alex's desk. He tossed his hat upon it and pushed the taller man into the wall behind him.

"Knock it off!" Alex shouted as he pushed Marquette in return, which only infuriated Marquette further. He shoved Alex again, this time so hard Alex thudded against the wall behind him.

"I cannot believe my father blessed this!" Marquette shouted into Alex's face. "You are probably the most selfish individual I have ever laid eyes upon—"

"Shut up!" Alex attempted to use his size to intimidate Marquette by looking down into his eyes. He gave him another shove. "You've always been such a lunatic!"

"You are a *blackguard in disguise!* You may have managed to fool my father and the rest of my family, but you will *never* fool me!"

"Oh, jeez, Marquette! You've been looking for an excuse to tear into me since I was a little kid, and now you think you've found one—"

Alex's office door opened, and his father peered inside.

"What on earth is going on in here?" he said with a frown.

Marquette shook his head, slowly backed away from Alex, and frowned at James. "Why do you not do something with your son?"

Sam suddenly appeared behind his father, moved between him and the door, and went to Marquette. He smiled nervously and suggested, "Hey, Marq, let's get a Coke."

"I do not want a Coke," Marquette growled. He took a deep breath, let it out, and reached for the hat he'd tossed on Alex's desk.

"Well, how 'bout a beer?" Sam asked. Marquette frowned and shook his head. Sam cautiously placed his hand on Marquette's shoulder. "Can we take a walk?"

Marquette pointed at Alex. "Fix this thing." And then he put his hat on and allowed Sam to lead him from the office.

James shook his head, closed the door, and looked into the dark eyes of his son.

Alex let out the breath he hadn't realized he was holding and dropped into his chair. "Boy, he's really nuts. They should have locked him up years ago."

"Alex, he's very concerned about his sister, as we *all* are."

"She's okay. What's the big deal anyway? This situation is temporary, and she understands. She knows how important it is to me. What I can't figure out is why the rest of you don't get it."

Carrie stood at the end of her mother's bed and watched Charise flash her photographs of her family members. Some she recognized; some she did not. Dr. Schneider had arranged the introduction of Dr. Bensen, a geriatrics specialist, and he'd said that Della would never walk again. She was lucky to be alive. *But is this really a life?* Carrie watched her handicapped mother attempt another photograph. Her speech wasn't that clear either, but Dr. Bensen had high hopes that, with therapy, she'd improve. Carrie doubted Dr. Bensen. After all, he'd taken only a minimal amount of money to keep quiet. Perhaps he was just a third-rate physician looking to score a few extra bucks. Maybe he didn't even know what he was talking about.

"She doesn't seem to remember anything," Mario said.

"Which is a very good thing for the rest of us," Carrie replied.

Mario nodded. "Carrie, I am so very sorry."

Carrie shook her head. "You couldn't possibly be sorry enough."

Mona was so deep in thought as she folded her laundry that she hadn't heard Joshua's car in the driveway. She jumped with surprise and nearly screamed when he came in the back door.

"Oh, thank goodness I didn't yell at you," she whispered with a smile. She put her arms around her husband and greeted him with a kiss. "Ty's finally asleep. Don't be too loud."

Joshua nodded with a smile and whispered, "I didn't see Carrie's car in the drive."

"She had to run some errands. I'm babysitting." Mona suddenly frowned and turned back to her basket of folding.

"And what's weird about *that?*"

Mona shrugged. "I don't know yet, but something doesn't feel right."

"Doesn't *feel* right?"

She sighed and shook her head again. "One time Daddy kept sayin' he had a strange feelin' that Old Man Wheelbig was up to somethin'. He didn't know what it was, but he knew Wheelbig was hidin' somethin' from him. Now, he and Wheelbig had been good friends for years and years. They even went to the same church together. Wheelbig was just such a wonderful, righteous man. He was even the head deacon! Why, Daddy felt guilty for suspecting him, and so he prayed and prayed about it. Well, one night Daddy woke up from a sound sleep. He said he felt like someone had touched his shoulder, but there was no one else in the room with him 'cept for Momma, and she was sound asleep. Daddy tried to go back to sleep, but he couldn't. So he got up to go sit out on the porch for a few minutes, on account of the fresh air might make him sleepy. Well, Daddy got out to the front porch, and in the moonlight he saw someone messin' around down by the boatshed…It was a full moon that night. So he trotted on down to see what was goin' on. There was his dearest friend, Old Man Wheelbig, hidin' his moonshine under Daddy's boat! And he was *so* drunk he actually offered Daddy a jug to keep quiet!" Mona giggled. "'Course Daddy said no, and Wheelbig started crying… you know, that awful, bawling drunkard crying." Mona shook her head. "I guess it was just awful."

Joshua raised an eyebrow in confusion. "So, do you think Carrie's making her own booze?"

Mona rolled her eyes in response. "*Joshua!* I'm not sayin' *that!*"

"Well, then, what *are* you saying, Mona?"

Mona sighed and explained, "I have a strange feeling Carrie's up to something. I don't think she's drinking again or anything like that, but it feels like she's hiding something from me."

CHAPTER 10

Election Day, November 1980

Tillie Martin sat in the window seat of her ma`ma's living room, watching the fluffy snowflakes fall. Glistening white pieces built a soft layer of brilliance, covering the ground and the leafless trees and rooftops in her old neighborhood. In the background, she heard voices on the television discussing the election and what the exit polls were showing at noon. Ronald Reagan was well on his way to becoming President of the United States, and Jackson Williams would surely serve another term as governor of South Dakota.

Her father and Burt had opened Angelo's II only three days before, and called periodically to discuss the election results with Rosa. Tillie heard her mother laughing at something Giuseppe said and couldn't help but smile...*Papa seems happier these days.*

The babies moved, causing an unfamiliar discomfort, and she placed her hand over them. Alex was gone again—last-minute campaigning for Governor Williams in Rapid City. She looked at the old photo in her hand and felt the ache of regret. It was a lifetime ago, and yet, if she allowed herself, she was there, smiling into his dancing blue eyes. She felt the strength of his arms as he held her and the wonderful softness of his first kiss. She closed her eyes as she recalled the warmth of his hand and the sound of his voice as he sang to her...*'Her brow is like the snowdrift, her throat is like the swan, her face it is the fairest that e'er the sun shone on...Annie Laurie...'*

The clang of Rosa's tea tray being set down on the table next to her brought Tillie back to the present, and she opened her eyes.

"My Angel," Rosa breathed as she stared at the photograph in Tillie's hand, "wherever did you find that?"

Tillie shrugged. "It was behind the door in my old room." She looked at the smiling faces of her and Noah, sitting together on some rocks at Roubaix Lake. She traced the outline of his face with her index finger and smiled faintly.

Rosa was startled, to say the least, because it was a *different* photo than the one she'd taken away from Giuseppe little more than a month ago.

"Why, Angel, you have not thought of Noah in years."

"Haven't had the time."

Rosa busied herself with pouring the tea. "Orange and spice," she said as she offered Tillie a cup.

"Thanks, Ma`ma."

Rosa took a seat beside Tillie and reached for the babies. "Are they busy today?"

Tillie shook her head with a soft frown. "They're a little quiet today, and I don't feel very good. I guess I'm just getting a little stiff and sore. They're so big now."

"How many more weeks?"

"Four," Tillie answered.

Rosa reached for the photograph in her daughter's hand. "May I?"

Tillie nodded and handed her mother the photo.

Rosa looked at the old photograph, guilt and regret filling her heart.

"Alex made me forget him," Tillie murmured as she looked out into the snow.

"I know, dear, but why would you think of him now?"

"Don't know. I hadn't thought of him until I saw that photo. It just popped out of nowhere. I thought you and Papa got rid of all that stuff."

Rosa swallowed hard. Unable to look into Tillie's eyes, she pretended to focus on the photograph in her hand. "We did," she lied. "But I do not go into your room so much anymore..." her voice trailed off.

"He was so different from Alex." Tillie took a sip of her tea and watched the snow. "So ordinary. Alex is so..." she hesitated. "Alex is so *extraordinary*. Like a flashy star or something."

Rosa forced herself to pretend a soft laugh as she squelched the tears attempting to escape her heart. *If only Angel could know how extraordinary a man Noah has become...if only I could have convinced Giuseppe...*

"I know this is difficult," Rosa said. "But Alex has promised that things will slow down after the election."

"I know, Ma`ma. And don't worry. He just kinda picked a rotten time to explore his political possibilities."

Rosa set the photograph on the window seat and took a careful sip of the hot tea. "Your brother Marquette is coming this afternoon, with Tara, of course."

"I thought he was in Peru or someplace crazy."

Rosa shook her head. "Bolivia. And they are both crazy, but they nabbed their culprits and called yesterday afternoon to say they were coming for a visit. He worries about you, you know."

Tillie smiled and shook her head. "Man, what a life. Wish I was him."

In Rapid City, South Dakota, Alex had just finished a motivating speech, rallying a crowd at the Howard Johnson's. Amid applause and cheering, Governor Williams took the stage, where they did their practiced handshake, and Alex hurried from the platform.

He was surprised to find Noah waiting for him in the lobby of the hotel, and he extended his hand in greeting. Noah took his hand and gave it a firm shake.

"Hey, what are you doing here?" Alex asked with a smile.

"I thought I'd save you some time. How about a lift?"

"Sounds good to me," Alex agreed.

Freezing rain had been falling on Rapid City and the outlying areas since early that morning. The roads were slippery, and many of the town's businesses had closed early.

"I'm sure glad I pulled my crews off the sites today," Noah remarked as they walked into the offices of Hansen Development, LLC. "They would have been miserable out there."

"I hope my charter can take off." Alex brushed the wet rain from his hair and off the shoulders of his black trench coat.

"I hope so, too," Noah agreed as he headed to the coffee machine. "I'm sure your wife is missing you."

Alex cringed. He'd been gone since Saturday but had spoken to Tillie every day over the telephone, including that morning. She said she missed him but everything was fine, the babies were fine, *everything was fine*.

Noah filled two mugs with coffee and handed one to Alex. "Come on, I gotta show you something." He walked off in the direction of his office and held the door open.

Alex had to smile as he entered the run-down little office, again noticing the dramatic difference between Noah's outer offices, where his staff worked, and the shabby little room Noah called his "shop." There was a wooden shelf lying on his desk amid the papers and messy files. Noah set down his coffee cup and picked it up.

"I made this for Carrie." He smiled as his rough, callused hands caressed the wood. "I got this really neat saw, and I made the cuts myself, sanded it all down, and finished it. She's gonna love it."

Alex stared with awe and amazement at the beautiful wooden creation Noah held so delicately in his hands. He was struck with the memory of Tillie's pretty hands and how they'd finished that old dining room set. She'd lovingly changed it into a work of art people couldn't stop commenting about.

Noah noticed Alex's intense stare and laughed. "Do you hate it, or what?"

Alex shook his head. "It's great, Noah..." He hesitated, looking again at Noah's rough hands, and thought of Tillie's pretty, delicate fingers, wondering briefly why she didn't paint anymore. "You remind me of my wife," he blurted out, and then he smiled and shook his head. "She has really pretty hands—"

"*I* remind you of your *wife?*" Noah laughed out loud and set the shelf down on his desk. He took a seat, looked at Alex, and attempted a very serious expression. "Buddy, you've been away from home too long."

Alex laughed at Noah's joke and took a seat in front of the desk. He sighed and began to nod his head. "I have, and one of Tillie's brothers and my entire family are very angry with me."

Noah nodded and gave Alex a coy smile. "Carrie would throw me out and have me tarred and feathered. I can't believe you get away with it."

"It'll be better after the election," Alex promised as he took a sip of his coffee.

"Life is just too short, Alex. You shouldn't fill your life up with so much stuff."

"I know," Alex agreed, and it was strange how easy it was to agree with Noah, yet argue tooth and nail with his family.

"You've been burning that candle at both ends since what now? August? You're missing the best part, Alex. For instance, when was the last time you felt those little babies moving around in there?"

The guilt weighing on Alex's heart over that particular situation actually brought a fine mist of tears to his eyes. He looked into his coffee cup to hide the emotion from his friend and took a deliberate gulp. "I don't even remember. She's asleep before I get home, and I leave before she gets up."

Noah looked horrified at Alex's confession. "What if something happens? Aren't you gonna regret it? And she's so young. Don't you worry about, *you know?*"

"Worry about what?"

Noah rolled his eyes. "*Other men,*" he whispered.

Noah's statement made Alex's mouth drop open in surprise, but he managed to rasp out a quiet reply, "Tillie's not like that."

Noah shrugged. "Loneliness will make you do crazy things. In fact, I never told you this, but I was gonna marry this girl once, back in '75, and she bugged out on me—for God only knows what reason—but I had it in my head she was coming back and we were gonna tie the knot, no matter what. Oh…" Noah groaned and rolled his eyes. "I completely went *crazy* and built that place up on Rimrock that I lease to Viv Olson. I must've carried the torch for that girl…well…" Noah scratched his head. "Right up until I married Carrie."

Alex remembered meeting Noah for the first time in 1975 and wondering about the terrible sadness in Noah's eyes. *But now his eyes are always smiling.* "When I first met you, you looked really terrible. I thought maybe it was the drinking."

"Thanks, buddy." Noah laughed. "No. It was the girl. Wonder where she is now. I wish I could tell her thanks. She straightened out my life and gave me a second chance. Heck, I wouldn't even have this business if it wasn't for her."

"What do you mean?"

"Well, she told me to go back to school and do something with my life—"

He was interrupted abruptly by Melinda, who entered through the open door of the office and put her hand on Alex's shoulder.

"I'm sorry, but Mr. Martin has an emergency phone call on line two. It's your mother and she's extremely upset."

Alex felt his heart begin to pound. It was unusual for anyone to bother him during a business trip, let alone his mother.

Noah reached for his telephone, pushed line two, and handed the receiver to Alex.

Alex cleared his throat and took a breath. "Hi, Mom."

"Oh, Alex," she softly cried on the other end, "we've taken Tillie to the hospital. Something's gone wrong. Please come home as quickly as you can."

"What's gone wrong? Is Tillie okay?"

He heard her swallow a sob, and she continued, "No, Alex, she's not okay. She's suffering from what Dr. Lewis calls placenta abruption. He says this is common in multiple births, like twins." Frances took a soft breath and whimpered, "You must come as quickly as you can, son."

Alex nodded. "I'll go to the airport right now and see if I can get a charter—"

"I know a guy," Noah interrupted.

"Noah knows a guy," Alex said. "I'm sure I can be there in just an hour or so."

"I'll tell her you're on your way," Frances cried. "Please hurry, Alex." And with those last words, the connection ended.

Alex looked at Noah as he started to get out of his chair. "I've gotta get to the airport. Something's gone wrong with Tillie's pregnancy."

Noah rose from his seat. "I'll take you."

"Hopefully someone will take off in this weather."

During their tea time, Tillie started to have contractions. They were soft and gentle at first but continued to grow in intensity until there was no break between them. Her abdomen above the babies was tender to the touch, and the pain became excruciating when the babies moved within her. By the time she got off the phone with Dr. Lewis she had started to bleed, and Frances Martin was called to rush them to the hospital.

Marquette and Tara arrived at the house shortly thereafter, only to find a note from Rosa explaining that she and Frances had gone to the hospital with Angel.

"The babes will be early," Marquette said as he and Tara hurried down the long hallway of the maternity ward at Sioux Valley Hospital. They saw Frances waiting near a nurses' station, wringing her hands.

"Mrs. Martin," Tara said, "Where is Rosa?"

"She and Giuseppe are in there," Frances answered, pointing toward a closed door.

"What is wrong, Mrs. Martin?" Marquette asked.

Frances shook her head and swallowed hard. Marquette saw her eyes fill with tears. "Tillie's losing a lot of blood."

Tara gasped, and Marquette took ahold of Frances' hand. "Have the babies already been born?"

Frances shook her head and began to weep. "Something's wrong with the placentas. Dr. Lewis will have to take the babies by Cesarean section…and…" She attempted to swallow her sobs as she looked from Tara to Marquette.

"What is it, Mrs. Martin?" Tara asked.

"The surgery will cause Tillie to lose even more blood," Frances continued. "She and the babies are very much in danger."

Upon hearing her words, Marquette felt the floor beneath him begin to buckle and swing, and he staggered backwards. He brought his hand to his forehead, closed his eyes, and moaned. Tara caught hold of his arm and attempted to steady him.

"Marquette!" she cried as she heard the faint weeping begin in her husband's throat. "*Please*, we need to stay strong for Angel. We must call out to the Lord."

He put his arms around his wife and leaned against her. "My baby sister."

As Tara held her husband in her arms, she questioned Frances, "Where is Alex?"

Frances looked away and tried to force away the fresh tears Marquette's dramatic reaction to her news had brought on. "Alex is in Rapid City. They're having freezing rain out there, and all the planes have been grounded."

Marquette cried in quiet, horrible, aching sobs, and he whispered to his wife, "First the blackguard impregnates her and then he leaves her to die alone."

"Angel will *not* die!" Tara snapped. She pushed out of his arms, pulled hard on his suit lapels, and frowned into his eyes. "Look at me, Marquette!" she demanded. "Angel will *not* die! Furthermore, she is *far* from being alone!"

The door Frances had pointed to opened, and two nurses dressed in surgical scrubs appeared. They pulled a hospital bed through the entrance, turning it toward the threesome near the nurses' station. On the bed lay a very still, pregnant body, covered in white blankets and wearing a blue cap on her head. Rosa was holding her limp hand and looking very serious, and Giuseppe was on the other side with Dr. Lewis.

Marquette stepped quickly to his sister, attempting to take her free hand into his own but noticing it was punctured with an IV tube. Her eyes were closed, and her lips were a strange bluish color.

"Angel," he whispered as they moved the bed along.

"She is sleeping, Marquette," Giuseppe whispered. "Dr. Lewis will take the babies now. You must let them go."

Marquette moved out of the way, and the doctor and his nurses hurried Tillie down the hall and out of sight.

Rosa slumped into Giuseppe's arms with relief, and he held her close. She had been so strong for Tillie and had not allowed her to see a single tear, even when the doctor's news had been so horrible. Tillie didn't bat an eye, didn't even panic, but instead gave Rosa a message for Alex, for when he finally arrived. *"Just tell him that I love him. Just in case."*

"Everything will be fine," Rosa had insisted.

And then Tillie had looked at Dr. Lewis and spoke with authority. *"You will save my babies, no matter the cost."* She had narrowed her eyes and instructed Dr. Lewis, *"Do not listen to my parents or my family, because they will make a decision from their hearts, and it will be deceitful and desperately wicked."*

"Oh, Ma`ma." Marquette shook his head and looked to his father.

"It is very bad, my son," Giuseppe said as he held his wife in his arms. "We may lose our Angel and her babies this day."

Marquette felt the floor spinning again, but Tara was quickly at his side. She put her arm firmly around him. "What happened?" she whispered as she looked to Giuseppe for an explanation.

He shook his head. "The doctor does not know how this happens, and I cannot pronounce it correctly, but the babies' placentas have come loose."

"Come loose?" Tara questioned in a whisper.

He nodded. "There is much blood, and the babies' heart rates are very low. And Angel's blood pressure is dropping." He reached for his son's hand and took a tight hold of it. "You must call your brothers, Marquette. Tell them to come here now."

"Yes, Papa," Marquette sobbed, and obediently backed away from his father. "I will find a phone."

"You may use mine," a deep, husky voice said from the nurses' station.

Marquette turned to see a male nurse, holding the receiver of a telephone in the air. He was extraordinarily tall and quite muscular. His skin was bronze and his shoulder-length hair the color of cream. His white teeth flashed a friendly smile, though he had the face of a warrior.

"Sit here," he said, indicating a chair beside him.

Marquette walked to the nurses' station and noticed that the man's nametag read "Angel." He looked into the man's eyes, and a soft sob escaped his throat. "That is what we call my sister."

The nurse slid the chair from beneath the desk top and gently put his hand on Marquette's shoulder. "Sit down, sir."

Marquette nodded as he sat down. He picked up the receiver and began to dial numbers.

"James and Sam and Becky-Lynn will be here shortly," Frances said.

Giuseppe acknowledged her information as he held his sobbing wife. "There, there now, my Rosa," he whispered, fighting his own desire to break down in screaming sobs. "Let us go to the chapel and pray."

Alex shoved his hands into his pockets and jingled the change around. "What am I going to do now?" he moaned. The airport had grounded all flights. There was no way to get to Sioux Falls within the hour he'd promised his mother.

Noah bit his lip and frowned in concentration. He snapped his fingers and enthusiastically suggested, "I know! I'll drive you there myself!"

Alex scowled. "That takes more than six hours on a *good* day, Noah. I have to be there sooner than that."

Noah shook his head and put his hand on Alex's shoulder. "What's done is done, Alex, and now you've got but one choice. Jump in the truck with me and let me take you back. Who knows, maybe the storm will clear up."

Alex sighed. "All right. Let's do it."

"I have to call Carrie first."

Carrie was just putting lunch on the table when the telephone rang in her kitchen.

"Carrie, it's me. Hey, I have to ask you something."

"Sure," she teased, "but first tell me why you're so late for lunch. I've been worried sick about you."

"Oh, man." Noah turned away from Alex so he wouldn't hear his words. "Alex has got himself in a fix. Tillie's having some big problems with the pregnancy and he has to get back to Sioux Falls today. The problem is everything is grounded at the airport. He can't even get a charter."

"Oh, dear," Carrie replied, catching her breath. "I suppose you want to drive him all the way back?"

"You read my mind. I think I can have him back to Sioux Falls by supper time and be back home to Rapid by midnight or so." He lowered his voice and spoke very quietly, "And I thought I'd call Josh and Mona to come over and sit with you, you know, in case *Stupid* comes creeping around or something."

Carrie giggled at Noah's choice of words. *Stupid* is how he had started to refer to Roy. She took a deep breath to quell her nervous heart. She couldn't deny that this was the last thing she wanted her husband to do, but it would be wrong to refuse him.

"Of course," she answered. "You guys go ahead and get on the road, and I'll call Mona…and we'll pray for Tillie."

"Thanks, Carrie. You're the best, and I love you."

"I love you, too. Drive careful."

"I will," he promised.

156

Carrie held the quiet receiver in her hand for a few moments before she hung it up and sank to her knees on the kitchen floor.

"Father, hear my plea. Protect my husband on his travels, and please don't let him find out about Angel."

Frances paused in the doorway of the chapel and watched the tiny couple pray together—at least she thought they were praying. They seemed to be speaking in their first language as they lifted their prayers and petitions to the Father. They held onto one another as they wept ceaselessly. It was a pitiful sight—one that Frances wished she didn't have to witness.

A tender hand was on her shoulder, and she turned to see her husband there beside her.

"How are things going?" he whispered.

She just shook her head.

"Have you heard from Alex?"

She shook her head again.

"Sam and Becky-Lynn went right upstairs," James whispered, "but I figured you'd be down here."

Frances nodded, leaned against her husband, and whispered, "If this had been Kate, I would have never forgiven Vincenzo."

James swallowed hard. "I know, Frances, I know."

"And that blackguard is nowhere to be found," Marquette growled through clenched teeth. He'd finally gotten ahold of Petrice after several transfers around the Russell Senate Office Building. "I guess that a friend will drive him back. We can only hope he dies in a crash along the way."

"Marquette!" Petrice scolded. "Please get control of yourself. Where is Vincenzo?"

"Kate sent a hand out to find him. She said they will leave Reata as soon as he comes in."

"Very well then. I will call my Ellie and tell her to pack up the children, and we will be on our way. I will have to call Dulles for an emergency flight plan, but I should be able to reach Sioux Falls before supper time."

Marquette drew in a soft breath, and his brother heard the tears in his voice as he said, "You cannot come quickly enough, Petrice. We may yet lose our Angel this day, and if we do, so help me God, I *promise* to make Alex pay."

CHAPTER 11

An hour into the surgery, Dr. Lewis sent his young assistant, Dr. Nygaard, to visit with Tillie's family. Dr. Nygaard found what few Casellis were at the hospital, along with the rest of the Martins. His tall, gangly frame was dressed in surgical scrubs, and a face mask hung loose around his neck. He took a seat in the chair in front of Rosa and Giuseppe.

"I'm Dr. Nygaard," he introduced, holding out his hand first to Giuseppe and then to Rosa. He took a deep breath. "Your daughter's still in surgery, but we got the babies out. Boy and a girl. One of each, just like she wanted. They're pretty small, less than four pounds apiece, but they'll be okay. We've got a pediatrician looking at them, and they're breathing on their own. They're a little further developed than we'd expected."

"And what of my Angel?" Giuseppe whispered.

Dr. Nygaard swallowed and shook his head. "We don't know yet. She's hemorrhaging significantly and we're giving her blood. If we can't get the bleeding under control, we're going to have to take her uterus. Dr. Lewis doesn't want to do that without her husband's permission. Do you know how much longer he'll be?"

"Probably another four hours," Sam said. "He called from Wall. They're having to drive back because of an ice storm out in Rapid. He couldn't get a flight out."

"She can't wait that long," Dr. Nygaard informed.

Giuseppe reached for Dr. Nygaard's hand and gave it a tender pat. "You take what you must, but save my Angel."

159

Dr. Nygaard nodded in understanding and left them alone to pray.

By the time Vincenzo and Kate arrived, everyone had returned to the waiting room in the maternity ward. Marquette threw his arms around his brother and cried.

"What has happened?" Vincenzo asked.

"They took the babies, a boy and a girl —" Marquette began.

"Took them?" Vincenzo interrupted.

"Cesarean section," Marquette answered. "We are waiting now for the bleeding to stop."

Vincenzo swallowed hard and looked into the grief-stricken eyes of his brother. "The bleeding?"

"Placenta abruption. Apparently the placentas pulled away from the wall of Angel's uterus before the babies were born, and this caused a lot of bleeding. They are giving her blood now, and Dr. Lewis is still with her. They have not let us see her —" Marquette's voice broke as he tried to swallow a sob. "And that *wretched* husband of hers is somewhere between here and Rapid City."

Vincenzo put a firm hand upon Marquette's shoulder. *I wonder how long it will be before he blows sky-high...but this is nonsense. Alex should be here for the birth of his children and to comfort his long-suffering wife.*

"What of Patty?" Vincenzo calmly asked.

"He and Ellie are on their way. They should be here around six o'clock or so."

Vincenzo felt his own anger rise. Petrice was able to come clear from Washington in a quicker fashion than the actual father of his sister's children? His face twisted into an indignant frown as he whispered, "What is taking Alex so long?"

"A friend will drive him here," Marquette answered. "Apparently all flights at Rapid City Regional were grounded because of an ice storm."

Dr. Lewis walked up the hallway, and Vincenzo and Marquette joined the rest of their family to hear what he had to say.

"I think she's stable now," Dr. Lewis announced with a sigh and a faint smile. "We didn't have to take her uterus, and I think she's going to be okay, but Dr. Nygaard and I are both on call tonight just in case."

"Can we be with her?" Giuseppe asked.

Dr. Lewis nodded. "Sure, but she's probably not going to be awake until morning. She's had a pretty tough time with the whole thing."

Giuseppe and Rosa followed Dr. Lewis down a long hallway and into a room.

The same nurse who had helped Marquette to make his phone calls approached the rest of them. His radiant smile reflected triumphant joy, and he said, "Dr. Lewis says you might like to see the babies."

They all looked up with surprise, for the little babies had been forgotten.

"You can follow me." He smiled as he led the way down the opposite hall. "They've both been moved into the regular nursery. You'll have to look at them from behind the glass, but at least you'll get to see them."

He led them to the nursery, where two babies, one wrapped tightly in pink and the other in blue, lay sleeping peacefully in clear acrylic incubators before a glass window. The Casellis and the Martins gasped with wonder, and some of them even managed small smiles.

"They're the only ones in there right now," the nurse said. "So they'll get *all* of the attention. And you can't see it right now because of the stocking caps on their heads, but they've both already got some little wisps of curly black hair." The nurse laughed and continued, "The little girl is so sweet and quiet, but her brother yelled until they gave him a bottle, and he gobbled it all up."

The Martins and Casellis laughed through their tears as they marveled at the miracle God had performed that afternoon.

"They are so small," Vincenzo said as he took a hold of Kate's hand. "How much did they weigh?"

"The girl was three pounds and thirteen ounces, and the boy was three pounds and fifteen ounces," the nurse answered. "But they're breathing and eating." He chuckled and added with a wink, "And pooping! So I think they'll be just fine."

"Will they get to come home with their ma`ma?" Marquette asked.

The nurse answered, "As long as everything keeps working like it is, they'll probably be ready to go home before she is."

They all nodded, and a few of them stepped closer to the glass for a better look, including old James Martin. He smiled at his new grandbabies and slowly shook his head. He turned to his oldest son and said with a serious expression, "Sam, let's go for a walk."

Sam obediently left his place at the window and fell in step beside his father.

"Now, this is how it's all gonna go down…," they heard James say as he and Sam walked down the hall, and their voices faded away.

Shortly before seven o'clock that evening, Petrice and Elaine arrived and were given the information of the day. Rosa and Giuseppe were still in the room with Tillie, and Dr. Lewis had allowed no one else.

"And that blackguard has yet to arrive," Marquette whispered to his older brothers as the three of them visited off by themselves. "Just think, she nearly *dies* bearing his fruit, and he manages to get himself stuck on the other side of the state!"

"I thought he would have been here by now," Vincenzo whispered. He stole a sly glance in the direction of Sam and James Martin, who had been joined by Pastor Andy Engleson by now, and added, "And he will find no friends in that corner. Whatever is being cooked up between the three of them is *not* good."

"They quiet themselves if we come too close," Marquette whispered. "Perhaps they will, at long last, do the job I have only dreamed of for the last five years."

Petrice shook his head and frowned. "I feel terrible about this, for it was I who referred Governor Williams to Alex for state matters."

"*You?*" Marquette whispered in astonishment.

Petrice affirmed, "Alex is a Harvard Law graduate, and Jackson needed someone he could depend upon. Alex assured me that he and Angel had discussed the matter thoroughly, so I gave my recommendation."

Marquette rolled his eyes and snorted. "You must be going senile."

"Marquette!" Vincenzo scolded in a whisper. He placed his hand on Marquette's shoulder. "Here come Ma`ma and Papa. Let us try to be civil—at least with one another."

Everyone got to their feet as Rosa and Giuseppe joined them.

"She is still sleeping," Giuseppe smiled faintly at the group before him. "Everything seems to be coming along fine."

There were several sighs of relief, and more footsteps were heard coming up the hall. They turned and recognized Alex in his long black trench coat, but who was the other man? He sauntered alongside Alex, dressed in a sturdy wool coat, jeans, and cowboy boots.

Rosa softly gasped, covered her mouth with one hand, and reached for Giuseppe's hand with the other.

"It is Noah," Giuseppe whispered into her ear as he squeezed her hand.

"Shall I throttle him now and get it over with?" Marquette whispered to his brothers as he took an angry step forward.

Petrice put his hand firmly against Marquette's chest. "Let us try to work this out," he whispered. "We are reasonable people."

As Alex and Noah walked toward the group, they saw the smoldering anger in everyone's eyes. Noah gave Alex an encouraging smile.

"You've got some comeuppance coming your way," Noah whispered as they walked along, and he elbowed Alex with a smile. "And you're gonna take it, too."

Alex swallowed hard as they approached the two families waiting for him. He and Noah had planned to come in together, thinking Alex might not get attacked in front of a stranger.

"This is my friend, Noah Hansen," Alex introduced.

As the introductions were made, Tara's heart began to race. She took a quiet breath as she recognized the man from Angel's photographs all those years ago! *And did Alex call him Noah?*

"How's Tillie?" Alex asked, and Giuseppe glared at his son-in-law.

"She's gonna be okay," Sam answered. He placed his hand on Alex's shoulder and guided him away from their hostile families. "I'll show you where her room is."

"Okay," Alex agreed, and he looked back at Noah, who smiled. "Thanks, Noah."

"No problem," he answered. Alex turned and followed Sam, leaving Noah alone before the angry group. He noticed their confused frowns, but he offered them a genuine smile in hopes of lightening the situation. None of them seemed to budge, and he was uncomfortable. Before he could stop himself, he began to ramble out his side of the story. "Well, he couldn't get a flight out," he explained in his friendly, easy-going way, hoping to soften the horrible thing his friend had done with some kind of an excuse. His eyes began to dance as he continued, "And they closed down the airport and he couldn't get a car, and so I said, 'Shoot, Alex, why don't you just let me drive you,' and I called my wife and she thought it would be a good idea, and Alex said, 'Okay,' and so we took off. The roads cleared up right around Wall, and we drove like crazy 'till we got here." He let out a nervous breath and became quiet. That was it; that was the explanation. He stood still and smiled at them, wondering what else he could possibly say.

Tillie's brothers stared in amazement at the roughly-dressed man who frantically explained before them, and they began to smile. Noah had delivered the story with an energy that unexplainably calmed the stressed and angry people.

"That was wonderful of you." Rosa broke free of Giuseppe's hand and reached for Noah's.

Noah took the tiny older woman's hand into his own, surprised at her obvious gratitude. "Is it Mrs. Caselli?"

Rosa nodded through her tears as she looked into the eyes of the man who'd loved her daughter so many years ago. *He is not a blackguard at all. Probably never was.*

"Will you drive all the way back tonight?" Rosa inquired, suddenly alarmed with the possibility that if Noah stayed there much longer, their secrets would soon have to be reckoned with.

Noah answered with his friendly smile, "I can make it back before midnight, so I should really get going. My brother and sister-in-law are gonna wait up with my wife until I get back. We're expecting, too."

"Oh," Rosa said as she tried to control her tears. "Congratulations."

"Thanks," Noah said as he reluctantly broke free from Rosa's grasp. There was just something so sweet and familiar about the little lady that made Noah want to stay.

"Could we buy you some supper?" Marquette suddenly offered. His angry expression was gone, and his eyes were alight with a curious shine.

"No, thanks." Noah smiled. "I'll just get a burger." He looked at Petrice and extended his hand. "Is it Senator Caselli?"

Petrice took Noah's hand in a firm grasp and smiled as he said, "So honored to meet such a fine man."

Noah chuckled and shook his head. "I just heard that Ronald Reagan is on his way into the White House. The last report on the radio said that Carter had already conceded, and there are still polls open."

Petrice smiled and his black eyes sparkled with delight. "That should please my dear brother very much," and he gave Marquette a friendly slap on the back.

"Me, too," Noah said as he looked to Marquette. "That whole pardoning of the draft-dodgers really ticked me off."

"Were you in Vietnam?" Marquette asked.

"Saigon. Sixty-nine to seventy-one."

Marquette smiled. "Saigon. Sixty-five to sixty-seven."

Noah's handsome face clouded over and only the soft sparkle in his eyes remained when he said, "Terrible place."

Marquette extended his hand to Noah. "It is a pleasure to meet you, and I hope we meet again."

"And you as well," Noah said as he began to reluctantly back away. He smiled and gave them a small wave. "I gotta go, but I'll be praying for Tillie and the babies all the way home."

They returned his friendly wave, said good-bye, and watched him turn and disappear down the long hallway.

The group stood silently still, looking from one to the other. Andy managed the first words, softly laughing while he said them, "For some have entertained angels unawares."

Tillie's brothers laughed. There was an unusual air of excitement just having been in the man's presence. What was it about him that made the tension melt so quickly from the room?

"What a wonderful man," Vincenzo commented.

"A *best* friend," Petrice smiled.

"A *perfect* knight," Marquette added.

Carrie managed to slip away from Joshua and Mona for a few moments and dropped to her knees beside her bed. She bowed her head as the tears she'd been holding back all evening rushed from her eyes and down her cheeks. She hadn't wanted Noah to take Alex to Sioux Falls, but there were no other choices available. She knew the possible consequences.

"Oh, Father," she pleaded, "please don't let anything happen to Angel and the babies. I don't know if Noah could bear the sadness of suddenly finding her, only to lose her again."

CHAPTER 12

A nurse was checking Tillie's blood pressure when Alex and Sam came into her room. Dr. Lewis was still with her as well. Alex went to the empty chair beside the bed and took Tillie's hand into his own. Her eyes were closed, as if she was in a very deep sleep, and her normally-dark skin was the color of ash. The red bag of blood hanging above her startled Alex, and he looked at Dr. Lewis.

Dr. Lewis sighed with relief. "Boy, I'm sure glad you're here."

"Eighty-eight over fifty," the nurse informed the doctor as she handed him the chart.

"We've been having a hard time keeping her blood pressure up," Dr. Lewis commented as he checked the chart. "I thought we were gonna lose her there for a little bit."

"What happened?" Alex frowned into Dr. Lewis' expression. *Apparently you're just too old to be taking care of pregnant women.*

"It's called placental abruption," Dr. Lewis answered. "The placenta detaches itself from the wall of the uterus and causes severe bleeding. It happens occasionally in multiple-birth situations, like twins."

Alex narrowed his eyes and angrily quipped, "Why didn't you tell us that something like this could happen?"

Sam was surprised at his brother's hot retort, and he put a heavy hand on his shoulder.

"But will she be okay?" Sam questioned gently.

Dr. Lewis frowned at Alex. "I think so. We've been able to keep her pressure above eighty now for the last two hours, but I'm on call along with another surgeon, and we'll hang around the hospital for a little while tonight, just in case."

"The babies?" Alex asked. He'd almost forgotten about his children.

Dr. Lewis offered a faint smile. "They're doing fine. They put them in some incubators. They're small, but the little boy is already able to eat. You got one of each."

He wrote further instructions on the chart and handed it to the nurse. "Listen, I'm going to get something to eat. I'll be back up in a little while. I'll just be in the cafeteria downstairs, so I can be paged if anything happens." And then he left Alex alone with his brother.

It was very quiet between the two brothers for a long time when Sam finally said, "Sure was nice of Noah to drive you back."

Alex took a soft breath. "Sam, I'm sorry."

Sam frowned at his brother and snapped, "She almost *died*, Alex, and all you can say is, '*I'm sorry?*'"

Alex shrugged and kissed Tillie's hand. "I really don't know what else to say, Sam."

"Well, I'm sure Marquette wanted to kill you, and I was about ready to let him," Sam stormed. He shook his head and snorted, "I can't *believe* you did this, especially to Tillie. You know, Alex, it's not like you're married to some naggy kind of a witch. She's a really nice girl, and she didn't deserve to have to go through this without her husband. Dad and I *told* you to stay closer to home. In fact, we *begged* you to spend more time with Tillie. Now the pregnancy is over, and you've missed the whole thing."

Alex clenched his teeth and frowned at Sam. "I'm not a little kid anymore, Sam. She's okay and we'll get through this without you leading the way."

Sam narrowed his eyes. "You're acting like a spoiled punk —"

"Hi, guys," James' voice was heard behind them, and they looked up to see their father.

"Hi, Dad," Alex said.

"How's she doing?" James put a hand on Alex's shoulder.

"Better," Alex answered.

"Hey, Sam," James said, "why don't you take the Casellis for some supper? They've been here all day…and Alex and I have to talk."

Alex felt like someone had dropped an anvil on him. *Here it comes*, he thought.

Sam rose from his chair with a huff. "My pleasure." And he left the room.

James shuffled himself into the chair next to Alex. "Son, I love you," he started as he tried to give Alex a smile. "I know you're a man now, but you're out of control. Choosing Tillie over a political life wouldn't be the *worst* thing you could do. In fact, it's what you *did* choose when you vowed to God and the rest of us. You promised to forsake all others. Did you think that statement just meant other women?" He smiled with a nod. "I've spoken with your pastor, and he seems to think the vow includes forsaking Governor Williams, as well as yourself."

Alex sighed, as if irritated. "Dad, I'm sorry. I just —"

"Save it." James put a gentle hand on Alex's knee and looked into his eyes. "I'm not gonna let you come back to work for a while."

"What?" Alex was astonished.

James shrugged. "You know how it works. You're not a partner yet. You work for me. That's how we have it set up. I can lay you off for a time."

"You can't just lay me off." Alex narrowed his eyes.

James nodded his head and smiled. "Oh, yes, I can, and you kids have plenty of money. You'll be fine."

"But Hansen Development —"

"I called Shondra, and she's got some associates that she feels are ready to handle it, with a little supervision of course."

"Who'll be supervising *them?*" Alex asked in quiet horror. "I'm the only one who's ever worked on those files."

"You will," James answered with a quiet nod. "I've seen your nice little office upstairs at home, and Shondra said she'll bring over files. Only as needed, of course."

"*As needed?*"

"Well, Sam and I and Shondra can probably handle the bulk of it," James answered. "So you won't be doing a whole lot." He smiled at his son and raised an eyebrow. "I want you to spend some time with Tillie and those babies. I imagine she'll have quite a recuperation period —"

"Rosa can help out."

James shook his head. "This is a treacherous thing you've done, and I'm more than a little worried it will change how she feels about you in the future. I know it's really changed her family's feelings about you."

Alex rolled his eyes. "Who cares?"

James took a breath and slowly let it out. He shook his head. "I had a friend, years ago now, but he taught me some of the most valuable lessons of my life. He was an attorney who got caught up in the young and famous lawyer thing, sort of like you. He paid absolutely no attention to his wife, who was the sweetest, prettiest little gal anyone could ever have. His best friend, who was a judge and lived just down the road, noticed all this was going on. He mentioned it several times to my friend but, of course, my friend wouldn't listen. He just pushed himself harder and harder, convinced that his wife would always be there for him.

"And she was a good girl and tried very hard, but she was also very young. This judge, who had lost his wife several years before, started to pay some attention to her. Naturally, she was flattered, and she tried to tell her husband about the overtures this judge was making. But my friend was so caught up in himself and his own life, he didn't give it a second thought. Naturally, this hurt her deeply, because she took it all to mean that he just didn't care. Maybe he didn't even want her anymore." He took a breath and continued, "To make a really long story short, Alex, she fell in love with that judge and nearly left my friend."

"Did they have an affair?"

James shook his head and smiled. "Heavens no. It wasn't like that at all, but the damage that had been done was not easily repaired. My friend wound up taking his wife and leaving town, trying to fix his marriage. His wife was just the most wonderful lady, and she believed in staying married and working it out, but my friend told me it was a long time before they were able to put the past behind them and truly start over."

Alex swallowed hard and looked into the sleeping face of his wife. "Is it Uncle Mac and Aunt Charlotte?"

James nodded. "How'd you know?"

Alex shrugged. "He's so attentive to her, and sometimes she seems very shy with him...as if she doesn't trust him."

James replied, "I imagine she's just waiting for the other shoe to drop. It's a very painful thing for a woman to be rejected by her husband, and especially when he decides he's got all the time in the world and doesn't share any of it with her. I believe God created woman specifically for a relationship with her husband. And when she's rejected, there's trouble."

Alex sighed heavily. "I don't want that to happen with Tillie and me. I think she understands that I just wanted to make a solid, secure future for us and the kids."

James moaned and rolled his eyes. "Oh, you did not, Alex! You were in it for yourself. And you *knew* this thing you were doing was going bad. Sam and I have been yapping at you for months about it, and let's not forget, you and Marquette nearly came to blows over the deal last September."

Alex clenched his jaw and looked away from his father.

James got up. "I gotta get something to eat. We've been up here all day." He put his hand on Alex's shoulder and said, "You pray about it, son. Pray a lot. God will tell you how you're supposed to handle your marriage." He pointed his index finger at Alex and gave him a small smile. "And remember, you're supposed to *lead* your wife; she's not supposed to *revolve* around you."

Alex nodded, and his father left him alone in the room with his sleeping wife. He kissed Tillie's cheek again and gently caressed the wild curls spread out around her head on the pillow. "I'm so sorry," he whispered. "I should have been here."

Tara could barely choke down her sandwich as she listened to the Martins and Casellis visit with animation about Alex's friend, Noah. *How in the world could they have bonded so quickly with a man they have just met?*

Vincenzo changed the tone of the conversation when he complained woefully about his ill-tempered stallion. "I just do not know what to do. I have tried everything to be friends with that animal, and it will just not have me!"

His brothers chuckled, but Giuseppe's expression was grieved. As he rose from his chair and offered Rosa a hand up, he said, "My, son, you have made a horrible mistake, but it is easy to mend. This melancholy you have for War Winds' lineage is all for naught. You bred that stallion with a lunatic mare. Now sell the beast and rid your spirit, and ours, of this worry." He looked at Rosa and said, "Let us go to the chapel for a time."

Rosa only nodded as if to agree, tucked her arm in the crook of Giuseppe's arm, and together they left the cafeteria.

Vincenzo's brothers razzed him a little more, and the Martins joined in on the good-natured teasing. Soon the conversation turned to politics, with the men discussing the election, and the ladies zeroing in on Elaine's next column. When Tara slipped away, no one even noticed.

From the doorway of the hospital chapel, Tara heard them whispering in Italian to one another, and she caught her breath. She had questions, no matter the consequences of revealing her own involvement. She made her way to where they sat, taking a seat in front of them.

"Hello, Tara," Giuseppe greeted with a small smile.

Tara looked from Giuseppe to Rosa, and they saw her round black eyes fill with tears.

"Is everything all right, Tara?" Rosa whispered.

Tara nodded. She searched their eyes, so lined with worry today but still twinkling with the passion she saw in her own husband's expression. Her tears rolled down her face as she whispered, "How long have Noah and Alex been friends?"

172

Giuseppe's head dropped into his hands, and he suddenly began to sob. Rosa put a comforting arm over her husband's shoulders.

"Papa?" Tara whispered as she looked at the top of her father-in-law's bald head, and her heart began to pound.

"Oh, Tara," Rosa cried. Tara looked to her mother-in-law and saw tears on her face as she confessed, "We have known for a long time."

"How long is a long time?"

"Before they were married."

Tara nearly fell from her chair with the surprise of their secret. She grabbed the wooden seat with both hands in order to keep her balance.

Giuseppe slowly lifted his head and looked into Tara's eyes. "What do you know of Noah?"

Tara took a deep breath and slowly let it out. "Papa...I..." she hesitated and shook her head as she looked into his eyes. "I helped to convince you to allow her to travel to Rapid City with Marquette and me. All I knew of was a man named Noah. I had no idea he and Alex were friends."

Giuseppe nodded and Tara watched huge tears drop from his eyes as he said, "They were not friends—at first. But their families have been connected for many years. The brother of Frances Martin was dear friends with Noah's father and his brother."

"Uncle Mac?"

Giuseppe nodded. "But that is not even the half of it, Tara dearest." His voice caught on a terrible sob. He lowered his eyes, covered his face with his hands, and cried horribly. Tara looked to Rosa.

Rosa managed to speak through her tears. "Tara, we have prayed for Noah for twenty years. We heard about him shortly after our arrival in America." She swallowed and shook her head. "He was a troublesome child who grew into a rebellious teenager, and eventually a dreadful drinker. When Angel returned and said he had behaved as a blackguard, naturally, we believed her."

Giuseppe lifted his head and looked into Tara's astonished expression. "Tara, please understand—" His words caught on yet another sob as he cried, "I am convinced that God's gift of Angel was meant for

Noah. After he met her, he dedicated his life to our Lord, stopped his drinking, and built a business." He drew a jagged breath and sobbed, "It was I who kept them apart. I have gone against God's will for my own daughter and His will for the man, Noah Hansen. Noah is more wonderful than you could ever imagine. There are so many things you do not know about Noah."

Tara raised a trembling hand to her forehead and wiped away the sweat beginning to soak her brow. "Did you ever tell Angel?"

Rosa and Giuseppe shook their heads as they stared back at poor Tara, who appeared to have been dealt a mortal blow. At their admission, she gasped and put her hand over her mouth.

"You should *not* have kept this secret," she whispered. Fresh tears rolled from her eyes as she looked at the two dearest, most loving people she had ever known.

Giuseppe was consumed with his quiet sobs again, and he hung his head and covered his face with his hands, while Rosa tried to comfort him. Tara watched them, realizing how they must have suffered, especially when Alex revealed his blackguardly tendencies. Her heart went out to them, and her gentle hands reached for Giuseppe's face, carefully drawing it upward so she could look into his eyes.

"God loves you, Papa," she said with a serious frown. "You are the *best* papa, and Angel is blessed to have you. You made the best decision you could, and God will bless this." She took a deep breath and began to shake her head. "I do not know how, but I know He will watch over and all will be done according to *His* plan."

Giuseppe put his old hands over Tara's and looked into her dark eyes. "You must *never* speak of this to my Marquette."

Tara nodded her head. *Never.*

The male nurse, who'd helped Marquette make his phone calls and had taken the Martins and Casellis to see the babies, now came to Alex. He suggested he should at least take a quick peek at his little children. Alex hesitated, afraid to leave Tillie for fear she'd awaken while he was gone. However, the nurse assured him Tillie would be sleeping through the night and that he might as well get acquainted with his little ones. Alex reluctantly followed him to the nursery, where he pointed to the tiny bundles in the incubators before the glass windows.

"If they maintain their body temperature for at least twenty-four hours," the nurse explained, "we'll be able to bring them out of the nursery for a little bit so you can hold them."

Alex smiled and nodded. When the nurse left, he stayed to watch the peaceful, little bundles sleep. *Real, tiny, little people. Thank God everything turned out okay…*

Alex heard footsteps and looked up, expecting to see Sam; however, it was Marquette's familiar shape. Alex cringed and turned his eyes back to his babies.

"I see you have found the babies," Marquette said as he took a position next to Alex.

Alex only nodded as he waited for the first strike.

Instead, Marquette stood quietly, watching the babies but saying nothing.

After a long time, Marquette put a friendly hand on Alex's shoulder. "Perhaps I have been wrong about you, Alex. Your friend, Noah, would not take up with you if you were as horrible as I have led myself to believe you to be."

Alex was surprised, and he looked at Marquette with caution.

Marquette looked into Alex's dark eyes, *the eyes his sister loved.* "Let us try again," he offered.

Alex was overcome by Marquette's sincerity, and offered Marquette his hand immediately.

Marquette smiled and took Alex's hand in a firm grasp. "For Angel."

Alex nodded. "For Angel."

Burt and Diane Engleson hurried up the long corridor in the maternity ward. Burt was still wearing his white apron, and Diane had attempted to hide her curlers beneath a blue nylon scarf. They found Giuseppe and Rosa sitting alone in a small waiting room.

When Giuseppe heard their footsteps in the doorway, he stood in surprise. "My friend! I forgot to call you with an update. Please forgive me."

Burt embraced Giuseppe with a smile. "Andy called us. Don't worry about it."

Diane took Rosa into her arms and gave her old friend a kiss on the cheek. "How are things going now?"

Rosa shook her head and tears fell from her eyes. "She is out of surgery, and Alex has finally arrived. He is in there with her right now. She will be okay."

"How 'bout the babies?" Diane asked.

"One of each," Rosa answered as she dabbed at her tears with a tissue. "Just as she wished."

"Well, where are the rest of your kids?" Burt inquired.

Giuseppe shrugged. "In the cafeteria, I think, still talking about the election." He firmly grasped Burt's shoulder. "Can you take a walk with me, my friend?"

"Of course."

Leaving Rosa and Diane behind, Burt and Giuseppe walked the long, lonely corridors of the hospital together.

"And it was Noah who brought him to her," Giuseppe cried. He shook his head and wiped his tears again. "And what a smile he had for all of us. I felt as if an old friend had come to comfort me. My sons, especially my Marquette, were all so taken with the man." He sighed mournfully and shook his head again. "What have I done to them? How terribly I have broken my family."

Burt shook his head in response, for there was nothing he could say.

Alex spent the remainder of the evening in Tillie's room, while her family members wandered in and out to give him the cold shoulder—except for Marquette, who had somehow overcome his hostilities in those few moments with Noah.

Even Alex's own family was chilly toward him when they came in to check on Tillie and pray quietly beside her bed. Around midnight, they all announced they were leaving, but Alex was to notify them if anything should change. He agreed, glad to see them leave for a while so he could be alone with Tillie and his thoughts.

All night long, Alex forced himself to stay awake as the nurses filed in and out to check Tillie's blood pressure, monitor the bags above her head, and examine her dressings. He wondered how much pain she would be in if she was awake, thankful for the peaceful rest she was getting now. His heart ached with the guilt of what he had done.

He cried as he remembered the delight in her eyes whenever he had come home early or if he said he was taking a day off. Toward the end, he hadn't taken *any* days off. He hadn't seen his wife the last week of her pregnancy, and his heart broke. *I thought I had more time.*

He suddenly recalled Andy's words during a special prayer at their wedding… *"Husbands, love your wives, even as Christ also loved the church, and gave Himself for it."* Alex broke down and cried as he thought about that. *Jesus loved me so much He gave His life…He laid down all selfish ambitions, even the temptation to be a king, and died so I could have everlasting life…and He wants me to love Tillie this way…Can I do that?*

He looked at her peaceful face and remembered the first time he watched her sleep in his arms. It had been their wedding night, and she had trusted him so much. He wondered if what had happened to his Uncle Mac would happen to him now.

Alex shook his head and put a tender kiss on her cheek. "I love her, Father, and I'm so sorry that I missed this event…but I don't know if I can do this the way that You want me to."

The sun was shining against the back of the heavy curtain on the hospital window when the last nurse of the night finished checking Tillie's blood pressure.

"Ninety-eight over sixty," he proclaimed with a smile to a still-sleeping Tillie. "Good girlie." He glanced at the tired man who'd fallen asleep slouched in the chair beside the bed. He shook his head with a smile. His tie was loose and crooked, and his starched white shirt was rumpled. He hadn't even left her to change his clothes. Hopefully this episode with his wife would make a difference in his life.

The nurse went to the window and opened the curtain, lighting the room with the brightness of the morning. Alex winced, covered his face with one hand, and struggled into a more seated position.

"Good morning, Mr. Martin," his deep, husky voice said with a smile. He went to Tillie and placed his gentle hand upon the pulse in her wrist. "Why don't we see if we can get the missus rolling."

Alex stood by the bed, took her other hand into his own, and frowned with concern as he looked into her sleeping face.

"Now, don't frown like that," the nurse chuckled. "This little gal is doing just fine, and we want her to wake up with no worries."

Alex looked at the nurse, noticing he was the same one who'd taken him to see his babies. He put on a smile and returned his focus to Tillie.

"Say her name," the nurse whispered.

"Tillie," Alex said, so quietly the nurse could barely hear him, and he laughed.

"Louder."

"I'm afraid she'll be mad at me." Alex took a nervous breath and looked at the nurse. "Everybody else is."

The nurse only laughed again and nodded his head. "Yep. Well, I was sent over yesterday afternoon, and I know all about you. But we've got those babies to think of now, so put your best foot forward and let's get rolling. You gotta start somewhere, and God's mercies are new every morning."

Alex was surprised at his forthrightness and took a deep breath. "Tillie," he said again, but this time he tenderly touched her face and leaned close enough to kiss her lips. "Tillie, wake up."

Slowly her eyes began to open, and she gave him a tired smile. "You made it," she whispered. "What did we get?"

"A boy and a girl," Alex answered as his eyes filled with tears of relief and joy. "Just like you wanted."

"Have you seen them?" she whispered. The pain was beginning to fill her body by now, and she remembered how they were taken.

Alex nodded with a smile and for the first time, she saw tears fall from her husband's eyes as he whispered, "Tillie, they're incredible."

"I want to see them," she slurred as she tried to blink the medication from the day before out of her eyes and somehow will away the pain in her middle.

"Pretty soon," Alex said as he took a careful seat on the edge of the bed and looked into her eyes. "But I have to tell you first how very sorry I am about being away these last few months…"

"Oh, Alex," she smiled, "it's okay. Let's just enjoy the babies."

"I love you so much," Alex continued. "I miss you and I want to make some changes. Well, changes have actually already been made."

He had such a peculiar expression on his face at that moment, it made Tillie laugh, and then wince with pain. "Oh, don't be funny today." She looked into his eyes and admitted, "I've missed you, too, Alex. I want it to be like it was before."

"It will. I promise." He suddenly remembered the nurse in the room with them, and he looked all around. "Where did he go?"

"Who?"

"The nurse," Alex said, a bewildered expression on his face.

"I didn't see a nurse."

Alex's eyes filled with tears again as he looked into the smiling eyes of his pretty wife. *God's mercies are new every morning…*

CHAPTER 13

Christmas 1980

Carrie watched Charise as she sat on the bed with their mother, paging through an old photo album and attempting to jog her memories. Charise's dark curls were tucked behind her ears, and her black eyes smiled at the old photographs. Sometimes Della recognized the pictured memories, and other times she didn't. Nonetheless, Charise continued to visit sweetly with Della, pointing at the different scenes and explaining what had happened in each.

Carrie shook her head and looked out the window of the nursing home. Only a week before Christmas, and already the Black Hills had seen nearly a foot of snow and subzero temperatures. She sighed as she watched the continuing snow. *Mom's the lucky one in all this...at least she doesn't have to lie to her husband.* The baby moved within her, and she placed a tender hand over her ever-growing abdomen. Her due date was still a week away, but she was ready to be done with this part.

The door to their mother's room opened, and Carrie turned to see who had joined them. It was Mario, and he carried two cups of coffee.

"Here you are, Carrie dearest," he said as he handed her a cup. "That should warm you."

"Thanks."

"How is he today?" Mario gave Carrie's stomach a gentle pat.

Carrie couldn't help but smile, and she delicately patted the baby. "He's feisty today."

"Already so much like his father," Mario said with a grin. He bent over Carrie's womb and said, "And you will grow into a fine man, just the same as your father."

Carried laughed, and the baby moved again. "Well, we don't know for sure that it's a boy—"

"But he certainly behaves as a boy," Mario reminded.

Carrie nodded and took a sip of the hot coffee. "Mmmm. That hits the spot."

"Antonio tells me everything went well for Noah in Sioux Falls. No mention of Angel?"

"Not a word, but that was a little too close for comfort."

"Yes, it was, but I still maintain Noah will be loyal to you *always*. He loves you and you alone. Do not forget, Angel left him without explanation. And you have given him children." He glanced at his wife and child together on the bed. "And that is something a man can never forget."

As if she'd felt his gaze, Della looked up from her album and smiled tenderly into the eyes of her husband.

"Hello," she greeted. "How long have you been here?"

Mario went to her bedside, took a seat on the edge, and drew her hand into his own. "Only a few moments, my love." He placed a soft kiss on her fingers and asked, "How are you this day?"

"I'm fine. Have you come to take me home?"

Carrie's eyes filled with tears, and she turned her back on them so they wouldn't see. *She always asks now…every time…* Carrie looked out the window again, trying to ignore the soft conversation behind her.

"But it's nearly Christmas," Della begged.

Mario pretended to make light of her statement. "And how do you know that, Della, my love?"

"See the snow? When the snow comes, here comes Christmas."

"But we don't celebrate Christmas," he reminded.

"Before you came, Carrie and I celebrated Christmas," she replied.

Carrie nearly choked on her coffee and turned around to face her mother. Della was looking directly into her eyes.

"You remember, don't you, Carrie?" Della questioned.

Carrie swallowed and slowly nodded. "Of course, I remember, Mom."

"We used to get a tree and hang lights." Della laughed, and her grey eyes suddenly sparkled with recollection. "Remember your first Christmas with Noah?"

Carrie swallowed again and slowly nodded.

"Oh," Della laughed again, "she was so surprised. Noah came home with a tree and all the decorations. He has always been so good to you, Carrie." Her eyes opened wide. "Can I see Noah?"

"No, Mom." Carrie shook her head. They'd had this discussion before as well.

Della frowned. "I just don't understand, Carrie."

Mario put a tender hand on Della's cheek, and she looked at her husband. "Do not fret so much about Noah, my love. He is very busy."

Della let out a sigh.

Joshua was surprised when he returned home that evening to find that Ty was with Mona again.

"Hiya, Tiger," Joshua greeted his little nephew. The happy red-headed boy went willingly from Mona's arms to his. Joshua kissed Mona and raised an eyebrow. "More errands?"

Mona nodded. "I just want to talk to her about it, and I've prayed about it, but I just don't feel right asking."

"Well," Joshua said with a thoughtful frown, "we're probably just getting older and weird—"

Mona giggled. "Speak for yourself, Josh."

"We're pert near fifty years old, Mona. We might start getting strange ideas in our heads."

"Whatever, Josh." Mona rolled her eyes and turned toward her stove. "As long as you're here, I'm gonna check my chicken." She opened the oven door and, with mitted hands, pulled out the roaster. "Estelle and I prayed for Angel today."

"Oh?" Joshua questioned, getting that peculiar feeling in the pit of his stomach.

"Yep. And I think she's doing better these days."

"Estelle?"

"No, Angel," Mona clarified. She put the lid back on the roaster, returned it to the oven, and turned around to look at her husband. "Estelle and I think there was something wrong last month…did I tell you about that?" Joshua shook his head, and Mona continued, "Well, we had this terrible feeling that something was wrong. So we prayed every day, sometimes over the phone."

Joshua looked at his wife with surprise. "Really?"

Mona nodded. "But we were talkin' about it today, and I think everything must be gettin' better for her."

Rosa Caselli sat in the window seat of her living room and gazed at the setting sun. Snow had been forecast to begin sometime that evening. *It is probably already snowing in Rapid City.*

"Father, be with him," she whispered. "And please comfort my Giuseppe. He suffers most grievously."

Christmas was nearly upon them, and Rosa was worried. Her sons planned on being in Sioux Falls to celebrate the holiday, but Giuseppe had yet to even speak to his son-in-law. Thanksgiving had been horrible, even though Tillie and Alex and their new babies came for dinner and stayed most of the day. Giuseppe obviously hated Alex and hadn't even attempted to hide it.

"This is so difficult, Father," Rosa whispered as she bowed her head. "Please have mercy on my heart, and forgive me for my part in this."

Estelle danced around the portrait with her feather duster, singing, "I'm dreaming of a white Christmas…" Her voice trailed off, and she smiled at Maggie. "And it's a gonna be a white one, Maggie May. Just look at that snow fly!"

Maggie laughed, and nodded as she watched her sister.

Estelle dusted Angel's photograph and smiled into the images. "I remembered some more words for you…" She cleared her throat and began, "Her voice is low and sweet, and she's the world to me, and for bonnie Annie Laurie, I'd lay me doon and dee."

Maggie chuckled. "Where'd you learn the rest of those words, baby?"

"Heard 'em on the radio, Maggie. Some old cowboy's gone and figured out the words and put 'em to music."

"And you sing 'em so pretty," Maggie complimented.

"Why, thank you, Maggie. I want to know all the words when she comes back."

Maggie took a deep breath and forced a smile. "That's a good idea, baby."

Mona bustled through her kitchen like a blur. It was Christmas Eve, and her family was due to arrive at any moment. She was delighted to have them all in her home at once. Carrie performed whatever duties Mona asked of her, and laughed hysterically as Mona shared one hilarious story after the next. Mona's family hadn't been to Rapid City since Carrie and Noah were married, so Carrie was looking forward to meeting the legendary family.

"Why are they staying at the Howard Johnson's?" Carrie asked as she buttered an enormous stack of homemade buns. "Between the two of us, we've got plenty of room."

Mona rolled her eyes. "'Cause Daddy has to have the whirlpool when he travels." She leaned closer to Carrie and whispered, "On account of his hemorrhoids…all them years drivin' truck, I s'pose."

Carrie giggled, and just then Joshua came into the kitchen and announced, "Daddy called and said they're on the way. They're all checked into the motel, and he's just tickled with the whirlpool."

"That's good, Josh," Mona acknowledged. "Did you remember to inflate that little donut Daddy likes to sit on?"

"Sure did, honey."

Noah and Ty came stomping through the back door at just that moment, covered with snow.

"We're done," Noah said with a smile, giving his snow boots a good stomp on the rug by the door. Ty stomped his little feet in the same way and smiled at Mona.

"We made a snowman, Auntie Mona," he said with a smile. "Come and see."

"Oh, dear, I just don't have time, Ty darlin'."

"Just peek out your kitchen window," Noah said. "You can see it from there."

Mona stood on her toes and glanced out the window above the sink. She laughed out loud. Noah's snowmen were always so precious. *Hard hat, safety goggles, and the saw and hammer...Wait, he's added something new this year...* She laughed again and shook her head. "I like the tool belt. Now, why don't you two get out of your wet clothes? My family will be here soon."

"Sure thing, Mona," Noah agreed, and he bent to help Ty.

"Did Daddy say how the plane ride went?" Mona asked as she stirred something on the stove.

"Oh, I guess Bubba had a little trouble once they got him up there," Joshua answered with a smirk.

"Now, which one is Bubba?" Carrie asked.

"Mavis' husband," Mona answered. "You remember...the one who ain't been the same since that accident with the UPS truck."

Noah and Joshua laughed, and Mona frowned. "Now, don't the two of you be laughin'. That could have happened to anybody."

Carrie laughed, and the baby moved. She reached for her huge stomach with surprise and reminded, "My due date's tomorrow. Maybe the Lord will bless and we'll get a new baby on Christmas."

Mona chuckled. "We can only hope—" She stopped what she was doing and looked at Carrie with concern. "Are you feeling okay, darlin'?"

"Just fine," Carrie answered with dismay. "Not even a twinge."

"*Tsk*. That's too bad." Mona shook her head and went back to what she was doing. "Maybe tomorrow."

"Maybe I'll just be pregnant happily ever after," Carrie grumbled.

Noah laughed and went to his wife. He patted her stomach and smiled into her eyes. "It can't last forever."

"It feels like it," she argued with a small smile.

Noah laughed again. "Well, I think you look great anyway."

Carrie raised an eyebrow and tried not to smile. "Thanks, Noah."

All the Casellis had arrived and were clamoring for a place to sit in Giuseppe and Rosa's living room. Even though everyone attempted to be in good holiday humor, they all noticed the coldness with which Giuseppe treated his only son-in-law.

After a sumptuous dinner and after everyone had opened their gifts, Giuseppe excused himself to the billiards room. His sons followed him in and closed the door behind them.

Giuseppe angrily racked the balls and aligned his cue.

Petrice cleared his throat and cautiously questioned his father, "Are we not even invited to play?"

Giuseppe looked at his three sons and a pain shot through his heart. *If only I had listened to my Lord, Noah Hansen would be standing here with the three of you.*

Vincenzo put a loving hand on his father's shoulder and attempted to encourage, "She loves him, Papa. I beg of you, please forgive him and try to move on. Angel has long forgotten the offense and does not waste one moment thinking of it."

Giuseppe hung his head and growled in defiance, "I cannot bear the thought of her wasting her precious life on a blackguard."

"Papa, he has apologized and is attempting to make things right with her," Petrice reminded. "He has not left her side since the babies were born, and does not plan to return to work until well after the first of the New Year —"

"I care not for his lame plan of repentance," Giuseppe barked. "He has shown his true colors, and I regret the day I gave her to him." He looked into the eyes of his astonished sons and promised, "And his self-love will show itself again when given the chance. Mark my words, a blackguard is *always* a blackguard."

"But, Papa," Marquette begged, "he has asked for forgiveness."

Giuseppe's face remained hard, and his sons were surprised. This wasn't like their father at all, and they silently committed themselves to pray for him.

PART II
CARRIE

CHAPTER 14

January 1981

Tillie and the babies had been home for just over two months, and Alex had been there with them. There were the occasional questions, and a few files from Shondra, but aside from that Alex spent his time helping his very stiff and sore wife. He lifted the babies, ran to the store, did laundry, and made meals. He did miss his work, but it was obvious Tillie needed him. She could scarcely take care of her own recuperating body at first, let alone two very demanding little ones.

They named the little boy Alex James Martin IV, but Tillie wanted to call him "A.J." because everyone needed a little originality, no matter the ancestral name. They named the little girl Laura Rose, after Rosa. They had Alex's olive-toned skin and dark eyes, but their hair was soft and curly, like Tillie's.

The babies had gained more than two pounds by this time and kept Alex and Tillie busier than they'd ever been in their lives. Feeding, changing, rocking, more feeding, more changing—and at all hours of the day and night. It was endless.

Feedings were particularly engaging because the babies were so small. They could hold only one or two ounces at a time, which meant they needed to be fed every couple of hours around the clock. And then there were the occasions when the babies continued to fuss, even after they'd been changed and fed. This perplexed Alex to no end.

Tillie had perfected the maternal sway on her nieces and nephews. She claimed it could "smooth over" any dilemma a baby might have. And, as soon as she was physically able to do so, she taught this method to her husband. She stood before him as she held one of the fussy little babies in her arms and swayed.

"It's all in the hips." She smiled into the baby's face and spoke in a very gentle, sing-song tone. "And in the tone of your voice. Now, don't cry. We love you so much, and you're just the best little baby in the whole world."

Alex held the other baby and attempted the same gentle sway. He didn't have a woman's hips, so it was a little difficult to master. However, he quickly figured it out, perfecting his own method of the maternal sway. Soon he could calm the babies as easily as his wife.

Being busy with two newborns left Tillie and Alex precious little time to themselves, and Alex regretted every day he'd been away during the pregnancy.

But Tillie never mentioned it. She'd picked up where they'd left off. She seemed to have forgotten he wasn't there for the birth of their children. Her spirit was content to take care of her new babies, and she was excited about whatever time Alex would be at home with them. She was truly and deeply in love with Alex, and it mattered not to her what had happened, but only that his babies were alive and healthy and that he was there with her now. It was what she had always wanted: a family.

On the outside, Alex appeared to be just as comfortable with her, but in his heart he feared everyday things would never be the same again. The guilt weighed on his conscience like nothing he had ever felt. He brought home flowers, comical cards, or other gifts whenever she sent him to the store for supplies. Her black eyes sparkled and smiled, the same as they always had, because there was no change in the way Tillie felt about Alex. The guilt of that, as well, piled upon him in a tremendous way.

One afternoon he returned home to find the house very quiet. Upon investigation, he found both of the babies sleeping at the same time. Tillie was lying on their bed, sound asleep as well. He looked at her for a moment and noticed that the outline of her body had returned to its original, slender shape. Another pang of guilt pierced him as he remembered Sam's words at the hospital, *"The pregnancy is over and you missed the whole thing.*" Alex swallowed hard and shook his head as he looked at his pretty young wife. How he hated what he'd done.

He remembered the felt box in his hands and recalled the gift he'd picked up on his way home. He went to the edge of the bed and took a seat. She awakened and smiled when she saw Alex sitting there. "What time is it?"

"About three," he answered.

Tillie's mouth dropped open with surprise. "Oh, my goodness! I've been sleeping for almost two hours! Are the babies okay?"

"I just checked 'em. They're sawin' logs."

Tillie laughed. "Did you remember the formula?"

"How could I forget?" He smiled, and then he held the felt box before her. "And I got *you* a little something, too."

"You have to stop spoiling me," she said with a smile as she reached for the box and opened the lid. Inside was a delicate pair of heart-shaped diamond earrings that matched the pretty pendant he'd gotten for her the past summer. "Well, okay. You can spoil me a little." She looked into his eyes. "Thank you, Alex. They're beautiful."

"You're not spoiled," Alex said as he looked into her eyes, wondering what was left in her heart for him.

She noticed his uneasiness and placed her hand on his cheek. "Alex, I love you, and I'll love you forever. Please let this thing go. We're okay."

Alex's eyes filled with tears of regret and guilt, and he slowly shook his head. "I am *so* sorry. How can I ever make things better?"

Tillie chuckled. "Alex, there is *nothing* wrong to make better. You asked for forgiveness and now it's over. The only person having a problem with this is *you*. Now, come on. I don't know what kind of a guilt trip my family has laid on you, but you're gonna just have to get over it."

"I can't. And I can't believe that you could just forgive everything that happened —"

"Alex," she said, placing her slender hand over his mouth, "it wasn't a big enough deal to dwell on. It was an *accident*. Everything turned out the way that I have always wanted it. Well…it would have probably been easier to have one baby at a time, but we can work with this." She looked earnestly into his eyes. "I'm so happy, Alex. I've always wanted a family. Please, share this joy with me and let it go."

Alex nodded his head and gathered her in his arms. "I love you, Tillie."

Although Tillie had forgotten Alex's absence during the birth of their children, her parents had not. They harbored silent resentment and anger toward their son-in-law that was not easily disguised. Giuseppe continued to be cold toward Alex, even though he did pray to forget what had happened. He saw that his Angel loved her husband, but he believed that it was her age of a mere twenty-three years that had actually saved the marriage. Her youth and innocence, combined with her tremendous devotion and affection for the man, had superseded all other feelings, and it embittered Giuseppe to no end. *Angel was meant for Noah, no matter her disobedience. She returned home that spring and repented of her sin, painfully and sincerely. Why did I allow her to suffer and believe she had just happened upon the man, after her mother and I had prayed for him for nearly fifteen years before the event?*

He knew he'd erred in keeping the two apart by making a foolish decision from his heart. He remembered over and over what Angel had said at the hospital when Dr. Lewis was about to take the babies: *"They will make a decision from their hearts, and it will be deceitful and desperately wicked."* And it was.

Giuseppe was consumed with the guilt of his omission by assuming Noah to be a blackguard. He hadn't even given him a chance to explain. *It was not mere coincidence that led Angel and Noah together in the first place.* That was painfully obvious when God allowed Noah to be the one to lead her straying, self-centered husband to the hospital that night.

Giuseppe sank to his knees in a pew in the back of Christ the King Church. He spent most of his mornings in the church now, seeking atonement and praying for God to right the horrendous situation he'd created. *Father, forgive me for the wretched thing I have done and for the miserable old fool I continue to be...I promise not to meddle another day...*

Alex was laughing as he came down the stairs and into the living room of his home. "Hey, that was Noah on the phone. Carrie finally had their baby this morning!"

"Oh, tell him congratulations," Marquette said with a smile from his place on the couch, where he was enjoying a morning cup of espresso. He and Tara had just arrived in Sioux Falls on a very early flight.

"Boy or girl?" Tillie asked. She and Tara were each holding a baby, giving them bottles.

"A boy," Alex answered with a smile. "His name is Jacob."

"I'll bet Carrie's happy," Tillie commented. "She was at least two weeks overdue."

Alex replied, "Exactly two weeks over. Noah said she's in a *really* great mood."

"We will have to stop and see Noah when we are in Rapid City," Marquette said thoughtfully. "Now that I know someone out that way."

"When are you going to Rapid City?" Tillie asked.

"In a few weeks. Tara and I are attending the Stockmen's Show with Vincenzo and his family. He plans on selling Liberal. Noah mentioned that he might be able to rid himself of the horrid beast at the horse sale. Did you know that Liberal has thrown our brother again?"

"Why does he keep getting on that horse?" Tillie shook her head with a smile. "I'm surprised he hasn't killed himself yet."

Tara shifted uncomfortably, wanting to change the subject. *It is unbelievable that Noah actually calls the house. Unbelievable that Noah has invited Vincenzo to the Stockmen's Show in Rapid City.* "I think A.J. needs to burp," she said. "How can I do this?"

Alex hurried to where Tara sat, positioned the white cloth diaper over her shoulder, and then assisted her with the repositioning of the baby. "And pat him, like this," he said, demonstrating the action for her. Tara nodded and began to pat the baby's back.

"I have to get more diapers and formula," Alex said as he walked over to the coat closet.

Marquette smiled and got to his feet. "Why do I not give you a hand?"

Alex tried to hide his look of surprise with a smile and a nod. "Sure."

Tillie masked her pleasant amazement by putting Laura into the burping position. She still couldn't get over Marquette's total turnaround when it came to Alex. It was as if he couldn't show him enough how he loved and appreciated the husband of his sister. She wished some of it would rub off on her father.

Alex bent over Tillie and gave her a soft kiss. "We won't be gone long." He touched each of his children and joined Marquette at the door. They were exchanging sincere pleasantries as they left together.

"I can't believe it," Tillie said with a shake of her head. "What on earth has come over my brother?"

Tara sighed and rolled her eyes. "He was very taken with Alex's friend and has decided that, if a man like Noah would take up with a man like Alex, he cannot be so bad after all."

Tillie's eyes were very curious and thoughtful, but she said nothing as she continued to pat her little baby until there was a loud burp. "Oh, look," she whispered, "they're both sleeping at the same time." She smiled into Tara's troubled eyes, thinking that she, too, was still very upset with Alex. "Let's lay 'em down so we can visit."

Tara nodded, and they got to their feet. They shuffled the babies down the hall and into the sweet nursery, laying them gently into their beds. Tillie covered Laura with a blanket and turned to make sure Tara hadn't forgotten to cover A.J.

"I would have liked to have had children," Tara whispered. She touched the soft black curls atop the baby's head, sighed, and smiled into Tillie's eyes. "But it is okay. The Lord has blessed Marquette and me in other ways."

Tillie put her arm on Tara's shoulder. "Come on. Let's have espresso while they sleep. This *never* happens."

Tara followed Tillie to the kitchen. They got themselves fresh hot cups of espresso from Tillie's pot on the stove, and settled on the couch.

"You look upset today," Tillie murmured over the top of her cup. "Is it the babies, or is it Alex?"

Tara shrugged and sipped at her espresso. "How are you feeling about him, Angel?"

Tillie smiled, and Tara saw in her expression the soft sparkle of a woman in love as she answered, "I love him, Tara. He's my husband."

Tara took another sip of her espresso and tried to swallow the resentment she harbored for Alex. *Of all people, why has God blessed him with this forgiving young wife and two beautiful babies?*

"Tara," Tillie said, trying to figure out why she and her parents couldn't let the thing go, "I know you're still really upset. I know Ma`ma and Papa are, too, but it would be a whole lot easier on me if you guys could just let it go." She smiled and added, "Even Marquette has done a one-eighty."

"I know." Tara forced a smile as she looked into Tillie's happy eyes. *Angel has totally forgiven Alex, and it makes me sick to think he could just take complete advantage of her good heart and pay absolutely no consequence…Noah would surely not have behaved this way.*

Tillie's eyes became mischievously curious. "Hey, I gotta ask you something." She lowered her voice to a whisper. "Now that we're *alone.*"

Tara raised one brow. "What are you up to, Angel?"

Tillie rose from her place on the couch. "Wait here a second. I wanna show you something." She hurried off to her bedroom, and Tara heard the closet door open and then the soft rustle of a box. Soon Tillie appeared again, holding a small red book with tattered corners. She took her seat on the couch.

"This is from my first semester at Augie," she shared with a smile, continuing nervously, "I found this at the college's bookstore. It has an old poem in it… 'Annie Laurie.'" She opened the worn pages to reveal a photograph tucked into the text of the particular poem. She took the photograph of her and Noah at Roubaix Lake and handed it to Tara. "I found this at Ma`ma's the day the babies came."

As Tara took the photograph she felt the tremendous weight of her secret press upon her heart, and briefly considered telling Tillie all she knew about Noah.

"Alex's friend, Noah..." Tillie whispered, for she could barely say the name without a soft smile.

Tara nearly fell from her place on the couch. *Does she know? Has she known all along?* She struggled to control every expression and reaction as Tillie continued.

"I've never met the man or spoken with him, but..." Tillie hesitated and sighed, "...and I don't know how it could be..." She looked into Tara's eyes as she bit her lip. Of everyone in her family, Tillie trusted Tara the most. She was solid and secure and would never betray a confidence. "Everyone saw him at the hospital that night, including you."

Tara dropped her focus away from Tillie and pretended to study the photo in her hands. She floundered with what was the truth and what had actually come to be. She wanted Tillie to know, and wanted it desperately. *But of what use would the information be? Noah is happy with another, who has just given birth to his son, and Tillie has vowed her life away to Alex...a blackguard in disguise. Marquette was right all along...*

Tara slowly began to shake her head as she decided to lie. "He is not the same man, Angel."

"I *love* this event," Marquette said as he munched a hot dog and sipped a Coke at the Black Hills Stock Show and Rodeo in Rapid City, South Dakota.

Vincenzo nodded with a grin. "And your Tara told me to keep an eye on you while you visited the food stands."

Marquette pretended a confused expression. "Whatever for?"

"Apparently there was an incident on a plane after our visit to Valley Fair last fall—"

"Oh, brother," Marquette interrupted with a roll of his eyes. "The pilot was flying like a maniac. It was not the food at all!"

Vincenzo laughed and glanced at Tara, who stood quite a distance from them, looking at Western-style clothing with Kate, Alyssa, and Angelo. He smiled and leaned closer to Marquette so he could whisper, "Is she feeling any better?"

Marquette's smile faded as he slowly shook his head. "It is very hard for her. She would so like to have had babes, but I also think she has come to the practical conclusion that God has chosen a different path for the two of us."

Vincenzo raised an eyebrow. "And what of her feelings toward Alex? Have they improved?"

Marquette shook his head. "Not that I have seen. We were there just a few weeks ago, and she was as cold as ice towards him."

"It is too bad. He has atoned for his sin, and she and our father would do well to let it go. It will only hurt Angel."

"Hi, guys," came a man's voice from behind them, and Vincenzo and Marquette turned around to see their new friend, Noah Hansen. He was with a lovely strawberry-blonde and a small, very redheaded little boy. On Noah's front was a pack that held a tiny baby.

Marquette and Vincenzo rose to their feet and extended their hands in greeting, first to Noah and then to his wife, whom he introduced as Carrie.

"And who is this little cowboy?" Vincenzo asked curiously as he bent over far enough to look the little boy in the eye, and he extended his hand.

"I'm Ty," he answered with a smile. "But Dad calls me 'Tiger.'" He took hold of Vincenzo's bigger hand and said, "How do you do?"

"Very well, thank you," Vincenzo answered.

Marquette was impressed with the little boy's grand manners, and he extended his hand as well. "I am Marquette. It is a pleasure to meet you."

"You have a very long ponytail." Ty giggled as he looked closely at the hair hanging down Marquette's back. "Longer than Mom's!"

Noah was taken aback. He hadn't noticed Marquette's ponytail at the hospital and, of course, had only spoken to him by phone when he and Vincenzo called to say they were coming to Rapid City together. Now Marquette was dressed in Western-wear instead of the black suit he saw him wearing before. His appearance had completely altered.

Suddenly it was like a slow-motion replay of an old memory he couldn't stop...*My brother, Marq...was in Vietnam...Marquette? Tall, dark guy with a ponytail...just happened to mention he was Angel's brother...He had some kind of a foreign accent...*

"He's two weeks old," Carrie said, and Noah managed to pull himself out of the old memory. "But," she continued with a smile, "we've never missed the Black Hills Stock Show and Rodeo, and I feel great, so we just thought we'd come down for a little while and see what they got."

"How are your sister's babies doing?" Noah asked. *Why in the world did she call herself "Angel" if Tillie is her real name? No. No way. It's not her, and it doesn't matter anyway if it is. I've got Carrie and the boys now, and I don't even want her anymore. Angel, if that really was her name, left me practically at the altar, and I don't care if I ever see her again.*

"Fine," Vincenzo answered, and then he patted the back of Noah's small son. "But they are not this big." He looked questioningly at his brother, "How much did they weigh when you were there?"

"Almost six pounds," Marquette answered with a smile. "I call them my teeny little sweetie people."

Tara noticed the group collect near the hotdog stand, and felt her heart drop into her stomach. She sighed and shook her head. *Marquette is oddly attracted to that man, and I can't figure it out. Perhaps it is just the commonality of Vietnam, but perhaps it is something more...*

Carrie saw the grief in Tara Caselli's long stare, and her heart pounded...*Either she knows I'm connected to the Ponerellos, or she knows about Noah and Angel.*

200

CHAPTER 15

March 1981

It was the middle of March by now, and the snow was flying in Custer, South Dakota. The little nursing home was perfect for her mother—out of the way and nestled into the Southern Black Hills, where no one would even think of looking.

Carrie spread the photographs on the table, and Della smiled.

"Oh, he's just beautiful, Carrie," Della whispered, touching the small faces. "How old is he now?"

"Nine weeks today," Carrie answered. "And look here, Mom, this is a new one of Ty and Noah. Don't they look great in their new cowboy hats?"

Della slowly nodded, but confusion filled her expression. "Now, why isn't Noah with you?"

Carrie shook her head and forced a smile for Charise, Mario, and Antonio, who were there in the room with her. "Noah's busy, Mom."

"Oh," Della said with a frown. "Then how did you get here?"

"I can drive myself, Mom."

Charise shook her head and leaned closer to Carrie to whisper, "The confusion *isn't* getting any better. If anything, it's *worse than ever*."

Carrie could only nod in agreement. Dr. Bensen had assured them she would steadily improve, but her head injury had been far more severe than they initially realized. Della couldn't keep her memories straight at all anymore, mixing them up with fragments of different times and details.

The physical paralysis in Della's upper extremities had improved. By now, she could feed herself, write, knit, and turn the pages of a magazine. Dr. Bensen credited that part of her recovery to Charise. At Christmastime she'd brought a puppy to the nursing home, and Della fell in love. Della named the puppy Katy, and started to reach for her immediately. She *never* forgot Katy's name, and she always reminded Charise to return with the puppy when she left.

The injury to Della's spine from the fall down the stairs, however, had left her legs useless. No amount of physical therapy would heal the damage, and Dr. Bensen told them Della would spend the rest of her days in a wheelchair.

Antonio took a deep breath and slowly let it out.

Carrie looked at him and frowned. "What?"

"You took a big risk exposing yourself at the Black Hills Stock Show and Rodeo in January, and then again last month when Marquette Caselli visited Noah," he murmured. "Both times his wife was with him. What if she were to recognize you?"

Carrie shrugged. "Well, she didn't. It's been almost six years, and my appearance has changed a lot since then. For starters, I was a fall-down drunk with hair in my face, and now I'm the wife of a man they admire and respect. I shower, wear clean clothes, and tote around two really cute little kids. Mrs. Caselli couldn't pick me out of a lineup even if she tried."

Charise bit her lip and shook her head as she watched their mother push the photographs around the table. "Is she going to be okay, Carrie?" Her concern wasn't whether Caselli would eventually find them, but how much of her mother they'd ever see again.

Carrie put her arm on Charise's shoulders and gave her younger sister a soft kiss on the cheek. "I think so. She doesn't seem to remember anything at all about Sal or the fall, and that's a *good* thing."

"We are close enough to keep an eye on you, Noah, and the boys," Antonio continued with a frown, "but I would prefer that you no longer take unnecessary risks."

Carrie took a deep breath. "Listen, guys, I'll do everything I can to keep this thing from falling apart, but I'm not about to start refusing to be with them. That would certainly make things look suspicious and draw attention to me. Right now they see me simply as 'Noah's wife.' Nobody will figure anything out."

Mario nodded and put a loving hand on his stepdaughter's shoulder. "You are right, Carrie dearest. And you have already done so much for us. Thank you for everything."

Noah and his accountant, Fred Taylor, met in Noah's downtown office in an attempt to do taxes for Noah's business from the previous year.

"So, what did you do with it?" Fred asked impatiently. "Maybe we can deduct it somehow. That's a lot of income tax, and it could make a big difference on your returns if we can deduct it for equipment or something."

Noah swallowed hard and stared at the figure before him. "I don't remember cashing out any stocks, especially not in *that* amount."

"Oh, come on," Fred laughed. "I get that all the time. Now, don't play with me, Hansen. I know you hate doing this, but we've gotta figure your taxes for last year, and we might as well get it done today."

Noah shook his head. "I'm tellin' you, Fred, I *didn't* sell those stocks last year."

Fred rolled his eyes, opened his briefcase, and hunted through it for a moment. He produced a piece of paper and laid it on the desk in front of Noah. Noah leaned over the paper to examine it, and his eyes froze on the signature at the bottom…*Carrie Hansen.* "That's my wife's signature."

"Well, they *were* the stocks you had put in her name only," Fred reminded. "We only needed one signature."

Noah felt like someone had knocked the air out of him. *What on earth would she need two hundred and fifty thousand dollars for?* "I'm gonna have to call her and ask about this," he said as he got to his feet behind his desk.

Fred rose to his feet and extended his hand to Noah. He raised an eyebrow and offered, "I can come back tomorrow..."

"Sure," Noah answered with a nod. *Carrie's bound to have an explanation for this.*

Fred opened the door to Noah's office, and they were surprised to see a sheriff's deputy standing there with Melinda. Melinda gave Noah and Fred a professional smile, turned, and went back to her desk.

"Well, I'll see ya tomorrow, Noah," Fred said. He smiled at the deputy and went on his way.

"Noah Hansen?" the deputy asked.

"That's me," Noah acknowledged, getting the most peculiar feeling in the pit of his stomach.

"I'm Deputy Kramer from the Custer County Sheriff's Office."

"Custer County?" Noah frowned.

"Sir, maybe you should sit down," he continued. "I'm afraid I have very bad news."

Noah's frown deepened. "What's going on?"

"I'm sorry, Mr. Hansen, but I'm here to inform you that your wife, Carrie Hansen, was killed this afternoon when her car slid off the highway and crashed in Custer State Park."

"What?" Noah whispered, staggering backwards and stumbling into his desk.

Deputy Kramer quickly reached for Noah and helped him into a seated position on his desk.

"Custer State Park?" Noah whispered as he rubbed the side of his face. "This must be a mistake. Why would she be down there?"

Deputy Kramer shook his head, and was about to speak when Melinda came into the office.

"Noah?" she asked as she reached for his arm. "Are you all right? What's going on?"

Noah shook his head and suddenly started gasping for breath. The deputy put his hand on Noah's shoulder and requested, "Get him some water." Melinda hurried to the water cooler in the outer office.

"Mr. Hansen, is there anyone I can call?" Deputy Kramer asked.

Noah started to cry. "Were the boys with her?"

"It appears she was by herself," the deputy answered.

Melinda appeared in the doorway with a paper cup of water and attempted to hand it to Noah, but he batted it away and put his hand over his face.

"Call Josh!" he cried. "Call Josh!"

Joshua was in his office at the church when the secretary told him Noah's office was on the line, and that it was an emergency.

"This is Josh," he answered.

"Hi, Pastor Hansen, this is Melinda. Can you and Mona come over here right away? I don't know how to tell you this, but Noah's just gotten some really bad news and he needs you guys."

"What's going on, Melinda?" Joshua asked as he stood from his chair.

Melinda swallowed her tears, surprised that she actually felt sadness at Carrie's passing. She'd always thought maybe she'd be more relieved. "Pastor, Carrie was killed in a car accident just a little bit ago. The sheriff's deputy is still in Noah's office with him. He asked me to call you."

Joshua's heart pounded with grief, and he sat back down in his chair. "I'll call Mona, and we'll be right down."

Melinda hung up the phone and noticed that someone was standing beside her desk. *Ben Simmons…I thought he was taking the day off.*

"What do you want, Ben?" she questioned with a frown, "and what are you doing here? I thought you were going to see your stepmother today."

"I was to see my stepmother." He drew an uncertain breath and cautiously inquired, "Did I misunderstand, or has Mrs. Hansen been in an accident?"

Melinda huffed out her air and coldly confirmed, "She's dead. Noah's in his office with the deputy. He won't let anybody else in there, not even me. Pastor Hansen's on his way."

Ben swallowed hard and whispered, "I must see him at once."

Melinda shrugged. "Whatever. Go get your head taken off, for all I care."

Without another word, Ben went to Noah's office, let himself in, and closed the door behind him.

Noah was sitting behind his desk with his head in his hands, softly sobbing, and Deputy Kramer was on the telephone.

"My friend," Ben whispered as he rushed to Noah's side and put a comforting hand on Noah's shoulder. "I am so sorry. What can I do for you?"

Noah shook his head. "Nobody can do anything for me now." He looked into Ben's eyes and cried, "I love her so much, Ben. She's everything to my life here on earth."

"I know." Ben impulsively put his arms around Noah. "Please know that I am here for you, whatever you may need, and your brother is on his way."

Deputy Kramer hung up the phone. "Mr. Hansen, the M.E. has your wife downtown now. Can you come with me?"

Noah slowly nodded and started to get to his feet. He looked into Ben's eyes again and whispered, "Please, Ben, please don't tell anyone that Carrie died in Custer State Park. I don't have an explanation yet, and I don't want people talking about her. She's just the greatest little lady."

"Of course," Ben agreed.

Noah reached for his handkerchief, dried his face, and said, "I'm gonna call Josh and tell him not to come. I have to go see Carrie now—"

"Perhaps you should allow your brother to be with you, Noah," Ben gently suggested.

Noah shook his head, "No. He'll ask too many questions and he'll never understand."

Instead of calling Mona, Joshua drove to their home. He didn't want to give this kind of news to her over the phone.

Mona was rocking Jacob in the living room when Joshua arrived, and Ty was watching afternoon cartoons.

"Hi." She smiled up at him when he entered the room. She noticed his downcast expression and frowned. "What's wrong, Josh?"

Joshua sighed as he took a seat on the couch. He put a tender hand on his wife's knee, and tears fell from his eyes.

"What's happened, Josh?"

"Oh, Mona," he whispered, "Carrie was killed this afternoon in a car accident."

Mona nearly dropped the baby in her arms. She gasped and sat up straight in the rocking chair. "Josh, are you sure? Have you talked with Noah?"

Joshua shook his head. "Melinda called me at the church, and she wants us to come down to his office right now. He's probably in pretty bad shape. She said the deputy was still there."

"The deputy?"

Joshua shrugged. "That's just what she told me."

"Well, what will I do with the kids?" she whispered in disbelief.

"They'll have to come with us —" Joshua began, but was interrupted by the ringing of their telephone. "Let me answer it," he offered, and hurried to the kitchen.

"Hello."

"Josh?"

Joshua recognized Noah's voice. "Hey, Noah, Mona and I were just on our way down to your place—"

"Listen, Josh," Noah interrupted in a soft sob, "I've gotta find the boys."

"They're both here, Noah. Now, just sit tight and we'll be right there."

"No, I have to go identify Carrie—" Noah's voice broke in a soft sob.

"Noah, I'll come with you," Joshua offered.

"No," Noah insisted, and if Joshua were there he would have seen Noah adamantly shaking his head. "I would rather do this alone. Now just stay right there with Mona and the boys, and I'll be right over. This shouldn't take too long."

"I don't know if this is such a good idea," Joshua tenderly protested. "I want to be with you."

"No. I'm going alone and that's final." And with that, Noah hung up the phone.

Joshua held the dead receiver in his hand and frowned at Mona.

"What's the matter now, Josh?"

Joshua shook his head and hung up the phone.

As Noah exited his office with the sheriff's deputy, Melinda put her hand on his arm and looked into his eyes with concern.

"What can I do for you, Noah?"

"Nothing," he answered as he continued. He suddenly stopped in his tracks and turned to look into her eyes. "There is one thing you can do for me, Melinda." He lowered his voice to a whisper. "Don't tell anybody that the Custer County Sheriff's Office was here—"

"Why not?"

"Because I said so. And if you tell anybody, so help me, I'll fire you on the spot."

Melinda slowly nodded her head, and Noah left the office.

The Custer County coroner had brought Carrie to the Rapid City facility because it was closer. She'd made it nearly to the county line when the slippery, snowy roads had caused her to careen off the highway, through a guard rail, and over a cliff. Deputy Kramer had said that the estimated time of death was at least three hours earlier.

Carrie hadn't gone through the windshield, nor had she been disfigured in any way by the crash. She appeared to have merely bumped her temple against the glass in the driver's side window, dying instantly. When the coroner uncovered her face for Noah's identification, she appeared to be sleeping, except for the bluish tinge on her skin.

Noah tenderly reached for a stray lock of her strawberry-blonde hair, and brushed it to the side.

"It's her," he whispered to the coroner. "This is my Carrie."

"I'm very sorry, sir," the coroner replied. "Would you like to have a few minutes with her?"

Noah nodded, and the coroner and Deputy Kramer left Noah alone with Carrie.

Noah placed a soft kiss on Carrie's cool forehead and looked at her sleeping face.

"How will we ever do life without you?" he whispered as the tears fell from his eyes. "How will I ever make it alone? I can't raise these boys all by myself." The sobs in his throat interrupted him. He touched one of her eyebrows and kissed her cheek. "And what was going on in Custer State Park? Why were you clear down there?"

No answers came from Carrie. Noah fell to his knees beside her and lay his head upon her chest. "I love you so much." And he wept and wept and wept.

"And you are certain she has died?" Mario questioned, quite shocked at the news of Carrie's passing.

"I am positive," Antonio affirmed in a whisper over the telephone. "Is it possible Sal learned of her identity and has killed her?"

Mario took a deep breath. "It is always possible, but I seriously doubt it. If he knew of her identity, he would have killed the rest of us by now." He sighed and continued, "Please follow up on this, my Antonio. We must learn for certain that it was just a slippery road."

"I will find out, Papa."

"And be there for dear Noah," Mario said as a sob caught in his throat. "Dear Noah is the kindest and best of men. Do what you can, my son."

"I will, Papa," Antonio promised, and then he hung up the phone.

Noah stomped his boots on the back steps, and Joshua went to greet him. He took Noah into his arms and held him while he cried.

"She's gone, Josh," Noah sobbed in his brother's arms. "She's gone, and I don't know what I'm gonna do."

"Noah, I'm so sorry," Joshua cried with him.

"How can I ever make it without her? I love her so much. It's like it's a mistake or something."

"I know," Joshua murmured, attempting to comfort Noah.

"And how will I ever tell my Tiger?" Noah whispered. "Josh, what am I gonna do?"

Tillie Martin was stirring a pot of her famous ravioli sauce when the phone rang in her kitchen. Tara was sitting at the table, giving Laura a bottle, and Marquette and Alex were in the upstairs office.

"Martins."

"Hey, this is Noah," came the gruff greeting on the other end.

Tillie nearly dropped the phone. She'd never spoken to Noah Hansen over the phone, and for the briefest moment she thought *her* Noah had managed to track her down.

"Noah?" she whispered into the phone, and Tara looked up with surprise.

"Yeah, Noah Hansen," he clarified. "Is Alex there?"

Tillie swallowed and took a breath. *What's gotten into me?* "Of course," she answered and lay down the phone. "That's for Alex," she explained as she headed for the stairs.

Tara nodded as she stared at the receiver on the countertop... *This is getting worse and worse...*

In a few seconds Tillie returned to the kitchen, hung up the phone, and went back to her sauce pot.

"I'm so terrible," she shook her head and frowned. "I thought the guy we were just talking about had finally tracked me down."

Tara nodded and pretended an amused smile.

"Anyway," Tillie took a breath and asked, "how long are you guys going to be in town this time?"

"Just a few days," Tara answered. "We have business in Washington that we have put off for far too long—"

She was interrupted by the hurried footsteps of Alex and Marquette coming down the steps.

"Noah's wife was killed this afternoon in a car accident," Alex sadly announced.

Alex and Marquette went to Rapid City for the funeral, leaving Tara and Tillie at home in Sioux Falls. The babies were still far too small to travel such a distance. When Marquette contacted Vincenzo, he wanted to come as well, so the three of them leased a charter.

Amid all the commotion and hasty plans, neither Tillie nor her brothers even mentioned to Giuseppe and Rosa what had happened to their new friend, Noah. Giuseppe came to Tillie's with some biscotti and was pleasantly surprised to see Marquette and Tara's rental car still in the driveway.

They must have decided to stay a few extra days after all, he said to himself as he came up the front steps and rapped on the door.

The door was opened, and Tillie gasped with surprise. "Papa! What are you doing here?" She let him in and helped him off with his coat.

"Oh, Doria was teaching our Angelo's II crew how to make some delicious biscotti, and I thought it was time for a break, so here I am." His black eyes sparkled as he inquired, "Is my Marquette here?"

"They're not back yet," Tillie answered as she hung her father's coat in the hall closet. "Do you want to have some espresso with Tara and me?"

"I would love some," he answered. "Where are those teeny, little, sweetie people?"

"They're awake," Tillie answered. "Tara's feeding A.J. right now, and I just finished with Laura."

"The hungriest duo in town," Giuseppe tittered as he followed his daughter into the kitchen.

"Hello, Papa," Tara greeted her father-in-law. She had A.J. in the burping position, and little Laura was in a small rocker on the table. "What brings you over on such a cold day?"

He delicately touched his new granddaughter's face with his index finger and smiled as he held up his package. "Biscotti. Care for some?"

"That would hit the spot," Tara answered.

Giuseppe settled himself in a chair and asked, "So where are the men today?"

"They're still at the funeral," Tillie answered as she poured her father some espresso from her fresh pot. "They probably won't be back until after suppertime."

"The funeral?" Giuseppe frowned with confusion. "Whose funeral?"

Tillie set the small cup down in front of her father and said, "Carrie's funeral was today, Papa. Did you forget?"

"Carrie who?" Giuseppe asked, obviously still very confused.

"Carrie Hansen," Tillie answered. "Remember? Noah's wife?"

Giuseppe softly gasped, putting his hand over his heart. "Do I misunderstand?" Tears sprang into his eyes. "Noah Hansen's wife has passed away?"

"Papa," Tillie said with concern as she reached for her father's hand. "Are you okay?"

Giuseppe swallowed hard. "I think I need a Rolaids, my Angel."

"Papa, did you not know?" Tara asked quickly. "I thought Marquette told you."

Giuseppe shook his head. "No one told me of this. When did this happen?"

Tillie hurried to her cupboard for the Rolaids, and Tara answered. "Just a few days ago, Papa. She crashed her car on a slippery road."

Tillie put the Rolaids on the table in front of her father, and Giuseppe immediately reached for the roll.

"Are you sure you're okay, Papa?" she asked. "Should I call Ma`ma?"

"No...I have had too much biscotti this day." He quickly dried the tears from his eyes and shook his head. He pretended a quick smile and rose from his seat. "I forgot something back at the ristorante. I must leave, dear ones." And with that, Giuseppe hurried for his coat, flung open the front door, and dashed for his car.

Alex, along with Marquette and Vincenzo, walked into the quiet church on South Canyon Road in Rapid City, South Dakota. They were met by a very grieved Mona, who was surprised to see them and reached out for Alex's hand.

"Mrs. Hansen," Alex greeted. "I'm so sorry." He gave her a gentle embrace.

"Thank you for coming, Alex," she said as she dabbed her tears away with a tissue. "I can't believe this happened to Noah. They were just so happy together."

Alex nodded and looked toward Tillie's brothers. "These are my brothers-in-law, Marquette and Vincenzo Caselli," Alex introduced. "They've recently become acquainted with Noah. Gentlemen, this is Noah's sister-in-law, Mona Hansen."

They both bowed, removed their hats, and reached for Mona's hands.

"How do you do," Marquette said, but there was no smile or shine in his black eyes today. In fact, his grief for the family was plain to see. For him, there could be no tragedy greater than the loss of his wife.

"Mrs. Hansen," Vincenzo said as tears escaped his black eyes, "this is a dreadful tragedy, and we are very sorry."

"Thank you for coming," Mona said. "Noah has told us so much about you. He's right over there." She pointed to a place not far from her where Noah stood, holding his new baby and visiting quietly with some friends. Ty was next to him, hanging onto his pant leg.

Noah saw them come in and turned his head to look at them. His eyes were downcast and sullen, and he simply shook his head. Alex embraced him first, and then Marquette and Vincenzo, who were crying quietly by now, unable to restrain their Italian emotions. Marquette bent over and scooped up little Ty to hold him close. Ty reached for his elegant ponytail, ran his little fingers through it, and looked into Marquette's black eyes.

"Mommy is with Jesus," Ty whispered.

Marquette's heart broke as he nodded, sending a fresh dose of tears down his face.

"Don't cry," the little boy said as he touched the tears on Marquette's cheeks.

"Noah, we're so sorry," Alex said as he embraced Noah again.

Noah shook his head sadly. "I just can't believe it. Everything was just going so great."

Mario Ponerello cowered in the back of the church as he watched Marquette Caselli enter with his brother. He pulled his hat further down, watching Marquette seat himself. *Unbelievable...I am sharing this room with my old nemesis and he is not even aware.*

"What will we do if Alex has brought his wife along?" Rauwolf whispered beside him. Rauwolf had disguised his appearance by dying his hair black and wearing a pair of glasses. He couldn't risk Noah seeing him there.

"Poor Noah will suffer most grievously," Mario answered, "and our lives will come apart very quickly." He watched Alex take a seat beside his brothers-in-law, noticing no lady with him. "I do not believe the Angel is here."

They both sighed with relief, and Rauwolf whispered. "We will have to find a way out as soon as we can."

Mario nodded.

Maggie was seated with Estelle and saw Alex, Marquette, and Vincenzo enter the sanctuary. Marquette turned his head to speak with Alex for a moment, and Maggie couldn't help but zero in on his familiar face. *I've seen him somewhere before.* She noticed his long, elegant ponytail and the stylish suit. The flash of his wedding band caught her eye as he carefully set his hat in the pew beside him. As if in slow motion it all came back... *"What'll ya have?" she'd asked. "Some information, if you please," he'd answered, and then he'd produced a photo of Ty's father.* Maggie lied her tail off that day. And then he'd noticed the painting.

She involuntarily shuddered at the memory. *Angel's brother…* *Marquette Caselli is Angel's brother…That means she's married to Noah's lawyer…I wonder if Noah even knows…I've gotta get outta here before he sees me.*

For March, the weather was unseasonably warm in the Black Hills of South Dakota. Carrie's interment took place at Mt. View, and Noah wept during the entire service. Alex, Marquette, Vincenzo, Joshua, Ben Simmons, and Harv Meyers carried her to her final resting place. Noah followed behind them. When her casket was placed on the platform, he laid his head on its cover and wept in agony. When the short service was over, it took all of them to coax Noah into the limousine that was to take them back to the church for a short reception.

Mario wanted to comfort his son-in-law but was forced to hide in the crowd, away from Marquette Caselli. He and Rauwolf made their escape during the processional back to the church, but had instructed Charise to make an excuse for Mario.

Mario wasn't the only one trying to avoid Marquette Caselli. Maggie slipped into the crowd around Noah, successfully hiding her own identity. She didn't know whether Noah was aware of Angel's marriage to his friend, Alex, and she didn't want to be the one to blow the whistle, especially not on this day. She'd be able to question him at a later time. On their way back to the church she pretended to be sick, and she and Estelle went home.

"This is my sister-in-law," Noah said as he introduced her to Alex, Vincenzo, and Marquette. "Alex, you remember Charise?"

"Of course," Alex reached for her hand and offered her a smile. "You were Carrie's maid of honor…you must have been only ten or eleven —"

"I was eleven that day."

"And very small next to Alex," Noah interjected. He looked at Tillie's brothers. "Alex was the best man —"

"'Cause Theo got arrested," Charise finished, and Marquette and Vincenzo chuckled.

"How old are you now?" Alex asked.

"I'll be sixteen in April."

"Where's your dad?" Noah asked. "I'd like him to meet some people."

Charise smiled openly and pretended to look around. "I know he's here somewhere."

"How 'bout Tony," Noah continued. "Did he make it?"

Charise smiled and nodded. "I saw him come in."

"I'd sure like to meet him." Noah glanced at Alex, Marquette, and Vincenzo. "You know, I've got a brother-in-law that I've never met."

"He's very busy," Charise explained. "Tony travels a lot."

From across the room, Melinda watched Noah as different people came along to visit with him and give him their condolences. She was surprised at all the single women in their church, and how many of them offered to take care of his boys. She rolled her eyes and shook her head. *As if he could be interested in any of those frumps! Gold-diggers.*

She let out a heavy sigh as she watched her grieved boss cry off and on during the day. He never let his little boys out of his sight, unless Mona was holding the baby or Ty wanted to go off with a Caselli. *This is going to take a really long time…I hope I have the patience for this.*

Giuseppe trotted through the front door of Angelo's II, nearly knocking down the hostess.

"So sorry," he said as he raced by her, heading for the kitchen.

He burst through the swinging doors, and Burt and his crew looked up in surprise.

"Hey, Giuseppe," Burt greeted, a confused expression on his face. "I thought you were going home for the day."

"Burt!" Giuseppe was breathing heavily as he reached for his friend's shoulder. "We must speak immediately!"

Burt frowned and nodded. "Of course, my friend."

Burt closed the door to the office in the back. "Sit down, Giuseppe. You look like you're about ready to have a heart attack."

"Perhaps I will," Giuseppe breathed as he took a seat in the chair by the desk.

"What's the matter?"

"Noah's wife has died," Giuseppe explained, and then he burst into tears. "What have I done, Burt? And what will become of Alex now?"

"Giuseppe, get a hold of yourself." Burt grasped Giuseppe's shoulder. "Nothin's gonna happen to Alex. What are you talking about?"

"I have wished my son-in-law dead for the last several months," Giuseppe confessed, "but Angel loves him and their new life with the babies. How could I have done such a thing? What is God doing?"

Burt took a deep breath and calmly explained, "Whatever has been done to Angel and Noah cannot be *undone* by you, Giuseppe. You need to give this matter over to God, once and for all, and submit to His will."

Giuseppe buried his face in his hands and cried. "Father, I am so sorry for what I have done!"

Burt patted Giuseppe's shoulder and silently prayed, "Please, God, help him. I don't know how much more poor Giuseppe can take."

CHAPTER 16

"The roads were very slippery that day," Charise attempted to explain to her mother. "It was an accident."

Antonio and his father watched with tears in their eyes as Charise gently conveyed Carrie's passing to her mother.

Della's old grey eyes filled with tears. "Can't she come anymore?"

Charise shook her head. "She won't be coming anymore, Ma`ma."

Della bit her lip. "Bring Noah to me. He'll straighten this out. He straightens everything out."

Charise shook her head as the tears fell. "Even Noah can't straighten this out, Ma`ma." She took a breath. "Remember what Carrie told us about Jesus?" Della slowly nodded, and Charise continued, "She's with Jesus now, Ma`ma. Carrie believed that Jesus died to forgive her sins, and she loved Him. She loved His Word and His ways. Carrie was very good and Jesus loved her, too. I know they're together in Heaven now—"

"And she doesn't have to worry about Sal anymore," Della interrupted.

Charise was quite shocked at her mother's words, as were Antonio and Mario. She hadn't mentioned Sal's name since her accident.

"Della, my love," Mario said as he took a seat on the bed and reached for her hand, "Carrie's accident was not because of Sal, this we know for certain. Antonio has thoroughly looked into the situation. We are quite safe once again. Carrie's accident was simply an accident."

Della nodded. "And now she's with Jesus."

"Yes, Ma`ma," Charise replied. "Now she's with Jesus."

Whatever Carrie had done with the money remained a mystery to Noah, and he instructed his accountant to pay the taxes and forget about it. It didn't matter to him what she'd done. He knew, had she been given the chance to explain, it would have all made perfect sense.

It was also a mystery as to why she was in Custer State Park. Mona told him Carrie had said she was running some errands and needed her to take care of the boys for the afternoon. And since Noah could not find an explanation for Carrie being in Custer State Park, he hid the details of her accident from everyone, including Joshua and Mona.

A few days after the funeral Noah received a reminder card from Jiffy Lube, saying it was time to change the oil in Carrie's Malibu. At first, Noah shook his head. The car was totaled in the accident, but of course Jiffy Lube wouldn't have known that. However, he happened to glance at the odometer reading on the card as he was throwing it away. *That's strange. She only used that car for errands. Why is the mileage so high?*

When Noah didn't think the mystery surrounding Carrie's death could get any worse, he received the bill for her gas card. She'd filled up with gas at a station in Custer, South Dakota, on the day she died. Curious, he hunted through the other bills in his office at home. He'd never checked them before because he'd never had a reason to. To his amazement, Carrie had stopped at the same gas station about twice a month for the last several months.

At first, Noah considered going to Custer to ask someone at the gas station if they remembered Carrie, and if they knew why she'd been coming to Custer so often. But then he decided he really didn't want to know. She'd hidden this from him for a reason, and his grief was already enough. He'd loved her so much, and to learn that maybe she'd been seeing someone else would have been too horrible.

Without Carrie's smiling face to come home to every night, Noah fell deep into a pit of despair. He was thankful for his little boys, but he desperately missed their mother. His life was suddenly back to the loneliness he'd gotten used to before they found one another. Part of him regretted ever having married her and dragging himself though the sadness her death had created. Then he'd look at his little boys and thank God that at least he wasn't left alone this time, like he had been when Angel left him all those years ago. Carrie had left behind some wonderful memories, but was it worth it? Was any amount of happiness worth the despair that came from having to say goodbye?

Joshua and Mona spent a considerable amount of time with Noah in the months following Carrie's death. She'd become such a remarkable part of their family, and it was agonizing to accept her absence. It was as if God had allowed her to stay for too brief a time, and when He was ready He called her home, leaving the rest of them behind.

Marquette and Vincenzo made several trips to Rapid City to comfort Noah. They prayed with him for long periods of time, and wept with him when the sadness in his heart needed somewhere to spill over.

"And she didn't know the Lord when we were first married," Noah told them one warm day in April. He smiled a small smile and shook his head. "But one day she up and says, 'I'm coming to church with you,' and I said, 'Okay.' Boy, Josh and Mona were really surprised."

Marquette's tears kept him from responding, but Vincenzo swallowed and said, "So now, because of your diligent witness, she is at home with our Lord and resting in His arms."

Noah slowly nodded. Even though he still wore a soft smile, tears ran from his blue eyes. *But I still miss her so much.*

Noah hired an older lady by the name of Vera Smith to come into his home and help with housework and care for the boys when Mona was not available. She lived alone, having been widowed for years, and was looking for something to do with her spare time. She was a friend of Maggie May's, and when Noah mentioned he might need someone to help, Maggie sent her over to meet him.

Vera's services weren't needed for much more than cleaning, laundry, and some grocery shopping. And even though Melinda frequently offered to help with the boys, Noah clung to his children and left the house rarely, if ever, for short meetings or site inspections. Alex directed a young associate in Rapid City to help Melinda and Ben with the general operations of the office, and James or Sam handled any legal crises that came along from the Sioux Falls office.

"Tiger is just so used to being at home with his mommy," Noah explained to Sam over the phone one day. "I don't know when I'll be able to come back to work. He's just not ready."

Sam agreed with Noah and made all kinds of arrangements so Melinda and Ben could operate Hansen Development in Noah's absence, for as long as necessary. It really wasn't important for him to be there anyway. There were so many sites already up and going. All they needed was a little supervision, and Ben could easily handle that. Sam noticed Ben's loyalty and devotion to Noah, and was thankful that Noah had hired someone like that.

And in Noah's absence from the office, Melinda slipped into the role of "Boss of the Whole Place," as Harv Meyers described it to Sam, along with Ben Simmons, over lunch one day at the Hotel Alex Johnson. Sam had come to Rapid City to make sure everything was operating smoothly, and to visit with Ben and Harv in person.

"She is *so* mean," Harv complained. "She tossed that young associate out on his ear the other day, and he was only doing his job."

Ben nodded. "She actually told me that *she* was in charge now, and that we would all have to start reporting to her."

Sam raised a dark eyebrow. "That's a scary thought."

Harv laughed. "And most of us are afraid *not* to!"

Ben chuckled, "And as long as the place is running as smoothly as it is, I see no reason to bother poor Noah with our difficulties."

"The next thing you know, she'll be calling me for a wage increase!" Harv snickered. "She doesn't need a raise. He's paying her too much the way it is."

Sam grinned and nodded. "Between the three of us, we should be able to keep Miss Melinda in line. We don't need to bother Noah with any of this." It was of far greater importance for Noah to be home with his children—especially Ty—than to be caught up with work.

Ty was not even four years old when his mother died. Naturally, he'd grown accustomed to her presence in the home. Sometimes he asked Noah so many questions, especially at bedtime, and Noah answered each one thoughtfully and gently.

"But when can I see her again?" the little boy persisted. His gray eyes were so full of curiosity; they made the child look just like his mother.

"When the Lord calls *us* home," Noah answered.

"But we *are* home, Daddy."

Noah nodded and answered gently, "But there's a better home where Mommy is now. That's Jesus' home, and you'll understand more when you're big."

Ty smiled and continued, "Big like you?"

"Yeah," Noah nodded with a small grin. "Big like me."

Jacob was only nine weeks old when Carrie passed so he didn't have any questions, which was a relief for Noah. He rocked his baby, gave him his bottle, and talked about the living memories of Carrie without having to go over again and again where she was and why she wasn't with them.

Ty called the baby "Jake" and he loved to spend time close to him, whether he was in his baby swing or just lying on a blanket on the floor. He brought his little cars and other toys close to Jake to play, even though Jake couldn't interact. Ty made engine noises for his cars and waited patiently for Jake to respond. When he didn't, Ty filled up the silence with conversation and instruction on what they were playing next.

Noah watched Ty play with his little brother and thanked God for these treasures Carrie had left behind.

CHAPTER 17

June 1981

It was Burt and Diane Engleson's anniversary, and Giuseppe had agreed to help out at Angelo's II while they went on a short trip. It was early morning, and he was counting the hostess' change order when the bell signaled someone had entered the restaurant.

"It is too early for business," he grumbled to the hostess. "You finish the change order, and I will see who it is."

She agreed, and Giuseppe went out into the restaurant to see who'd come in so early.

When Giuseppe and Burt opened Angelo's II, they'd enlarged a number of Giuseppe's photographs from his beloved days in Italy. They'd carefully framed and hung the photographs on the very rear wall of the restaurant. Spot and track lighting illuminated the area, bringing out some of the best details of the photos.

Giuseppe rounded the corner to enter the restaurant and saw a man in a ball cap, with his back to Giuseppe, looking intently at the photographs on the wall.

"Can I help you, sir?" Giuseppe inquired.

The man turned, and Giuseppe was surprised to see an almost-familiar face. His eyes were downcast and he'd grown a beard, but Giuseppe would have recognized Noah Hansen anywhere.

"Is it you, Noah?" he greeted as he walked toward him, hand outstretched.

Noah nodded and took Giuseppe's hand in a firm shake. He managed a small smile. "I was in town to close on a lease over there on 41st Street. Thought I'd stop by and see how the place was looking."

"Of course," Giuseppe acknowledged with an open smile. "You never saw the finished restaurant, did you?"

Noah shook his head. "I was pretty busy when you guys were building it."

Giuseppe felt a pang of remorse as he remembered how excited Noah was only the year before, awaiting the birth of his child.

"Thanks for the card," Noah said. "I really appreciated that."

Giuseppe suddenly embraced Noah and held him close. "You have our deepest sympathies, Noah, my friend. Please know that you are always in our prayers."

"Thanks, Mr. Caselli," Noah replied, pleasantly surprised by Giuseppe's open compassion.

Giuseppe backed out of his embrace. "And where are your boys this day?"

"They're over at the hotel with Josh and Mona," he answered. "We all came to town, 'cause I'm just not ready to leave 'em yet."

"Understandable." Giuseppe took a deep breath and swung his arm before him. "Well, what do you think of the place?"

Noah nodded as he looked all around. "I like it." He turned his attention back to the wall of photographs and asked, "Where'd you get these?"

"I took them myself. When we were still in *Italia*."

Noah pointed to a photo of two men standing together, dressed in farmers' clothing but wearing identical peaked, feathered caps. "Is this you and your brother?"

"Yes."

Noah allowed a small smile as he remembered Angel's and Giuseppe's words and spoke them aloud, "And you were *powerful warriors*."

Giuseppe swallowed hard and nodded.

Noah took a breath and pointed to the only sketch on the wall. It was of a man who resembled a younger version of Giuseppe, sleeping in an easy chair with the newspaper resting on his lap. "This one doesn't look like a photo."

Giuseppe shook his head and swallowed hard again. "Something that was given to me."

Noah nodded. He'd noticed the signature in the corner: *Angel, '75.* He looked into the familiar sparkle of Giuseppe's expression but said no more.

Tillie eased the bedroom door shut and crept down the hallway and into the living room. She breathed a sigh of relief. Those little stinkers had *finally* fallen asleep, and she was headed to the couch for a nap.

It was mid-June, and Alex had gone back to work, leaving her home to mind the twins on her own, which she'd mastered quite well. Every now and then, however, the two of them would get what Giuseppe called a "little wild hair" and raise Cain for hours on end. They were seven months old now, and "scooted" through the house, leaving small disasters in their wake. Laura loved eating the dirt from the houseplants, and A.J. particularly enjoyed cramming wads of newspaper into his mouth. The toy pileup was uncontrollable and the house was usually a mess, but it didn't bother Tillie at all. If she could just keep up with the laundry the two produced, she was satisfied.

She happened to glance out her front window as she headed for the couch, surprised to see Vincenzo's pickup pulling into her driveway. Marquette and Petrice were with him, and she smiled as she watched the three of them get out of the truck and walk to the front door. She quickly opened her door and whispered, "My babies are sleeping, so be very quiet!"

Petrice embraced his sister with a whisper, "We had a chance meeting in town and decided to stop over."

"Where are your wives?" Tillie asked.

"They are not with us," Marquette smiled, giving her a kiss as he passed through the door.

Vincenzo brought up the rear and kissed Tillie's cheek. "We are on the loose!" he teased, and his brothers stifled their laughs. Someone stepped on a squeak toy, and they all froze in their tracks.

"Oh, dear," Petrice whispered, his eyes wide with anticipation. He knew the importance of keeping a baby asleep. His brothers attempted to squelch their laughter as they waited for the crying to begin. However, nothing happened, and they all sighed with relief.

"Well, how about some iced tea?" Tillie whispered. "And let's sit on the patio. I have to keep those two little ones sleeping. I really need a break."

Her brothers silently nodded with understanding smiles. While Marquette and Vincenzo found their way to the comfortable furniture on the patio out back, Petrice helped Tillie get the tea and the glasses together. They soon joined their brothers and took seats under the umbrella at the table.

"That oak becomes more beautiful with every season," Vincenzo commented as he looked at the huge shade tree above them.

"I know," Tillie agreed, and she looked curiously at her brothers. "Now, what brings all of you around at once?"

"We may be going into business together," Vincenzo started, and he looked at Petrice. "The Senator knows a gentleman in Texas, and we are looking at a possible investment there."

"Sounds interesting," Tillie replied as she looked around the table at her brothers.

"We have such busy lives," Marquette said with a tender smile. "But, Angel, we think of you so very often."

Vincenzo reached for Tillie's hand and smiled into her eyes. "And I know I am closer, but Reata keeps me so busy."

"I know," Tillie said as she looked back at her brother with a curious frown. "Are you worried about something?"

"What we mean to say," Petrice took a breath, "is that we always want what is best for you. Even though you are a grown woman now, we still feel like we should somehow keep an eye on how your life is going."

"Angel," Marquette said, "what we want to know is if Alex is staying closer to home this time."

Tillie was surprised at the question and smiled nervously as she answered, "He barely puts in an eight-hour-day, guys." She looked around at the three of them, saw their concerned expressions, and was touched by their thoughtfulness.

"It's not like it was before," she said. "He comes right home after work and helps me with the house and the kids. Most of the time he winds up making dinner for us." She smiled and added, "Things are going great."

Her brothers all nodded, and Marquette responded, "We just needed to know."

With a heavy sigh Giuseppe slumped into a chair at his kitchen table. Rosa was just coming down the stairs and, seeing the anguish in his expression, went to her husband. She seated herself in the chair nearest to him and took his hand into her own.

"What is wrong, my love?"

"Noah was in to see me today," he answered.

Rosa's heart pounded as she squeezed Giuseppe's hand. "How is he?"

"He saw Angel's sketch."

Rosa gasped. "Did he say anything?"

"Not a word about it." He rubbed his bald head and went on, "You know, Rosa, I never expected to see Noah Hansen in my ristorante. Why on earth would he show up there?"

Rosa shrugged her small shoulders.

Giuseppe was quiet for a long moment, and then he spoke again. "Without Noah Hansen, Carrie's first baby would not have had a father. Despite my sin and deception, God used that man to do something wonderful."

"Yes, He did," Rosa agreed.

Marquette and Tara took a short break at their home on Como Lake in Italy. Tara awoke in the morning to find her husband not in the bed with her, and she ventured out onto the veranda above the lake, to his favorite place near the marble railing. The soft breeze blew his long, wavy black hair, which was free from its usual ponytail. His eyes held a very thoughtful and distant expression as he watched the boats on the peaceful waters below him.

As she watched him, Tara thought how handsome he was and how the last thirteen years with him had passed all too quickly. The adventures they'd been on and the things they'd done with their life together had been quite remarkable. He was right. Even though the Lord had not blessed them with babies, He had blessed them in other ways. Tara had finally found contentment in having *just* Marquette. His passion for her alone was unending, and she thanked God for Marquette's unconditional love and devotion to her.

Marquette felt her watching him and turned to see his Tara smiling at him. "Good morning, my love."

She went to him and took a seat on his lap. She softly kissed him and looked into his eyes. "What were you thinking just then?" She brushed a stray lock of his hair away from his face.

"Oh," Marquette sighed and looked out over the lake. "Pray for me, Tara. I must make my peace with Alex."

She looked at him in surprise. "But I thought you had—even long before me."

Marquette shook his head. "I put on as if I have, because I want so much for it to happen. And Angel seems to love him so much. She is truly happy with her babies and her life, and Alex seems to be trying so very hard for her."

Tara nodded. "Yes, he does, Marquette, and they have promised God forever with each other. We were witnesses in the matter."

Marquette slowly shook his head and frowned. "But something still nags in my heart, and it is difficult to put aside, Tara. Why do Ma`ma and Papa seem to dislike him?"

"I think Ma`ma and Papa have completely forgiven Alex."

Marquette shook his head again, and his frown deepened. "They are keeping something from me, Tara. I feel it to the depths of my soul."

"Oh, Marquette." Tara feigned a smile. "They would not keep anything from you."

"Where Angel is concerned, I fear they would keep a secret for the devil himself if it meant protecting that marriage."

"My dear Marq," Tara stroked Marquette's forehead and looked into his eyes, "you make your peace with Alex quickly, for where that marriage is concerned there is nothing anyone can do about it now. We watched them promise God forever with one another, and you should no longer wish her out of it."

Noah stepped into Maggie May's for the first time in nearly three months. Maggie, Estelle and Mel all looked up in surprise. His dancing blue eyes were as sad as could be, and a ragged beard covered his handsome face. They hadn't seen him look this way in a very long time.

"What'll ya have, stranger?" Maggie asked in her gruff voice. "Mel made some killer chili. It's been sellin' like hotcakes."

"Just a Coke," he answered as he stepped up to the bar and took a seat.

Maggie opened the bottle and placed it before him.

"Thanks, Maggie," he said, and took a long gulp.

Estelle went to his side and put a loving arm over his shoulders. "We've missed you, Noah. How have you been?"

Maggie hoped Estelle could keep quiet. Poor Estelle never seemed to remember Carrie, let alone the fact that she'd passed away.

"Not too bad," Noah answered. "How 'bout the two of you?"

"Can't complain," Maggie answered quickly and then, in an effort to bypass any of Estelle's questions, asked, "Where are you off to today?"

"I'm meeting Josh and Mona over at Canyon Lake Park," he answered. "Today's Tiger's birthday."

"How old is the little Tiger now?" Maggie inquired before Estelle could comment.

"Four."

Maggie nodded and continued, "How was Sioux Falls last week?"

"Good. I saw that new restaurant we put up over on the east side of town. Looks pretty nice."

Maggie drew a deep breath and mustered all the courage she had. "So, did you see any of those famous Casellis?"

Noah chuckled. "Only Mr. Caselli. The senator and his brothers were visiting their sister."

"Oh," Maggie acknowledged, "and how is Mrs. Martin?"

"Pretty good, I guess," Noah answered. "The babies are growing."

"Now, did we meet her at the funeral?" Estelle suddenly inquired, and Maggie felt her heart fall into her stomach. *I'm trying to be subtle...*

"Nope," Noah answered. "The babies were too little to travel."

"I see," Maggie replied.

"Is she tall like Alex?" Estelle asked with wide eyes, suddenly very interested in the turn of the conversation.

Maggie rolled her eyes, "Is *who* tall like Alex?"

"Mrs. Martin," Estelle clarified. "'Cause he's *really* tall."

Maggie looked at Estelle and raised an eyebrow. *Thanks, baby. That's the perfect way to find out if he's ever seen her, or if he knows— and it doesn't sound a bit strange coming from you.*

Noah couldn't help but chuckle at Estelle. He patted her shoulder and answered, "You know, Stellie, I don't have any idea if she's tall or short, or even what she looks like. I've never met the woman. I've never even seen a picture of her."

Maggie let out a relieved breath. *So you don't have any idea. Well, it's better that way, especially now.*

Della cried, and Charise dabbed at her tears with a soft tissue.

"Don't cry, Ma`ma," she begged.

"I just don't understand why I can't see Carrie anymore. I just don't understand."

"I know, Ma`ma, but she's with Jesus—"

"I know all that," Della retorted.

Charise shook her head and looked at her father. "I don't know what to do anymore."

"Call Noah," Della demanded. "Call him this instant. Tell him I want to see him."

Charise shook her head. *This is getting impossible.*

The June sunshine warmed the park at Canyon Lake. Mona had made sandwiches and Ty's favorite Jell-O salad for his birthday. She'd also decorated chocolate cupcakes and brought along a thermos of milk for the celebration. She brought bread crumbs for the ducks and geese, and Ty and Joshua fed the excited birds while Noah gave Jake a bottle.

"He looks like you," Mona commented as she watched her tiny nephew sleep peacefully in his father's arms.

"Yeah, especially when he screams," Noah joked with a faint smile.

Mona chuckled as she took a seat beside Noah on the blanket. Sometimes he seemed to be feeling better, and then there were his bad days.

"How are you today, Noah?"

"Better, I guess—"

He was interrupted when Ty rushed over to the blanket and plopped himself down in front of his father. Joshua was close behind him, but he didn't make quite such a loud landing.

"Daddy, did you see that big goose chasing me?" Ty panted.

The sleeping baby wasn't even disturbed by Ty's commotion, and Noah couldn't help but smile.

"I saw it, Tiger," he answered. "How'd ya get away so fast?"

"I *ran!*" Ty giggled. "And I ran faster than the goose."

"And faster than Uncle Josh," Joshua noted with a smile.

Noah chuckled at his son, but Ty saw the masked sadness in his father's expression. He stood up and placed his tiny hand on Noah's cheek. "What's wrong, Daddy?"

"Nothing," Noah lied through a smile.

Ty slowly nodded and smiled into his father's eyes. "Auntie Mona should tell you a story. Her stories are *so* funny!"

Noah looked at Mona. "Okay, then, Auntie Mona, do you have a story for us today?"

"Umm," Mona hesitated, casting her gaze into the heavens as if thinking of something, and then suddenly looked at them all with wide eyes. "I know one I haven't told for a long, long time—on account of it's controversial."

"What's *that* mean," Ty asked with a soft frown.

"Means you can't tell it to church people," Joshua said with a stern expression.

Ty only nodded in understanding, but Mona and Noah laughed.

"Tell it," Ty coaxed, taking a seat on his auntie's lap.

"Well," Mona began in her rhythmic Southern drawl, wrapping an arm around Ty's middle, "you know, we lived out in the country when I was little and we had this country mailman—"

"What's a country mailman?" Ty asked.

"He has to use his own car to deliver the mail," Mona answered. "Anyway, his name was Garner McCoy, and he was sort of a drinker, so sometimes we'd get our mail, and sometimes he'd just up and forget about us. Why, there were times we didn't get mail for a whole week, and the lights pert near got turned off when we didn't pay the bill, 'cause, of course, we didn't get the bill." She took a deep breath. "So a bunch of the neighbors jumped old Garner McCoy one day and took him over to the detox—"

"What's detox?" Ty questioned.

"It's where you take people who drink too much —"

"Drink too much of what?"

Mona sighed with a smile. "Too much soda, and it makes their teeth fall out."

Ty nodded as if he understood, and Noah and Joshua snickered.

"So they took him over to the detox," Mona continued. "Now Old Man Fletcher, the school bus driver, volunteered to deliver the mail while Garner was in the detox, and it was the best mail service we ever had. Pretty soon, though, Garner was ready to come home and get back to work. And he was such a good mailman for a long time, but then he started to forget us again, and my daddy thought he ought to have a talk with Garner the next time he saw him." Mona paused to take a breath. "So one day Daddy was out by the road—'cause you know we lived on a gravel road—and he was pulling the weeds outta Momma's petunias down by the mailbox. Here come Garner, swerving up the road like a lunatic, and Daddy knew something was up. Daddy jumped into the ditch just so that Garner wouldn't run him over, and as Garner went by, somethin' hit Daddy right in the side of the head. Daddy was knocked nearly unconscious. And as he staggered out of the ditch, he saw what had hit him —"

"What was it?" Ty asked.

"Why, it was an empty bottle," Mona answered, and Joshua and Noah broke down in laughter.

"Wow," Ty shook his head. "He went back to the soda. Did he lose any teeth?"

"Lost 'em all," Mona answered, and Joshua and Noah laughed even harder.

Noah put his hand on Mona's shoulder and smiled into her eyes. "Thanks, Mona. I don't know what I'd do without you."

PART III

OBEDIENCE

CHAPTER 18

March 1986

It was that time of year again, and Vivian Olson sat herself down in front of Noah's old wooden desk to hammer out the details of yet another lease on Angel's Place. He was still in the small, dingy office he'd been in since 1976, and this was the third three-year lease she'd come over to negotiate.

"So, what do you think?" she asked as she raised one black-penciled eyebrow.

Noah raised his own eyebrow and half-smiled. *What do I think? I find it unbelievable that you're still alive, let alone spry enough to harass me for another three-year lease.* "I can't believe you want another lease." He pretended his tone gruff and cross. "Why don't you just *buy* the thing?"

Vivian shook her head and looked at him. He'd grown a terrible beard five years ago after his wife had passed away, and it made him look older than his thirty-four years. His sandy-colored hair had thinned slightly on top, and there was just a touch of gray at his temples now. His eyes were lined with sadness and weather, and seldom did Vivian ever see them dance.

She smiled, and her older eyes glinted with a dreadful mischief. She opened her briefcase and dropped a file onto his desk. "I know you won't read that stuff, but you know I'm not gonna buy the place. Now, you can threaten all you want that you're gonna sell it out from under me, but you don't want to sell it any more than I want to buy it."

"Oh, Viv," Noah scoffed and shook his head, "you know that's simply not true. I've been trying to unload that place for years."

Vivian rolled her eyes with a snort and pointed a very wrinkled index finger at Noah. "*That's a lie.* I wanted to buy it in '83, and you wouldn't budge."

Noah had to look away from Vivian to hide the smile tugging at the corners of his mouth. He rubbed his bushy whiskers and tried to muster the most thoughtful expression he could. "Okay," he pretended to relent. He turned his eyes toward her again and said, "I'll let you lease it for another three years, but after that, either you buy it or I sell it to someone else. This is your *last* option period, Viv. I've got people standing in line to buy that property."

Vivian shook her head disgustedly, picked up the file, and put it into her briefcase. "I suppose that rotten Alex Martin will be calling me?"

"Actually," Noah said with a clever shimmer in his eyes, "he'll probably be stopping by to see you. I'm meeting with him this afternoon."

"Oh, joy," Vivian muttered as she got to her feet.

Noah stood behind his desk and offered Vivian his hand. She took it and gave him her regular, awkward shake. "Love doing business with you, Hansen."

"Me, too, Viv," he said, and then he watched her little feet stomp out of his office.

The sting of Carrie's death had softened over the years, but Noah still missed her. He kept her photograph on his desk at home. Sometimes in the evenings, when the boys had gone to bed and he was by himself, he let his memories wander. They'd shared a beautiful life together, but it had ended way too soon. He still hadn't brought their pontoon boat out of storage, though Vincenzo Caselli had nearly convinced him last summer to do so. He'd promised the Casellis maybe in the spring, but now he was hoping they'd forget about it.

For more than a year Carrie's scent had lingered in their home, especially in their closet. Noah kept all her clothes exactly where she'd left them until Mona made him give them away. He argued that Charise might be by for something, but that assumption proved to be false. Noah hadn't seen any member of Carrie's family since the day of the funeral.

Hansen Development, LLC, had grown in leaps and bounds over the past five years. Noah now owned the entire building he'd formerly leased parts of, and he'd expanded his construction crews to nearly one hundred people. He kept Alex Martin and several of his associates extremely busy. The accountant they'd hired so many years ago had to hire extra people just to handle Noah's finances.

Ty would turn nine years old in June, and he had grown into a tall, thin boy with a wavy mane of red hair. His eyes were the same captivating gray of his mother's, and how Noah missed her when he looked into them. He was a soft-spoken, gentle person, and the best pitcher Timberline Little League had ever seen. His teammates loved his nickname, "Tiger," and Mona sewed the name onto the back of his jersey.

Jake, on the other hand, was everything opposite of Ty. He had turned five years old that January, and was he ever a handful for Noah. He got into things Ty never dreamed of doing, and his happy-go-lucky attitude reminded Noah so much of himself. His hair was sandy-colored like Noah's, and his blue eyes sparkled and danced, much the same as his father's had when he was younger.

The only thing Noah's boys had in common was their undying love for baseball. Jake idolized his older brother and never missed one of Ty's games. Jake would get to start T-ball this year, and he was excited about that.

Maggie May's was still the best place in town to get a decent lunch, and Noah stopped by nearly every day to get a bite to eat and visit with his oldest friend.

She watched him as he came through the doorway. His stride was slow and thoughtful, as it had been for many years now. He looked so terrible with that scraggly old beard she wished he'd just shave. How Maggie longed for the young man who used to ride in on his motorcycle and skip up to the counter with yet another plan of how to find

Angel. She sighed at her memories and wondered, *what happened to all the years?*

She watched him for a moment as he stopped at Angel's painting, as he had started to do on a regular basis, and gazed upon every stroke. He looked at the yellowed photograph still tucked into the frame, and endearingly touched Angel's face with a callused index finger. He smiled, sighed, and seated himself at the bar. How Maggie longed to tell him that she'd found Angel, but it never seemed to be the right time.

"Hello, Maggie May," he greeted. "Whatcha got for me today?"

"Mel made ribs," she answered as she filled out a ticket and quickly placed it on the wheel behind her.

"Leased Angel's Place for another three years today," he continued with a pretended frown. "That Viv, she just won't buy it."

Maggie snorted and shook her head. "Like you'd ever sell it." She poured him a cup of coffee and set it down in front of him.

"I'd sell that place in a heartbeat," he argued as he took a sip.

"Brother," Maggie muttered and shook her head. *Should I show him? I want to talk about this…*

She reached under the counter for the envelope and slid it to where Noah sat. She'd kept them for the last ten years—the photos Noah had taken during the building of Angel's Place. Every now and then she'd take them out, look at them, and let herself remember. Perhaps it was her age. Maggie would be sixty-one come summer. Or perhaps it was something else. Whatever the case, she'd started to regret the passing of time, and it was difficult for her to let certain things go.

"What's this?" he asked, smiling with curiosity as he reached for the envelope.

"You gave me those at least ten years ago. I saved 'em."

Noah chuckled as he opened the envelope, seeing the old photographs. First the empty meadow, then the hole, foundation, frame… Angel's Place.

"Wow, Maggie," he said with a smile. "I didn't know you still had these." He nodded toward the painting. "I thought that was the only one you had."

"Nope," Maggie answered. "I saved 'em. Saved 'em all."

"Man," he chuckled again, and shook his head, "I was so crazy about her. What in the world came over me?"

Maggie shook her head. "Don't know, but she was really somethin' special."

"Maggie, you talk about her like she was real or something. She had to have been an angel."

Maggie was steamed. They'd had this disagreement before, but she wasn't about to back down. "Noah, that girl was as real as real could be, and she stood right here in my bar and Stellie took her picture."

"Maggie, the Bible says, 'Be not forgetful to entertain strangers: for thereby, some have entertained angels unawares.'"

Maggie frowned. "In a bar, Noah? God sends his angels into *bars?*"

"Why sure, Maggie," he grinned. *I can still get to the ol' girl after all these years!* "And I was a young idiot who needed help." He placed the old photos back into the envelope and handed them to Maggie. "You keep these to remind me if I ever do anything that insane again."

Maggie took the envelope and tucked it into its place beneath her counter. *One of these days I'm gonna tell him...*

About a year ago, when she could no longer squelch the urge to paint and sketch, Tillie gave in to her God-given creativity and began again with her favorite piece, *Obedience*. She had intended it to be just for practice, but as she painted, the portrait of Rosa and Delia came to life upon her canvas. It was the same scene as before, but the colors were brighter and more vibrant. She gave the characters in the painting feeling and personality that were not there before.

This painting was very special because she planned on giving it to Alex for his thirty-sixth birthday, which was in a few days. He had loved the painting and had begged her to allow him to hang it in his downtown office. She'd refused, as she saw the work as immature and filled with flaws. She permitted the original to hang in his office at home, where only he could see it.

Her five-year-old twins giggled as they watched her box it up in preparation for its transportation to Alex's office downtown. The painting they'd watched their mommy hide all over the house was finally finished, and would soon belong to their father.

"Can I have one for my room?" Laura asked.

Tillie laughed at her little girl. "I don't know, Laura. It took Mommy an awfully long time to finish *this* one."

"That's because you had to keep hiding it from Daddy," A.J. said. He raised an eyebrow and looked so much like Alex it made Tillie smile.

"When are you going to tell him?" Laura's black eyes sparkled, and Tillie was reminded of her father's expression.

"On his birthday," Tillie answered. "So you have to keep this secret just a little bit longer."

"We will, Mommy," the two answered in unison, and it made them all laugh. Tillie looked at her precious little children and wished again that she and Alex were able to have more. However, the scarring from their birth was so extensive that even surgery hadn't helped to correct the problem. Over the past five years, Tillie had gracefully learned to accept that two babies were all she would be given.

She set the large box aside and gathered her two little ones into her arms. "I love you guys so much," she whispered while she held them. They giggled while they hugged their mother and gave her kisses.

"As much as you love Daddy?" Laura asked.

Tillie laughed at her little daughter. "Yes, as much as I love Daddy."

Alex made it to Noah's office downtown, despite the snow that had started to fall in Rapid City. He took the earliest charter he could in order to meet with Noah, rattle Vivian Olson a little, and then fly home to his family by supper time.

Noah noticed that Alex was distant that day, even when they'd gone over to see Vivian about the lease. Normally, Alex loved to tease the cantankerous old landlady, but today his heart just wasn't in it.

"It's for Scott McDarren," Noah said with a frown. Alex didn't seem to hear him at all, and so he obnoxiously cleared his throat and spoke a little louder. "Alex! Should I keep going, or turn around and talk to the wall?"

"What?" Alex shook himself out his half-daydreaming state. "What did you say?"

Noah frowned and shook his head. "What's with you today? You haven't listened to me all day long. Is everything okay?"

Alex looked at his friend and slowly shook his head. "I have to tell Tillie something tonight, and I'm worried about how it's gonna go."

"Oh, brother," Noah muttered. He frowned at Alex and scolded, "What have you been up to now?"

"Noah!" Alex laughed. "I haven't been *up to* anything."

"Well, then, it can't be so bad."

Alex rubbed his forehead and leaned back in the old wooden chair. "Dad and Sam have asked me if I would move to Rapid City and manage the office here. Aunt Charlotte's health is really bad, and Uncle Mac would like to move south permanently instead of just taking her there for the winters."

"So you'll be moving to Rapid City?"

Alex nodded. "And Tillie and I live in this incredible old house she practically rebuilt with her own hands." He sadly shook his head. "I don't know how I can even ask her to leave it."

"And I suppose Sam and Becky-Lynn aren't interested in relocating to the *Wild, Wild West?*"

Alex shook his head. "Sam and Becky-Lynn are too busy taking care of her mother. She's been sick since Becky-Lynn's dad died. Of course, they could put her into a nursing home, but they don't want to do that."

Noah moaned. "Wow. You've got a little bit of a problem."

Alex agreed, fishing out a flat box from his suit-coat pocket. "But I got her this over at O'Berg's." He opened the box to reveal an elegant diamond bracelet. "Hopefully it will soften the blow."

Noah softly whistled at the bracelet, shook his head, and said with a lopsided grin, "I don't know about that. That looks like a guilt gift to me."

"It's not a guilt gift," Alex said with a frown. He closed the lid and put it back into his pocket. "And then, of course, there's this whole thirty-sixth birthday thing. Here I am, crossing over the midway point of my thirties and I have this twenty-eight-year-old wife who is absolutely ageless and beautiful." He shook his head and looked past Noah out the window at the falling snow. "I feel really weird."

Noah laughed out loud. *A little mid-life crisis, right here in my office!* But Alex's hair was still as blue-black as it had ever been, and his dark eyes were not lined with the age Noah saw in his own mirror every morning. His eyes narrowed with mischief, "Alex, are you sure you even have a wife? I mean, I've never even met this woman you talk about constantly."

Alex smiled and pulled out his wallet, where he kept a photograph of Tillie and his children. "I've got a picture right here," he said, starting to thumb through it.

Noah leaned over for a better look, but Alex couldn't find a photo of any woman in that wallet. Noah began to laugh again. "That's what I thought."

"I know it's in here somewhere." Alex laughed nervously, perplexed as to where the photo had gone to.

Noah laughed again. "Yeah, right, Alex —"

They were interrupted when the door to Noah's office opened, and Melinda came in with a tray of coffee. Noah frowned curiously at his ruthless assistant. *That's kinda nice of you, Melinda. Is it poisoned?*

"I thought you guys might need a little warm up," she said with a sweet smile, casting a shy glance in Noah's direction. Noah didn't seem to notice but Alex had, and when she left he brought it to Noah's attention.

"She likes you."

"No, she doesn't," Noah scoffed. "That woman doesn't like *any-body*, not even herself."

Alex raised one eyebrow. "Shondra's *never* looked at me that way."

"That's because you don't have this great beard."

"You should ask her out," Alex suggested. "She might be fun. She's really pretty, and you know she's smart. She practically runs the place for you."

Noah shook his head. "No way. I'm done with women. I was left at the altar and widowed. Why on earth would I put myself through that again?"

James Martin was eighty-seven years old now and still practicing law with his sons. His hair was as white as snow, but he stood tall and broad-shouldered, like his sons, and his mind was as sharp as a tack. As he stood in Sam's doorway, he noticed how silver his oldest son's hair had gotten. Sam was forty-eight years old now, but only showed his age in the color of his hair. He and Alex looked almost exactly alike, except for that one marked difference.

Noticing that there was someone in his doorway, Sam looked up and smiled at his father, observing the strained expression on the older man's face. James held a copy of the *Sioux Falls Argus Leader* in one hand and his glasses in the other.

"What's up, Dad?"

James frowned and stepped into Sam's office, closing the door. He shuffled to a seat in front of Sam's desk and tossed the newspaper in front of him. "Your brother met with Jackson Williams over at Minerva's yesterday. Did you know anything about this?"

Sam shook his head as he picked up the paper. "He didn't say anything to me about this." He groaned when he saw the photo on the front page. The ex-governor of South Dakota and Alex smiled into the camera that had taken the shot. Below the photograph was a simple caption: *Williams May Choose Martin as Running Mate.*

"He can't be serious," Sam said as a feeling of sickness began in the pit of his stomach.

James shrugged. "He's already committed to moving to Rapid City."

"Which we thought would slow him down. But the governor's primary is more than a year away."

James sighed and shook his head. "Where is he today?"

"Rapid," Sam answered as he skimmed the article. "This says Alex hasn't made a decision yet, and that he *may have other irons in the fire for the '86 election year*." He shook his head disgustedly. "What other irons? Wonder if Tillie's seen this yet."

"I wonder if she even knows," James added.

Jake's reward for getting his room picked up was for Noah to read him a story before he went to bed. The name of the book was *The Littlest Angel*, and the story was one of Jake and Ty's favorites. The three of them snuggled into Jake's bed while Noah read to them, transfixed on the wonderful story.

When the story ended, Ty yawned and gave his father a soft kiss on the cheek. "I'm going to my own bed, Dad. Jake kicks."

Noah smiled and nodded as his oldest son wriggled from the warm bed. "Okay, son; I'll be in to kiss you in a minute." Ty nodded, yawned again, and left the room.

Jake yawned, snuggled into his father's arms, and angelically protested, "I don't kick." He yawned again and asked in a very sleepy voice, "Daddy, do angels have names?"

The question took Noah by surprise. "Well, God named Gabriel and Michael, so I'd have to say yes, Jake, angels are given names." He got out of the bed and tucked Jake's covers all around him, kissed his forehead, and turned off the light beside his bed. "Good night, son," he said as he headed for the doorway of the room.

On his way out of the bedroom, Jake asked a question that stopped Noah in his tracks. "Daddy, have you ever seen an angel?"

Noah turned in the doorway and looked into the darkened bedroom where his little son lay. He swallowed away the sudden emotion in his throat and answered, "Yes, Jake. Once. And it was a very long time ago, even before your brother was born."

"What did it look like?"

"Oh, she was beautiful," Noah breathed.

"Do you think I'll get to see one someday?"

"Maybe," Noah answered, waiting for the child to question him again, but no more words came from Jake. He had fallen asleep.

Noah shuffled into Ty's room, tucked the boy all around the same as he had Jake, and kissed his forehead. "Goodnight, son."

"Goodnight, Dad," Ty said with a yawn. "I heard you talking about the angel. Is that true?"

"True as I'm standing here."

"Cool," Ty said with a giggle.

Noah smiled and left Ty's room. He wandered into his office off the kitchen, settled himself in the chair behind the desk, and stared into the darkness out the window. *Why have I started to think about that again?* He slowly opened the top drawer on his left, reached to the very back, and pulled out the framed photograph he'd saved. He almost threw it away once, but Carrie told him it was important to save. He hadn't looked at it for nearly ten years, but now that Carrie was gone, he felt a strange compulsion to recall that whimsical weekend in April of 1975.

He gazed into the photograph of him and Angel in Maggie's bar. He leaned back in the soft leather chair and closed his eyes, resting the framed photo against his chest. He was instantly lost in their kiss at the waterfall, the softness of her hand in his, the sparkle of her black eyes when she looked at him, and the tenderness in her voice when she told him she loved him.

Noah sighed and opened his eyes. *Maybe I just need to start dating or whatever they call it these days. Alex is happy in his marriage, except for having to tell Tillie they're moving...He thinks maybe Melinda likes me. Maybe I'll give it a try.*

CHAPTER 19

"What's *this* all about?" James demanded as he tossed the previous day's newspaper onto Alex's desk. He clenched the bow of his glasses tightly between his teeth and waited for an answer. He frowned as he thought, *Alex is thirty-six today, and obviously returning to a sin he's long forgotten!*

Alex looked up at his father and back down at the paper. He shook his head and frowned. He'd had no idea the photo or the story was going into the city newspaper. "Listen, Dad, this isn't what it looks like—"

"Well, what is it then?" James snapped. "'Cause it looks an awful lot like politics to me. And did you bother to tell Tillie? Is she okay with this?"

Alex swallowed hard. Obviously, Tillie hadn't seen the article because she hadn't said anything to him when he returned from Rapid City the day before. "I haven't talked to her about it yet, because it was just the one meeting." He narrowed his eyes and frowned at his father. "And besides, if I want to run for office, I'll do it. It's my life, not yours."

"I can't believe you." James shook his head. "You'd take your perfect life and wreck it with this nonsense. You *know* you can't handle it."

Alex shot to his feet and pointed his index finger at his elderly father. "*I* can handle it just fine. It's *you* and probably *my brother* who can't!"

They were interrupted at that point when Shondra knocked softly on the door outside, and let herself in. She smiled at Alex, noticing his horrible scowl. She saw James rise from his seated position, and she quickly closed the door behind her.

"Happy birthday, Alex." She glanced from father to son. "Please calm yourselves down as quickly as you can. Tillie is on her way this moment with a gift for Alex. *Please* don't wreck it." She quickly left the office and closed the door behind her.

James shook his head and was about to speak when they heard another knock, and the door opened. Tillie smiled at Alex as she pulled in the huge box, complete with a red bow.

"Happy birthday, Alex!" She smiled lovingly into her husband's eyes.

Alex smiled and stepped to where she stood. "What's this?"

Tillie's sweet laugh broke James' old heart, but he forced a smile and waited to see what the gift would be.

"Open it up," she encouraged with a smile.

Alex fumbled with the wide ribbon and opened the large box. He gasped with anticipation when he saw the corner of the frame. "Is it what I think it is?" he asked excitedly, forgetting the confrontation with his father for the moment.

Tillie laughed again. "Pull it out."

Alex grabbed hold of the frame and drew it from its box. It was his favorite piece, *Obedience*. He smiled with satisfaction, and then he frowned curiously at the painting. "Honey, this is a different painting."

"I was never completely satisfied with the first. I did this one especially for you."

Alex looked into her pretty black eyes and gave her a soft kiss. "Thanks, honey. It's beautiful."

He took down the old painting of his great-grandfather, Arturo Martinez, and hung *Obedience* in its place. Now Tillie's new painting would be the first thing anyone saw when they came into his office.

On their way to Denver in April, Marquette and Tara stopped in Rapid City. These visits always made Tara nervous, but she did her level best to steer their conversations away from Marquette's family, *especially* subjects concerning his sister. For five years she'd done this, and no one was the wiser.

The weather was unusually warm for April, and Noah suggested they take the boys to Canyon Lake. They picked up deli chicken and salads from Albertson's grocery store and brought along a blanket to sit on. After their impromptu picnic, Ty and Jake headed to the small lake's shore for some fishing, but the adults stayed back on the blanket to visit.

"I used to live right over there," Noah said, pointing across the lake at the old rental cabins.

Marquette raised an eyebrow, a smile on his lips. "You have certainly moved up in the world, Noah."

Noah nodded and chuckled. "Yep." As he gazed across the lake at the run-down little cabins, the memories washed over him. He closed his eyes, took a deep breath, and sighed with a smile. He opened his eyes and looked wistfully at Marquette and Tara. "Me and the artist were gonna live over there."

Oh, dear, here we go again, Tara thought. Noah hadn't mentioned meeting *the artist* until just last year; however, the frequency with which he brought her up was increasing. In the last six months alone, he'd mentioned *the artist* during every visit. Rarely did he speak of Carrie anymore, and Marquette had even started to wonder about the elusive girl who'd left Noah at the altar.

"Have you heard from her?" Marquette asked.

Noah shook his head. "She won't be coming back around. I was a big loser back then. Must've scared her away."

"Well," Marquette scoffed with a shake of his head, for it was how he comforted Noah, "she cannot possibly be worth having. She sounds flighty and undependable."

Noah shrugged. "I don't know. She didn't seem flighty to me. She had a real good plan for her life, and I think she was afraid I'd screw everything up."

Marquette smiled. "Would she not be surprised to see you now?"

Noah took a deep breath. "Maybe."

More than you could ever imagine, Tara thought.

"But maybe she wasn't even real," Noah offered, surprising both Marquette and Tara.

"Why do you opine such a thing?" Marquette questioned.

"Because she was here and gone, and my whole life changed in those few days. How is that possible?"

Tara swallowed. *What is he going to say next? This is something new.*

"She told me to call her 'Angel,'" Noah continued, "and I think she was one."

Tara's mouth dropped open in surprise. *That is the first time he has ever said her name!*

Marquette frowned curiously at Noah. "Perhaps. I do believe angels come along and take human form when we need their help. For instance, when my sister was near death during the birth of her children, a certain nurse, a strong, warrior-like man, attended to us. He helped me to make phone calls, he made sure we remembered the babies, and he stayed with Alex that terrifying night."

"I believe in angels," Tara blurted out. She was alarmed, to say the least. Marquette was skirting dangerously close to saying his sister's nickname.

Noah smiled at her. "I did get a picture of her while she was here. I'll bring it along the next time you're in town."

Tara's stomach felt like she'd just fallen over the edge of a very high cliff as she listened to Marquette reply, "I would love to see it."

Maggie heard the familiar singing in her bar and knew that Estelle must be busy dusting the old picture again. She shook her head. *Poor Stellie.* The confusion hadn't gotten much worse over the last five years, but it was still difficult for Maggie. Sure, Estelle still waited tables and was very productive, but a lot of her memories were a jumbled-up mess. The only thing she consistently remembered was Angel.

Maggie walked to the counter to watch Estelle dust the picture.

Estelle was smiling as she sang the haunting words, "And like the winds in summer sighing, her voice is low and sweet. Her voice is low and sweet, and she's all the world to me, and for bonnie Annie Laurie, I'd lay me doon and dee…" Estelle looked at Maggie with surprise. "How long ya been there, Maggie?"

"Just a few seconds, baby," Maggie smiled. "Whatcha doin'? You just dusted her off yesterday."

"Oh," Estelle moaned and clutched at her heart, "the Lord has pressed upon me to pray for Angel again."

"Again?" Maggie frowned as she remembered the last time she had to deal with this issue five years ago. "What for now?"

Estelle shook her head. "Don't know, but I think she's in some kinda trouble again."

Maggie snorted and rolled her eyes. *Yeah, right. Married to a millionaire and spoiled rotten. She's got troubles alright.*

Noah hastily looked through the pile of mail that had collected on his desk at work. It was really a disaster lately. He couldn't tell the difference between the mail he'd received last week and the mail delivered that day. He glanced at Melinda, whose desk was in perfect order, and bit his lip. *Well, I can ask….She might kill me.* He paged her on the intercom, and she hurried right in.

"Would you please sort this stuff for me?" he asked as he moved bits and pieces of the paper around on his desk. "I've got a meeting to get to, and I'm afraid I'll miss something in this mess."

"Of course. I'd be happy to do that for you."

Happy? That's new. Boy, she's sure been nice lately. Maybe she does like me. He looked at Melinda and noticed she was dressed very nicely. She had on a professional-looking red suit with black trim on the sleeves and collar, and she *did* look attractive. "New suit?"

"No," she answered.

"Well, you look very nice," he said with a smile.

"Thanks," she said, and smiled in return.

Noah frowned and scratched his head. *Maybe I'll give it a whirl. What's the worst thing that can happen? She could say no and quit her job, but Alex says she likes me. Besides, Melinda's never married or dated. Maybe she could use the company, too. And I know she's a Christian because she's been coming to our church for at least ten years.* "Say, Melinda," he began, his face flushing beneath his beard, "how 'bout dinner sometime?"

"I'd love it," Melinda replied without hesitation. "How 'bout tonight?"

"Okay," Noah agreed, surprised at her forwardness. *I thought maybe we'd just talk about it for a few weeks before the actual event.*

"Can you pick me up at six-thirty?" she asked.

Noah slowly nodded. *Boy, she doesn't waste any time.* He got up from behind his desk and eased himself toward the door.

"Sounds great," he answered as he grabbed his coat and dashed out through the outer office. He didn't slow down until he reached the sidewalk outside. *What in the world came over me in there? Am I really that desperate? I'm through with women.* He rolled his eyes. *Oh, well, it's just one little dinner. What could it hurt?*

Finally! Melinda thought as she watched Noah frantically exit the building. *I can't believe he took this long to crack.* She smiled and sighed with satisfaction. *And the first thing I'll change around here is that stupid Ben Simmons' employment status.*

Tara soaked herself in luxurious bubbles, covering her from her chin to her toes. She leaned back into the soft pillow behind her head and closed her eyes. *Finally, some time off to think!* She and Marquette had recently come across some old notes and files regarding the Ponerello case. *Marquette must be so vexed*, she thought as she soaked. For five years, they'd learned nothing of the Ponerellos. It was as if they had finally managed to vanish from the face of the earth.

When she heard the bathroom door open, she peeked out of one eye to see her husband in the doorway, holding the familiar pink stationery. "You have heard from Angel," she smiled, closing her eye and resuming her relaxing soak.

Marquette silently acknowledged his wife's comment and took a seat on the edge of the tub. Had Tara's eyes not been closed, she would have seen the dreadful frown on his handsome face when he said, "And she does *not* sound happy at all."

"What is the matter?"

"It seems that *Mr. Wonderful* is moving them to Rapid City," Marquette sarcastically informed her.

Tara's eyes flew open and she glared at her husband. She was *so* tired of the recurring malice towards the husband of his sister when they were by themselves. However, when he was with Alex, it was an entirely different thing altogether. He acted as if he were Alex's best friend. "Marquette!" she snapped. "You must stop this one-sided sparring with Alex. Have you not made your peace with him yet?"

Marquette jumped from the side of the tub and threw his arms into the air. "No! Did you pray for me as I asked you to?"

"I have prayed without ceasing for you, Marquette! Perhaps you are disobedient!"

"I am *not* disobedient," Marquette mumbled as he turned away from her and headed for the bathroom door. *Why can she not understand?*

She took a deep breath and quieted her voice as she continued, "You must let this thing go, Marquette."

He turned toward her as he backed his way out the door. "I do not know if I can." He slammed the door behind him.

"Humph!" Tara sank deeper into the bubbles. Eighteen years she'd been with Marquette, and he had only one fault: the inability to forgive the husband of his sister.

Tara nearly slipped beneath the bubbles as she momentarily forgot Marquette's outburst and remembered something he'd said...*Rapid City? They are moving to Rapid City?*

Tillie sat behind Alex's desk in his office at home and stared at his favorite painting. He loved the new version in his office downtown even more than this original, and she was pleased about that. She remembered selling one of the originals to Maggie, the black bartender, and then seeing it in her bar just a day or so later. She wondered if it was still there and why she'd even care.

"Penny for your thoughts."

Tillie startled at Alex's voice and looked to see him in the doorway. He slowly walked to where she was seated, knelt beside her, and looked into her eyes.

She smiled at him and looked back at the painting. "Why do you love that picture so much?"

Alex turned his focus to the piece and scratched his chin. "Its mystery."

Tillie nodded and looked back at her husband. "I called the movers today. I told them it was going to be about mid-August, and they said they'd be over to give us an estimate."

Alex saw the sorrow in her eyes and said, "I know this is hard. You made this little house a home, and you'll make our next house a home, too."

Tillie smiled sadly. "I know, but it's *special*. It was our first place."

Alex touched one of the curls near her face. "But it's special because *you're* special."

Tillie nodded as she felt the strange weight dragging in the bottom of her heart. She fought hard to keep the tears away. *He'd never understand. That's why I've never told him.* "I don't want to go there," she said so quietly he almost didn't hear her.

"I know you don't." He looked into her eyes and searched for whatever it was she couldn't bring herself to tell him. "Why?"

Tillie shook her head and turned her eyes away from her husband. "I don't know. I just don't want to go."

Rosa Caselli sat in her window seat alone, sipping a cup of tea. She gazed to the west and thought, *Angel and the babies will be going soon.* She shook her head. *What will become of them now? How will God reveal all that we have kept secret?*

Giuseppe saw his lovely Rosa and came up behind her to plant a delicate kiss upon her cheek.

"I heard you," she smiled at him, patting the cushion next to her.

"You must have ears like an elephant," he grumbled as he sat down. "I see you are in your thinking place."

Rosa smiled into Giuseppe's eyes. "And what do you think I am thinking about?"

"Rosa, nearly fifty years have I shared my life with you. I can read your mind."

"Then read it."

Giuseppe's black eyes shone like marbles, and the lines on his face were suddenly very downcast as he frowned into Rosa's eyes. "You are afraid for what will happen when Angel sees him again."

Rosa nodded. "And what will she say when she realizes our deception?"

Giuseppe shrugged and shook his head. "Hopefully she will understand we did what we felt was best at the time."

Rosa took a soft breath and whispered, "Perhaps they have forgotten by now. Eleven years is a long time."

Giuseppe agreed. "Perhaps." He hesitated, and then asked, "Has she spoken of him at all?"

Rosa shook her head as a tear rolled down her cheek. "Not for many years, Giuseppe. Should we tell her before she goes?"

Giuseppe put his arms around his wife and held her close. "No. We will let God deal with it from here, my dearest Rosa, as I should have in the beginning."

"Will she ever forgive us?"

"I pray so." Giuseppe caressed Rosa's back. "And I pray for it every day."

Noah waited patiently in the outer offices of Martin, Martin & Dale. When he saw Shondra's familiar face come through the wooden doors, he got to his feet.

"He's finally done," she informed with a smile, holding the door open for him. "We couldn't get rid of that noisy bunch from Texas. Thanks for waiting."

"No problem." Noah followed Shondra through the doors and down the hall. "How are the moving plans going?" he asked, knowing that Shondra Payne was making the move to Rapid City as well, to assist Alex in the management of the large office.

"Well, Alex and Tillie have already sold their house," Shondra answered. "Now if I could just sell mine."

They reached the door to Alex's office, and Shondra did her usual polite knock to signal she was about to enter. To their surprise, Alex swung the door open and smiled.

"Noah," Alex said as he stretched out his hand, and Noah took it in a firm shake. "What did you think of the site?" He opened the door further to allow Noah to pass, and Shondra continued on down the hall.

"It was great," Noah answered with a smile as he walked past Alex and into the familiar office. Suddenly, Tillie's new painting came into full view. Noah stopped in mid-step, frozen to the place where his feet had carried him, and stared at the painting. He could hardly catch his breath, and Alex noticed his hesitation.

"Where did *that* come from?" Noah whispered.

"My wife painted that for me for my birthday," Alex answered, noticing the startled look on Noah's face.

Noah swallowed hard. "*Your wife?*"

Alex thought Noah was getting ready to tease him some more about not ever having seen his wife. "Yes," he chuckled, and took Tillie's photograph from the corner of his desk. "See, I really *do* have a wife!"

Noah turned his eyes to the photograph Alex had produced. *Angel?* He staggered into the seat in front of Alex's desk, his eyes on the photograph of Angel. *She probably couldn't wait to dump me back in '75. Why would she want a loser like me when a Harvard Law graduate awaited her return?* All these years, Noah had looked at the back of that frame and never once thought to look at the photo. *Why didn't I check it? Especially when I knew in my heart Mr. Caselli was her father.*

"I'm really sorry," Noah said as sincerely as he could muster. He struggled to his feet and looked again at the new painting on Alex's wall. He noticed it was signed *Angel, '86*, and frowned. "I thought your wife's name was Tillie."

"Well, her given name is actually Matilde," Alex answered. "But her brothers nicknamed her 'Angel' when she was little. It's kind of a long story."

Noah swallowed, and noticed that his mouth had gone dry. "I think I'm gonna go, Alex. We can have this meeting another day. I just remembered something I have to take care of before I leave town."

Alex nodded, a confused look on his face. "Are you okay?"

Noah took a soft breath and replied, "I'm fine." He shook Alex's hand and hurried out. He found his rental car parked out front and sat in the driver's seat for a long time.

He sighed and shook his head. *All these years. She's been right here, having his children and loving him. How can that be possible? She loved me first, I just know it. How can Angel love someone like Alex? Sure, he's a nice guy and a great lawyer, but he's a terrible husband.* Noah shook his head again.

The conflict rose within Noah as he sat there and thought about the man he considered his best friend, and then about the woman he'd loved. Just to see her again would undoubtedly draw him back into the emotion he'd shared with her before.

The right thing to do with this information would be to avoid her and any situations involving her. She probably doesn't have a clue and has long forgotten me, anyway. I should just tell Alex what happened, make him promise to keep it to himself, and we'll all go on happily ever after...I'll sure be keeping my big mouth shut in front of Marquette and Vincenzo after this. They obviously don't have a clue.

Noah shook his head, willing away his righteous thoughts; in his heart he stepped over the line a knight must *never* cross. He took a deep breath and felt a tingle that began in his toes and spread all the way to the top of his head. A smile played on the corners of his mouth. *Okay, really, now...What could it hurt? I can handle this. I'm not a kid anymore, and I've got a lot of questions for that girl...*

TO BE CONTINUED...

A Special Message for the Reader

Carrie started out much like the rest of us before we discover the Kingdom of God. She spent her life on her own pleasures, not giving the slightest care for anything or anyone else. Then along came Mona, who put the message into no uncertain terms: "Carrie-darlin', you gotta pray. You're in some sin here..."

Through the kindness of her unselfish husband Noah, Carrie came to know the Lord. She confessed her sin and took Jesus as her Lord and Savior, which changed her in ways that no one had ever thought possible. She set aside her excessive drinking and lustful ambitions. The desire to nurture a family and husband was born in her heart. She studied her Bible to learn about the relationship our Savior wants to have with all of us.

Did Carrie sin after all that? Yes. Though she'd become aware of God's love and His special rules to govern her life, she chose to grieve the Holy Spirit of God by deceiving her husband and his family—she broke the Ninth Commandment (*Thou shalt not bear false witness against thy neighbor*—Exodus 20:16). But, the Lord Jesus had already sealed (guaranteed) Carrie's salvation and forgiveness through the same Holy Spirit (*And you also were included in Christ when you heard the word of truth, the gospel of your salvation. Having believed, you were marked in him with a seal, the promised Holy Spirit, who is a deposit guaranteeing our inheritance until the redemption of those who are God's possession—to the praise of his glory*—Ephesians 1:13-14 NIV). The day she careened off the cliff in Custer State Park, the Lord Jesus was there with her and she was escorted to Heaven—the reward for her relationship with an all-forgiving Savior.

Beloved, if you're in a situation where you've made horrific mistakes and you think your sin is too much for God, *think again*. "God is faithful and just to forgive us our sins, and to cleanse us from all unrighteousness" (I John 1:9). God says what He means, and He means what He says. Just ask Him to forgive whatever you've done. Pick up His Holy Word and study His promises. Then, like Carrie, you'll know the Lord Jesus, and your eternal future will be assured.

Other Books in The Caselli Family Series

Book I
The Pretender: A Blackguard in Disguise

Book II
Pit of Ambition

Book III
A Blackguard's Redemption

Book IV
The Gift: The Story of Annie Laurie

Book V
The Truth: Salvatore's Revenge

For future release information,
please visit www.TaMaraHanscomBooks.com

PREVIEW

BOOK III – A BLACKGUARD'S REDEMPTION

June 1986 – Rapid City, South Dakota

Maggie May West was sixty-one years old and still wearing her hair in the puffy beehive style she'd pinned around her head since 1963. Her jet-black hair was sprinkled with streaks of silver swirled within the old-fashioned hairdo, and her old black eyes had begun to line with age. Still, she thought, me and Estelle look pretty darn good for two old black women, running a tough business on our own, without husbands.

Maggie was cleaning off her bar when she saw Noah's pickup park out front. He jumped out and trotted through the door. That's weird. She frowned as she watched him. Normally, his regular stride was slow and purposeful, as it had been for many years now, but not today.

Noah's sandy-colored hair had started to gray slightly at his temples, and his young eyes were lined with weather and grief. He had grown a terrible beard after losing his wife, Carrie, five years before, and it made him look older than his thirty-four years.

But there was a lightness in Noah's step today, and a certain sparkle in his blue eyes that had been absent for too many years. Maggie's heart skipped a beat when she saw the renewed expression. Something's happened, she thought as she watched her oldest friend settle himself on a stool before the bar and gaze fondly at the old painting that had hung on the wall for the last eleven years. Maggie's sister, Estelle, was lovingly dusting it today, always so dedicated to taking care of her most-prized possession.

"Hello, Noah," Estelle greeted him with a smile. "I'm keeping her pretty for you. She'll be so surprised."

"Thanks, Stellie," Noah replied, and he smiled at Maggie. "What's your special today, Maggie May?"

He'd asked that question a thousand times over the last twenty years, but somehow today it was different. His tone, his eyes, the spring in his step…

Estelle noticed it, too, and she slowly walked to where Noah had seated himself and stood next to him.

"Cheeseburgers," Maggie answered quietly. She narrowed her eyes and stared him down as she asked, "And what's gotten into you?"

Noah laughed and gave the counter a loud slap, making Estelle jump with a startle. He looked at the painting hanging in Maggie's bar, and then he glanced from one lady to the other. "You're never gonna believe it," he said with a wink. That was something they hadn't seen in at least a decade.

Estelle narrowed her stare and studied Noah's expression. She watched his eyes sparkle and dance with the delight of youth, and her heart began to pound. He's finally found her! Italics for this last sentence.

"Ha!" Maggie mocked a laugh. "Let me guess," she said as she looked him over. His eyes had always been a dead giveaway, and they danced now in a way they hadn't in years. They still held the sadness and grief that had been there since Carrie's passing, but today his eyes sparkled as Maggie had only seen in his expression one time before. And all at once Maggie knew! She struggled to swallow the ball that had gotten into her throat.

"You've seen Angel," Estelle whispered as she watched the joy in his expression.

Noah laughed out loud again, nodded his head, and took a deep breath before he answered. "Almost, ladies. I saw her picture when I was in Sioux Falls."

Estelle gasped and covered her open mouth with her hand. She had prayed for Angel to return for so long, and now it was finally coming true.

"Where did you see that, Noah?" Maggie asked seriously. The hair on the back of her neck prickled, and she reached below the counter for her favorite whiskey. Noah had been terribly depressed and lonely since Carrie's death. *Perhaps he hasn't seen anything at all. Perhaps he's only imagined it. There's just no way.* Even though Maggie attempted to deny the revelation, she'd known for many years that it was only a matter of time before he found out.

She poured herself a shot and quickly belted it down. She remembered all too well the young lady who'd called herself "Angel." She was a beautiful girl Noah met in the spring of 1975, the artist who'd painted the cherished painting titled Obedience — the very one hanging in Maggie's bar. A ycllowed snapshot was still carefully tucked in the corner of the frame. It was a photograph taken by Estelle, of Noah and Angel standing before the bar. In the photo, Noah was giving her the most tender of kisses upon her beautiful cheek.

Noah had spent an entire weekend with the young lady, and then she'd returned to her home, wherever that was. She'd promised to come back and marry Noah, but the arrangement never materialized. Noah went on a search for her that consumed the next eighteen months of his life. He drove hundreds of miles, searching small towns throughout South Dakota for the girl he was supposed to marry. He even built a monstrous house, expecting to find her and bring her back. Tragically, he never located Angel; eventually he married a young woman by the name of Carrie. What had happened to Noah, however, after that single weekend with Angel, had never stopped amazing Maggie and Estelle. Noah hadn't had a drink since that time, and had completely changed his life. He went back to school and built a successful business developing and selling property.

Maggie took another shot, then let out her breath with the confession, "Listen, Noah, I've known for the last five years —"

Noah and Estelle gasped at the same time.

"I know, I know." Maggie rolled her eyes.

"But how…?" Noah began.

"At Carrie's funeral," she replied. "Marquette Caselli was that guy who came around in '75 looking for Ty's father...Remember that?"

Noah nodded. "You thought he was a Fed or something."

"Thought he was gonna take down the whole town and you with 'em, so I lied my butt off for you," Maggie continued. "Anyway..."

"But you kept it to yourself?" Estelle accused with a scowl.

Maggie frowned at her younger sister. "What good was it gonna do anybody? Gimme a break." She looked at Noah and pointed her index finger at him. "She's married to your best buddy, and you were all busted up about losing Carrie. I just didn't think it was the smartest thing in the world to tell you."

Estelle gasped softly again, made a "tsk" noise between her teeth, and shook her finger at Maggie. "You shoulda told us, Maggie May."

Maggie rolled her eyes again and shook her head.

"I guess I should have known." Noah thoughtfully scratched his head and said, "I knew I saw one of her sketches in her father's restaurant in Sioux Falls, and it was even signed 'Angel.' I've thought forever that Mr. Caselli sure looked like Angel, but then, there were things that were different. Like she told me that she wanted to be an art teacher, and Alex's wife studied Russian history and comparative literature."

Maggie wrinkled up her nose. "What's that?"

"Beats me," Noah answered with a shake of his head, "But I had to go over to Sioux Falls and meet with Alex, and when I walked into his office there was the painting..." He pointed to the one over the bar. "I asked him where he had gotten it and he told me Tillie had painted it, and then showed me her photograph." Noah shook his head. "I nearly passed out."

"That's her name?" Estelle's old voice tried to croak out. "Tillie?"

Noah nodded. "Her family's nickname for her is 'Angel.'"

Maggie swallowed hard and looked woefully at the whiskey bottle in front of her. She wanted another shot, but two was her limit. She reluctantly capped it and put it back in its place under the counter.

"They bought a house here," Noah blurted out.

"What?" Maggie whispered in astonishment, and Estelle could only gasp again.

Noah replied, "I know they were in town a couple of days ago and bought a house up in Carriage Hills. They're moving here, ladies."

"Well," Maggie began in her shocked whisper, "have you talked to her?"

Noah shook his head, "I've completely avoided her." He bit his lip and sighed. "I wanna see her again so bad, just to ask her why she didn't come back."

"Well, you deserve an explanation," Estelle encouraged with a frown.

Maggie swallowed and looked into Noah's eyes. "Have you told Alex?" Noah shook his head and looked away from Maggie as she asked, "Have you told Josh?"

"No," Noah shook his head again. "I'm not telling him about this, and hopefully I can keep it from Mona. They'll just get worried and think I'm flippin' out or something —"

"Well, maybe you are," Maggie interrupted.

"No, I'm not, Maggie," Noah insisted. "Besides, I've got a few questions for her. Like why she didn't at least call me and have the decency to let me know she was gonna dump me for a Harvard Law graduate."

"Yeah," Estelle snorted and nodded in agreement. "He deserves an explanation, Maggie. Look how long we've wondered what happened to her."

"And don't be telling Mona on me when you see her for your Bible study," Noah instructed as he shook his finger at Estelle. "Promise?"

Estelle nodded.

Maggie slowly shook her head and swallowed. "Noah, I don't know if it's such a good idea. Something happened in here eleven years ago." She hesitated, and shook her head again. "I don't know. Something really strange." She looked into Noah's eyes with a sigh. "I just don't want to see you get hurt again. It was really hard for you. Don't you remember?"

Noah rolled his eyes, obviously dismissing Maggie's warning, and he shook his head. "I'm totally over all that, Maggie. Don't worry."

Maggie wanted to agree with him, but a strange weight suddenly pressed upon her heart. If she believed in God, she would have gotten on her knees at that moment and prayed.